FOUR WEDDINGS AND A SWAMP BOAT TOUR

BOYS OF THE BAYOU

ERIN NICHOLAS

ISBN: 978-1-952280-10-8

Editor: Lindsey Faber

Cover photo: Wander Aguiar

Cover design: Angela Waters

THE SERIES

Boys of the Bayou
My Best Friend's Mardi Gras Wedding
Sweet Home Louisiana
Beauty and the Bayou
Crazy Rich Cajuns
Must Love Alligators
Four Weddings and a Swamp Boat Tour

Connected series...
Boys of the Bayou-Gone Wild
Things are going to get wild when thee next batch of bayou boys falls in love!
Otterly Irresistible
Heavy Petting
Flipping Love You

Boys of the Big Easy
Hot single dads in the sexy city of New Orleans
Easy Going (prequel)

The series

Going Down Easy
Taking It Easy
Eggnog Makes Her Easy
Nice and Easy
Getting Off Easy

ABOUT THE BOOK

She's been proposed to five times.
Five.

She even said yes to one of them.
And then broke his heart when she called it off. Not to mention
her mother's heart. And her grandmother's. And his mother's.
And...you get the picture.

Paige Asher has now officially sworn off all dating. Diamonds
give her hives.
All she wants is to be a yoga-doing, cat-collecting, vegetarian in
peace. Away from her marriage-crazy family and all their
expectations.

So when her weekend fling turns into a real friend and offers
her a place to escape, she finds herself on his doorstep in
Louisiana. And right in the middle of not just one family
wedding, but three. Of course.

Charming, sexy bayou boy Mitch Landry gets stuff done.

Whatever anyone needs. From alligator-sitting to getting a buddy drunk to showing a woman a good time to fixing a swamp boat, he's the man. No problem. No drama.

But he wants a hell of a lot more from Paige than a temporary friends-with-benefits arrangement. He wants to take care of her. And her five cats. He also really wants other men to stop asking her to marry them.

But if a roommate and a few orgasms are all she wants, that's what he'll deliver.

He can just be her friend and not commit the greatest sin of all...asking her for forever.

Probably.

1

There were five reasons why just showing up on her hot holiday fling's doorstep was a bad idea.

"Reason number one," she told Bernie, the black and white cat perched on the passenger seat of her car, watching the scenery go by. "I personally hate surprises. So what am I doing surprising someone like this?"

Bernie didn't know. Or he wasn't willing to say, *your mother finally drove you officially over the edge.*

Paige appreciated Bernie's diplomacy.

Fred, the long-haired orange cat, huddled on the floor on the passenger side, absolutely *not* interested in the scenery outside the car, was not afraid to tell her how he felt about the whole thing, however.

As he'd been doing for the past nearly one thousand miles.

His meow was more of a pitiful wail, however, explaining that this road trip sucked, and she was the worst cat mom ever, than a helpful analysis of her thoughts and motives.

"Okay, I could have planned better," she admitted to the unhappy feline.

Fred's answering meow was full of blame and a reminder

that her "plan" had basically consisted of throwing a few things together—including Bernie and Fred—getting in her car and heading south.

She hadn't even plugged Autre, Louisiana, into her GPS until after she stopped for the night just outside of St. Louis. Autre was *well* south of Appleby, Iowa, and she'd known she had a long way to go before she had to worry too much about specific directions.

So, yeah, the this-is-really-a-bad-idea realizations hadn't started until she'd passed New Orleans and was on her way to the bayou.

Now those thoughts wouldn't leave her alone.

"The number two reason this is a bad idea," she told Bernie (and Fred, though he was talking right over her), "is that I don't even know this guy well enough to know how he feels about surprises."

Bernie looked over at her.

"Right, he might hate them," she agreed. "I also don't know if he has a criminal record. Or if there are any unsolved missing person cases or murders around his general neighborhood. Or if he keeps a chainsaw in his shed."

Fred agreed, loudly, that showing up on a potential murderer's front step was a bad idea.

Or maybe he was just telling her that he resented...well, everything about this car trip. Again.

"Okay, that's not true," she told both cats. "I'm *sure* Mitch Landry has a chainsaw in his shed. He can fix anything. Apparently. And I'm guessing, sometimes, that means he needs a chainsaw."

Fred wailed.

"Well, he single-handedly saved the Apple Festival last week," she argued with the indignant animal. "He heard there was a problem with the electrical wiring in the town square, he headed over to check it out, and the next thing we knew, there were lights and music, and the apple cider and popcorn were nice and hot."

Fred did *not* care about apple cider or popcorn.

"And he did tell me that he's the general fix-it guy for his family's businesses. So yeah, there's a ninety-nine percent chance he has a chainsaw," she told the cats. "And honestly, him being so capable with those big hands and all those muscles..." She looked at Bernie. "I know what you're thinking. Cutting people up with a chainsaw would take muscles too, and I'm sure you're right, but I can't help that him being the super-hero to the town, and the idea of him in a toolbelt, is kind of hot."

Bernie looked back out the window. He, clearly, didn't share her attraction to blue-collar-works-with-his-hands men.

"Oh, you barely met him," she told the cat. "You saw him for, what, three minutes when he came to the yoga studio? You don't know what you're talking about."

The cats both lived at her yoga studio. Though she did let them into her apartment over the studio at night if they wanted to come snuggle. And sometimes a couple of others came up too. But even she knew letting twenty-three cats hang out in her apartment was a lot.

The rest of the cats stayed downstairs in the yoga studio that doubled as a cat café and adoption center. Fred and Bernie and three other cats were hers and weren't up for adoption, but most of the time they hung out with the others on the lower level where there was more room to roam.

The cat adoption center saved her, just barely, from being an official crazy cat lady.

In her mind anyway.

"And," she went on, making her case to Bernie. And Fred if he'd shut the hell up for two minutes. "Mitch was so cute at the festival. He was like a little kid with the snow, and the way he played the games and tried all the apple ciders and cookies and cakes, and the way he chose the biggest caramel apple."

She smiled, remembering him taking it all in. They didn't get a lot of snow in Louisiana. They certainly didn't have six inches of it hanging out around for days at a time. And watching him at the festival with all the apple foods and crafts, she would have thought they didn't have apples in Louisiana either.

"I mean, can a guy who lights up at the sight of snow and loves caramel apples hack someone up into little pieces with a chainsaw?"

Fred yowled, and she really thought he was saying, *Of course. Why not?*

Paige blew out a breath and gripped the steering wheel tighter.

Her car made an awful grinding noise again as she slowed down for a stop sign. Again. She shook her head.

"*That* is reason number three this is a bad idea," she told the cats. "That noise every time I use the brakes is *not* good and probably means we can't just turn around and drive back home."

Fred did *not* like that idea. Bernie seemed indifferent.

"Reason number four this is a bad idea," she said, turning onto Cedar Street—Mitch's street, according to Bud at the gas station on the edge of town. "I didn't tell anyone where I was going."

She'd texted her mom, friends, and two sisters *I need a vacation, see you in a few weeks, I'll call soon.*

"And yeah, okay, I could tell them now," she said when Fred proclaimed that the dumbest of all the things she'd done. Well, next to putting him in a car and driving him a thousand miles away from home. "But I also don't want a lecture."

He meowed loudly, and she frowned.

"A *human* lecture."

4

But she really should tell someone she was here. Her mom and her sisters would be worried. Her friends a little too, but less so. Piper and Whitney knew that Mitch had come to town and rocked her world. They might be shocked that she'd chased him all the way to Louisiana, because Paige never chased guys anywhere at all, but they wouldn't necessarily think it was *bad*.

Yeah, she'd tell them.

But *not* her mother. Not yet.

Though her making this impulsive trip would not be number one on Dee Asher's list of *Things Paige Has Done That I Do Not Understand*.

"Nope, number one on that list would be me calling off my wedding a week before walking down the aisle," she told Bernie. "But this trip might be number two."

Fred meowed. It was a little softer this time. Maybe because the car was moving slower now as she looked for numbers on the houses. But there was no canned tuna to be seen, and his favorite pillow was still back in Appleby by his favorite window so, that meow was definitely still disgruntled.

"You're right," Paige told him. "Refusing to get back together with Garrett when he finally spoke to me again would be number two."

Garrett was her mother's best friend's son. The women had been thrilled that their kids were getting married. Paige hadn't just broken Garrett's heart when she called off the wedding. Her mom still wasn't over it four years later. Neither was Garrett's mom. Or Paige's grandmother. Or her aunt. Or... Okay, Paige was maybe the only one in her family who was over her canceled wedding.

"Turning down Stephen Corbett's proposal would be number three," she told the cats. "Turning down Adam Lawson's proposal would be number four. Or maybe four and five." Adam had proposed twice. "So that puts this trip at probably number six and the cat café-yoga studio at number seven on the list of things Mom just does not get about me."

Fred meowed in response.

That wasn't true. He was just meowing because he was pissed. He didn't care at all what Paige was going through. Typical cat.

"Yep," she said to Bernie, since he, at least, wasn't yelling at her. "Dee might put this trip above the cats and yoga, but not above rejecting perfectly nice men with great jobs who would give me a good life." She even mimicked her mother's voice when she said the words she'd heard dozens of times.

The white house with the right number on it was the next one. Paige felt her nerves start jumping as she rolled to a stop across the street from the house Bud had described to her.

So this was where Mitch Landry lived.

Her heart kicked against her ribs as she thought about the guy she was here to see. Then she laughed lightly. She wasn't just here to *see* him. She wasn't stopping by for tea. She was hoping to freaking live with him for the next few weeks.

She definitely should have called ahead.

But now that she was finally here, looking at his house, the truck in the driveway, the work boots on the front step, she realized Dee Asher might actually think this was a great idea.

Mitch had spent less than thirty-six hours in Appleby, Iowa, but he'd won the town over. He'd saved their big Apple Festival. Single-handedly. He'd also charmed everyone he met. He was good-looking, friendly, able to fix anything, and, seemingly, thought Paige was amazing.

The living a thousand miles away in Louisiana was certainly a checkmark in the "con" column, but Dee wanted Paige married and settled down. She might be willing to overlook the fact that the guy who had finally gotten Paige to put her toothbrush in his bathroom would take her baby girl so far from home.

Paige rolled her eyes. Actually, Dee might appreciate that too. Paige was a huge pain in Dee's ass.

"Okay, this is it," she said to the cats. She pivoted to look into the back seat where Calvin, Eddie, and Tiny Tim were sleeping.

Initially, the other three had agreed with Fred on her Worst Cat Mom of the Year nomination, but they'd given up yelling about it two hundred miles back or so.

It had been a *long* trip.

Paige turned back to study Mitch's house. Her heart knocked against her ribs again, and she blew out a breath.

He said he's crazy about you. You were planning to be here in another three weeks for the wedding anyway.

She had agreed to be his plus one for his cousin's wedding to one of Paige's friends, Tori.

Tori, Paige's now ex-veterinarian, was an Iowa girl who had fallen for a Louisiana boy and moved her life to the bayou. Mitch had tagged along with Tori and her fiancé, Josh, last summer on the trip to fetch a bunch of animals Tori couldn't leave behind. Paige and Mitch had met over the back end of an alpaca when Paige had stopped by to say hello.

There had been instant sparks, and Mitch hadn't needed to sleep on the couch in the den at Tori's mom's house that night.

It had been the perfect fling. He'd been hot and funny and charming and had done things to her body that she feared had ruined her for other men. Then he'd been gone the next morning by six a.m. No awkward breakfast conversation, no learning how she liked her coffee, no chance of running into her mother and getting hopes up about wedding dress shopping.

"Tori wouldn't be friends with a guy who hacks people up with a chainsaw," she told Bernie.

Bernie finally meowed in return.

Paige nodded. "You're right. I definitely wasn't worried

7

about any murderous tendencies when we were having the hottest sex of my life."

Fred yowled.

"Hey, I don't need your judgment," she told the cat. "He's also been texting. So he hasn't forgotten about me. Or written me off entirely. Hell, he mentioned moving to Iowa to see what this might turn into."

Her stomach flipped at that. She wasn't sure if it was a good flip or a bad flip, though. When he'd showed up in Appleby two weeks after Christmas, again with Tori and Josh, Paige had been shocked by how happy she was to see him. And how intense their chemistry was the second time around.

Then he'd mentioned that he wouldn't mind relocating to Iowa, and it had freaked her out. She did *not* want a serious relationship, and a guy leaving his family and job just to "see what could happen" had seemed like a kind of major commitment.

And now, here she was, about to knock on his door and ask if she could stay for the next three weeks. Or three months.

He was so going to take this the wrong way.

"Reason number five that this is a bad idea," she told the cats. "Mitch Landry is going to think I want to be his girlfriend."

Bernie meowed again. So did Calvin. As if they agreed with her.

Dammit.

"The way my luck goes, he'll be proposing by Wednesday," she told Fred, who had climbed into her lap to look out her window at the house too.

Fred looked up at her and meowed.

"Okay, I won't turn around and get right back on the road," she promised. "But I'm warning you now, the second he pulls out a ring, we're out of here."

She put Fred on the seat next to Bernie, rolled the windows down partway, shut the car off, took a deep breath, and got out.

She was here. In spite of the five very convincing reasons, this was a bad idea. Not to mention Fred's general opinion about the whole thing.

She ran a hand through her hair and looked down at the t-shirt and capris she had on. It was January. It had been twelve degrees when she'd left Iowa. Twelve. She was now standing here in a short-sleeve baby blue t-shirt and denim capris. It wasn't *hot*. Not at all the steamy weather she associated with Louisiana. But it was in the mid-fifties, and for a girl who'd grown up in Iowa, this felt downright balmy right now.

So, good weather in January. There was a *good* reason for this trip.

It was nice to know there was one.

She started up the front walk.

Please be home. Please be happy to see me. Please don't let this be worse than the time I almost died choking on the chocolate cake when Stephen proposed at Vincenzo's.

It couldn't be worse than that. Right?

She never reacted well to being proposed to. Always because it was a shock and always because *no way, thank you very much, no matter what.*

But yeah, that time she'd almost inhaled cake into her lungs in a fancy restaurant in front of fifty people, and the resulting hacking and coughing and watering eyes and smeared mascara had not been pretty.

She coughed lightly now, her lungs giving her a little hey-don't-freak-out-and-suck-anything-into-us reminder.

Yeah, well, *she* wasn't the one who was going to be shocked that she was standing on Mitch's front porch today.

Okay, okay, she was a little surprised that she was here. That she'd done this. That she'd thought about running away from home, and he was the person she ran to. But he'd be shocked to see her too. She was going to just focus on that and not all of the *what is it about this guy?* that kept swirling through her mind.

She took in the details of the house. It was nice. Simple. Small. White. Well kept. There was a huge tree in the front yard that she thought was likely a magnolia tree. She didn't have a lot of experience with magnolia trees, of course, but she'd seen a lot of them as she'd scrolled through the results of her What You Need To Know About Louisiana search last night on her laptop in the roadside motel.

She eyed the front of the house. Did she knock on the porch door, or did she go onto the porch and knock on the front door? The front door, surely, right?

But when she opened the light screened door to the porch, she felt almost as if she was stepping into a living room.

The porch was adorable. Sure, it belonged to a hot, sexy, alpha male who gave her eye-crossing-toe-curling orgasms. But he had a freaking adorable porch. There was no way around it.

There were potted plants everywhere, hanging from baskets overhead, sitting on shelves, and even on the floor. On one end of the porch, that stretched the entire length of the front of the house, was a porch swing long enough to fit two or three adults. It faced the street and would be the perfect place to sit and rock and watch the neighborhood go by.

She glanced around. Of course, not much was going on in this neighborhood. It was very quiet. The houses were set back from the street several yards, and there were wide expanses between them. This was the far end of town, furthest from the highway and closest to the bayou. The houses were older. The front walks cracked and uneven, the plants and trees very established. There was also an overgrown field that stretched out behind this house and the two to the west. It spread out all the way to the line of trees in the distance.

She couldn't see or hear it from here, but she knew the bayou was on the other side of those trees. Less than a mile from the houses. She hadn't known which house was Mitch's, but she'd checked out the town of Autre online.

That wasn't super creepy. Was it? It wasn't weird that she'd looked the town up since she was moving here. Temporarily, of course, but she was going to be staying for a couple of weeks. Or three. Or for the summer. Which was still several months away.

Okay, when she'd first considered coming to Louisiana for the summer, it had been because she thought that was when Josh and Tori's wedding would be.

Instead, they were getting married on Mardi Gras. Which was a Tuesday. In February.

Even once she'd heard it was a Mardi Gras wedding, Paige had still assumed it was a few months away. She wasn't sure why she'd thought of Mardi Gras as a warm weather holiday, but she did. Probably the plethora of naked breasts associated with the celebration.

Anyway, she knew where the bayou was from here. And where the highway was. In case she needed to head back north.

This porch, though... she wasn't in a hurry to go back north suddenly. She didn't have a porch there. She definitely didn't have a porch with a hammock in it.

But Mitch did. The hammock was hooked onto the house and onto a post that seemed to have been secured to the floor of the porch specifically for that purpose.

Paige could already imagine lying in that thing on a rainy day with a good book. Or maybe with a hot, laid-back, Louisiana boy. Or both. A hot guy and a book? Yes, please, sign her up. Specifically, Mitch Landry and a dirty romance.

Okay, she could knock on this door if that was how she was going to get a couple of afternoons in that hammock.

She knocked and waited, holding her breath.

She heard footsteps inside, and her stomach swooped.

A second later, the door swung open.

And a gorgeous brunette, with streaks of pink in her hair and tattoos that ran the entire length of her left leg and her left arm, opened the door.

Paige knew that the leg tattoo went from ankle to hip because the woman was wearing nothing but a t-shirt. As in, no pants. The shirt was at least three sizes too big for her and covered everything important, but it still left a lot of skin bare.

Paige could only assume it was a man's shirt. As in Mitch's. The man who lived here–who would have t-shirts here.

Paige's swoopy stomach knotted, and the breath she'd been holding came whooshing out.

Dammit.

This kind of...hurt.

"Hi," the woman said, looking at Paige with a combination of surprise and curiosity. "Can I help you?"

"Um... yes, if you can tell me this is *not* Mitch Landry's house."

That would be good. Sure, it looked exactly as Bud had described it, but maybe there were two white houses with big trees in the front and a screened-in front porch. None of those things were particularly unique.

The woman smiled. "No, this is Mitch's place."

"Dammit," Paige muttered.

"You okay?" the woman asked.

"I mean...maybe. I could be. If you told me you're his sister."

Though that would mean the woman was lying to her.

She and Mitch had been texting for nearly six months between his two visits to Appleby and they'd shared about their families. Mitch was from a big, loud family that all lived within about ten square miles of one another. But he was an only child to a single dad. He had lots of cousins and aunts and uncles, but no siblings.

The woman leaned into the doorjamb. "Not his sister," she said with a knowing smile.

Paige nodded. "Yeah, I figured."

"Cousin."

Paige nodded again but then paused. "Oh."

The woman smiled. "Yeah." She stuck out her hand. "I'm Kennedy."

Paige took it. "Paige."

Kennedy's eyes widened, and her hand tightened on Paige's. "Iowa Paige?"

Paige felt her brows arch. "He told you about me?"

"He told Chase and Owen who told Sawyer who told Juliet who told me," Kennedy said. She tugged on Paige's hand. "Come on in. I can't even tell you how awesome it is that I get to meet you first." She pulled Paige into the house. "I mean, I do get to meet you first, right? You haven't seen anyone else? Because I haven't gotten any texts or calls."

Paige had no choice but to follow the chatty woman through the living room. "Um, just Bud, at the gas station."

Kennedy nodded. "Good. Okay. I mean, he'll tell someone. Or call the bar. But I get to *meet* you first." She gave Paige a grin. "That's very good."

"Oh. I..." Paige had no idea what to say.

Kennedy had thrown a lot of names at her. Chase she recognized. He and Mitch were good friends. The others she had heard of, but she wasn't sure who they all were exactly and how, or if, they were even all related. As far as she could tell, everyone became a part of the Landry family once they spent about five minutes with them.

Ah, and that would be reason number six that this is a bad idea.

She had her own big, meddlesome family. She was trying to get *away* from them and have some space. Why had she come to Louisiana where she knew that Mitch's family would be up in her business too?

Because you have a thing for that hot Louisiana boy, and when you thought of escaping and hiding out somewhere for a few weeks, you immediately thought of him and how nice it would be to let him take care of you the way he says he wants to.

Temporarily, of course. She didn't need taken care of in the long-term.

Probably.

She'd never actually been on her own. She'd lived in the same town that her entire family had lived in all their lives. She knew everyone in Appleby. There wasn't a single thing she could need that her family and hometown couldn't and wouldn't provide.

Except peace. And solitude. And independence.

That's what she wanted. That's what she was looking for.

But in the short term while she made a plan for all of that independent solitude? Yeah, hanging out with Mitch would be nice.

No one could blame her. The guy was good with his mouth. When he was doing delicious dirty things with it and when he was using it to sweet talk her or charm her entire hometown.

And he knew the score. She'd told him about her plethora of proposals, and he'd seen her family in action. He knew where she stood on relationships and overly involved families.

A short-term getaway and a little friends-with-benefits on the side with Mitch had sounded perfect.

But now, one of Mitch's relatives was already pulling her through his house and into his kitchen.

"He did *not* tell us you were coming today," Kennedy said, nudging Paige into a chair at the kitchen table and crossing to the fridge. She pulled out a pitcher of what looked like iced tea and then went to a cupboard.

She stretched for a higher shelf, and Paige was relieved to see the edge of a pair of denim shorts peek out from under the bottom of the big t-shirt she wore.

"We were working on the otter enclosure today, and the board I was standing on shifted, and I ended up on my ass in the water." Kennedy laughed. "Came in here to wash and dry my stuff and clean up. He's still down there."

"Oh, should we call him?" Paige asked.

"Hell no. Not before I have a chance to grill you," Kennedy said. She looked at Paige over her shoulder. "I mean, get to know you."

That sly grin did *not* say that there was going to be anything quite as polite as "getting to know each other" going on. Kennedy wanted to get some dirt.

Or maybe give it.

She brought two glasses to the table. "Peach sweet tea," she said, setting one down in front of Paige. "I'll happily buy you a beer when we get to Ellie's, but I have to wait for my bra to dry. And I want to be the first to hear all about Iowa."

Kennedy plopped into the chair perpendicular to Paige's and tucked a foot up under her butt.

"Ellie's?" Paige asked.

"Our grandma's bar," Kennedy said, taking a drink of her tea.

Right, his grandma owned a bar. Paige knew that.

"You'll meet everyone at dinner," Kennedy said. "Unless they hear you're in town or see your car and end up here before that."

"Everyone has dinner together?"

"Most nights," Kennedy said with a nod.

"How many people is 'everyone'?" Paige asked with trepidation.

Kennedy tipped her head and appeared to be counting in her head. "It varies a little but fifteen, maybe twenty."

Paige barely kept from groaning. This was so not going to be a laid-back, relaxed getaway. She'd pictured a little cabin on the bayou, out in the trees, crickets and frogs singing at night while she sat on the front porch with... okay, the sweet tea fit that little daydream. And that porch swing.

The hammock though... that was next level.

A big noisy family that was all too curious about her and Mitch and what it meant that she'd driven all this way out of the blue to be with him was *not*.

"You know, I'm more of a grilled-cheese-all-by-myself-for-dinner girl," Paige said.

Kennedy laughed. "Okay."

"Is it?" Paige asked skeptically.

"Sure it is," Kennedy said with a nod. "As long as you're good with not having any of that while you're in Autre."

Paige sighed. That's what she'd figured. "You don't have cheese down here?"

"'Course we do. What do you think we put on our chili cheese fries?"

"So then your family just doesn't believe in people being alone? Ever?"

"Not my family, not most of the people who live in Autre, not most of the Cajuns I know from anywhere."

Paige thought about how far she could get if she got in her car and started driving again right now. She'd have to stop for the night again, but she could put Autre pretty far in her rearview before that. She could head back to Iowa. Or she could head to Colorado, which was her plan for six months from now. Or she could just drive and see where she ended up.

But her car was making a really bad noise...

"I can't believe Mitch thought he was goin' to keep you bein' here a secret," Kennedy said.

"Oh. Um." Paige lifted her glass for a sip.

She tasted the sweet, peach-flavored tea and... sighed. But this time with pleasure. Damn, that was good. She took a bigger drink before setting the glass down again. "He doesn't know I'm here. I wasn't supposed to show up for another three weeks."

Kennedy's brow lifted. "Is that right?"

"Yeah. I... was coming for Josh and Tori's wedding, but... I decided to come early."

"I see." Kennedy lifted her glass again.

"It's not like that."

"Like what?"

"Like what you're thinking," Paige said, taking another drink and wishing for some peach schnapps to add to her glass.

"What do you think I'm thinking?" Kennedy asked.

"I think you think that I'm either a crazy stalker or I'm madly in love with Mitch."

Kennedy nodded. "If the spectrum is crazy stalker to madly in love, which end are you closer to?"

Paige set her glass down and regarded Kennedy. She didn't know this woman. If she *was* madly in love with Mitch and was planning a future with him, she might think that she should try to make Kennedy like her.

But...

"I'm just here for the hot sex, the otters, and the wedding cake. Someone *else's* wedding cake."

Kennedy's grin was quick and bright. "That is—"

She was cut off by the sound of heavy footsteps thudding across the back porch.

Paige's heart thudded just like those footsteps.

The door opened, and then there was a pause.

"This is going to be sooo good," Kennedy said, lifting her tea glass again.

2

"**P**aige?"

The sound of Mitch's voice sucked the air out of her lungs. God, she'd missed him. It had been one stupid week. *One.* And she'd missed him to the point that him saying her name made her heart flip.

She turned on the chair, trying to smile, but afraid that her expression was a combination of oh-my-god-I-want-you and what-the-hell-am-I-doing-here?

She swallowed hard. "Hey."

He was in a pair of jeans and a fitted gray t-shirt. His hair was wet. He didn't have any shoes on. And he looked stunned.

"Surprise," she said, again trying the smile. And again, pretty sure it looked more like a grimace. "I was just—"

Before she could even finish the *thought*, not to mention speaking the sentence, he was there, pulling her up from the chair and cupping her face.

His mouth covered hers, and she melted.

Everything is going to be okay.

That was the only thought in her head as he kissed her.

Mitch was kissing her right now, his tongue sweeping into

her mouth, his hands holding her possessively, his big body hot and hard against hers, and there really wasn't anything else she wanted to think about right then.

He kissed her and kissed her and kissed her. She kissed him back, of course, but she was aware they had an audience so she didn't grip his shoulders and climb up his body to wrap herself around him the way she wanted to.

"Maddie, you are never going to guess where I am and what's happening."

Kennedy's voice infiltrated, and Mitch lifted his head.

He kept a hold of Paige's face with one big hand, staring into her eyes, but he reached over and plucked the phone from Kennedy's fingers.

"Hey!" she protested.

He hit the button to disconnect the call. Then tucked the phone into his back pocket.

"Give me a fucking break, Ken," he said, still looking at Paige. "I need a little time here."

Paige wet her lips. "Time for what?"

"Time to absorb you myself before I have to share you."

Her heart flipped. Again. Because of the tone of voice and the look in his eyes. But then she registered the actual words. "Share me?"

"How did you find my house?"

"I asked Bud. At the gas station."

He nodded. "So not the bar or the garage or the tour company or Landry Construction or Landry Accounting or Landry... anything?"

That was a lot of Landrys. "No."

"You didn't talk to anyone with Landry or Boys of the Bayou on their shirt?"

"No."

He smiled. "Then we probably have about ten more minutes...maybe fifteen...to get out of here."

"Get out of here?"

But Mitch had already taken her hand and started for the back door.

"Hey! Phone!" Kennedy called after him.

"No," Mitch said simply, pulling Paige across the back porch and down the steps.

"How about a ride home?" Kennedy yelled.

"No," Mitch called back.

"I'm taking all your beer when I leave!" Kennedy told him.

"Don't care."

"Then I'm taking your pickles too!"

"Touch my pickles, and I'll tell Bennett about the time you told Jason Guillory that you wanted to have six babies with him."

There was a beat of silence. Then Kennedy yelled, "I was seven!"

Mitch just laughed.

"And Bennett will think that's adorable!" Kennedy added. "He's obsessed with me!"

Mitch stopped by the dark green pickup and pulled the passenger door open, turning to Paige.

"Pickles?" she asked. "That's a threat?"

"I love pickles, and I don't share. Especially Alice's."

"Who's Alice?"

"Lady over in Bad."

"And how did you meet Alice?"

Was she feeling jealous of the pickle queen? Yep.

"I met her when she was waitressing at the café over there. I drive through a lot. I stopped for lunch often. She quit waitressing about two years ago, so now I stop and check to see if she needs anything. Leaky faucets fixed, oil change on her car, that kind of stuff. She pays me in home-canned pickles."

"And she's young and blond and thinks you're amazing."

He chuckled. "She is seventy-two and used to be a brunette. But yeah, she thinks I'm pretty great."

Paige had no trouble believing that. Any of it. She hadn't known him long, but what she did know made it very easy to imagine Mitch stopping to check on an older lady just because he wanted to be sure she was okay.

"Bad?"

He grinned. "Bad, Louisiana. About ten miles up the bayou."

"That's a... strange name."

"Long story." He shrugged. "They're our rivals in just about everything. Football and stuff. But some of the guys over there are pretty great."

"Do they call themselves the Bad Boys?" she joked.

"They do."

She laughed. "It would be a huge, missed opportunity if they didn't."

"That's what they say. *We* call them bad at everything. It's been a long-running, very obvious, but still a funny joke."

"Do they have tourist businesses to compete with too?" It was clear that Mitch was friends with some of the guys from Bad and that immediately made her curious about them. She wanted to know everything about Mitch and the things and people he liked.

She supposed that was normal. When you were interested in someone, you wanted to *know* them. But she'd never really felt that way before. Then again, she'd known most of the guys she hung out with for years, if not her whole life. The things and people they liked were things and people Paige liked too.

It probably did make sense that she would marry one of them. But she just couldn't deny the feeling of *ugh*—that was really the best way to describe the emotion—the idea brought on.

"They do not have tourist business," Mitch said. "In fact,

ERIN NICHOLAS

that's something they give us shit about. They think we're selling out by bringing all these strangers down here to tromp around, disrupt the wildlife, and make easy money off of boat rides."

Paige lifted a brow. "Is any of that true?"

"Nah. They're just mad because they're not creative enough to do what we do."

"And is Bennett one of the Bad boys?"

"Nope. Our girls don't fraternize with those guys."

"Really?"

He laughed. "That's what we like to say. It's not true, of course. But Bennett is Kennedy's fiancé. He's from Savannah and is one of the owners of Boys of the Bayou. Probably one of our next state senators too. And he is, in fact, obsessed with Kennedy and thinks her crazy shit is adorable."

Before Paige could come up with a response, Mitch moved in close, again cupping her face in both hands.

"Speaking of adorable, crazy shit—I'm so damned happy to see you," he said gruffly.

She couldn't help but smile. "Am *I* the adorable, crazy shit, or is my just showing up here the adorable, crazy shit?"

"A little of both," he said with an affectionate smile. "Though I don't know if I'd call you crazy. I think you're just..."

"Difficult?"

"Hard to get," he said diplomatically.

She would accept that answer. She smiled but said, "I should have called."

"You don't have to call."

"I shouldn't have just shown up."

"You can just show up anytime, darlin'," he told her with a slow grin.

She swallowed. "I'm glad she's your cousin."

He looked confused for a moment. Then understanding dawned. "You thought I had another girl over?"

22

She shrugged. "Maybe."

"Paige." He shook his head.

"Well, we're not exclusive," she said. "We live a thousand miles apart. I wasn't supposed to be here for three more weeks, and that was going to just be for the wedding. I mean..." She shrugged. "It would be okay."

No, it fucking wouldn't! But her voice was wrong. It would be fine. It would probably be *good* because she and Mitch were not going to be serious. This wasn't a long-term thing. He'd made her no promises, and she shouldn't expect anything from him.

And vice versa.

"I told you that I haven't been with anyone else since I met you last July," he chided softly, lifting one hand to her face again and drawing his thumb back and forth along her jaw.

She swallowed. He had said that. And it had freaked her out. That was pretty intense.

But she hadn't been with anyone else since then either.

She'd been shocked when he'd texted her after their one-night stand. It had taken her days to respond because...what was she going to say? She wasn't looking for a relationship and certainly not a long-distance one. But she'd finally been unable to resist. And they'd texted for six months. No calls. No video chats. No emails. Just texts. But she'd loved it more than any of the dates she'd been on in the two years prior.

Then he'd showed up again a week ago. And dammit, he'd gotten to her.

To the point that she was now standing behind his house in Louisiana, dealing with the realization that she'd actually been jealous over him.

She never got jealous.

"Maybe you were just saying that to get me into bed," she told him.

"I got you into bed without having to say much of anything

the first time," he reminded her, his voice getting husky and his eyes hot.

Well, that was true enough.

"So you said we had about fifteen minutes to get out of here?"

"Maybe twenty. It'll take Kennedy ten minutes to walk to my grandma's bar now that she doesn't have a ride. Or her phone." He grinned unapologetically. "Then they'll all have to get the details, load up, and get over here."

Paige felt a shot of *uh-oh*. "Her bra is still in the dryer. She said she couldn't go to the bar until then."

He chuckled. "Well, then we might have a little more time. But you never know with Ken. She will *love* having been the first to meet you and to see my reaction to seeing you. My guess is she's headed there now to brag."

"She did mention how happy she was that she met me first." Paige was feeling a little overwhelmed. And like her this-is-a-bad-idea list would have been *a lot* more helpful if she'd gone over it somewhere around Memphis instead of New Orleans.

But God, she was so happy to see him. To *feel* him. Which she did now, running her hands up his arms to his shoulders and then to his chest.

"Yeah, I definitely need some time with you before my whole family wants to meet you." It seemed her touch made his voice a little gruffer.

Her eyes widened slightly. "And when you say *whole family*..."

"Dozens of loud, unfiltered, fun-loving Cajuns," he said with a nod. And a grin.

Dozens. Oh boy.

She'd known about the big family thing. And the up-in-your-business nature of that big family. But she hadn't really thought about it when she'd been running away from home.

She wasn't their family or their business. And sure, if she were Mitch's girlfriend, then maybe she would matter more to them. But she wasn't. And wouldn't be.

Right?

"Hey, Paige?"

"Yeah?"

"Get in the truck."

He probably knew exactly what she was thinking. She hadn't been shy about telling him that she was *not* looking for anything too serious or involved.

She nodded and climbed up onto the seat. "Where are we going?"

"Away from here. Where no one can find us for... a while."

See, the he-surely-has-a-chainsaw-in-his-shed thing should make the idea of driving out to where no one could find them creepy.

The hot look in his eyes, his big, work-hewn hard body, and, dammit, the way she'd missed him over the past week, made it all sound like exactly what she needed though.

"How long is a while? Because a solid week or two would be great. If there's like a cabin out there somewhere..." She waved her hand in the general direction of the bayou. "I'd be down for that."

His eyes went hot again, and he leaned in to kiss her quickly. "That sounds like heaven on earth."

Tingles raced over her body. This guy had a powerful physical effect on her that she still wasn't used to.

"So we can do that? Right now?"

He chuckled and leaned back. "I wish. But there aren't many corners of the bayou that my family doesn't know. And the corners with cabins, they're definitely aware of."

"Damn." It had sounded too good to be true but still, damn.

"But," he went on. "They won't chase us out to where I'm takin' you. They'll wait for us to come back."

"They'll be sure that we will?"

"Well, there's no seafood pot pie or bread pudding out there." He slammed the door closed.

She watched him round the front of the truck and then slide behind the wheel. "You'll always come home for seafood pot pie and bread pudding?" she asked.

He gave her a grin. "Always." He started the truck and shifted into drive, starting around the side of the house.

"It's that good?"

"It's good. But it's an even better cover."

"Cover?"

"For how much I just like bein' at home, sittin' around with all of them."

She lifted her brows. "This from the man who was going to move to Iowa last week."

He stopped at the end of his driveway and gave her an assessing look. Several seconds ticked by. Then he nodded. "Makes you really think about what Iowa had that I wanted so badly, huh?"

Whoa. She frowned. "Dammit, Mitch. I told you I didn't want anything serious."

"Yet, here you are." He pulled onto the street.

"I came for the wedding. Like I said I would."

"Three weeks early."

"I got proposed to again."

He stomped on the brake, stopping right in the middle of the street. Her hand flew up to brace against the dash.

"*What?*" he demanded.

She nodded. "At Josie's wedding. A guy I've known forever. Asked me to dance, and then worked his way up to 'you know, we're both single'."

Mitch shoved a hand through his hair. "Jesus," he muttered.

"I turned him down," she offered.

Mitch lifted a brow. "You better fucking have."

"Oh yeah?"

"Yeah."

There was something about that firm, possessive answer that made her wiggle on her seat. Not out of discomfort but because she felt stirrings of desire.

Guys being jealous and possessive did *not* turn her on.

Supposedly.

"So, you got proposed to." He said it as if disgusted and resigned at the same time. "You said no. Got in your car. And came here."

"Pretty much."

"So you're hiding out."

She swallowed. "Pretty much."

"Do they know where you are?"

"Whitney and Piper will. Eventually."

"What about your family?"

"I'll tell them I'm in Louisiana."

"Will you tell them why?"

She lifted her chin. "I'll tell them I came down here for Tori's wedding and decided to stay a little longer."

"What will they think about you being here with me?" he pressed.

She wet her lips. "I'm not sure I'll mention you."

He blew out a breath and focused his gaze out the windshield. "You're staying with me."

It wasn't really a question, and she again felt ribbons of heat. Mitch Landry was laid-back. He was the definition of easy-going. He was charming and wanted to pitch in to help however he could. He'd been in Appleby for about thirty minutes before he'd been volunteering to help fix a furnace, a few roofs, and the wiring in the town square. He'd also been accepting of her relationship rule. Which was *No Relationships*.

Well, her *two* relationship rules. One: No Relationships. Two: No Marriage Proposals.

In her experience, it didn't actually take a relationship for her to get a marriage proposal.

But now, the more possessive and bossier Mitch was kind of doing it for her.

She nodded. "I'd like to stay with you."

He looked at her again. "Spare room or my room?"

Okay, so he was just going to lay that out there. "I've only been here for a few minutes. Should we talk about—"

"Are you here because you want a friend or because you want orgasms?"

Her eyes widened. Then narrowed. Fine. If they were just going to dive right in here...

"Both," she said. "Friends with orgasms."

He held her gaze for several beats. "Okay."

Just okay.

She'd never been around a guy who was so accepting of what she wanted. Ever.

He started to shift the truck back into drive, but her gaze landed on the car parked across the road from his house. Her car. That was full of cats. Oh, crap. He'd totally distracted her from her *cats*.

"Mitch." She grabbed his arm. "Wait."

"We're T-minus eight minutes here," he said.

"I know. I... brought some..." She'd brought cats. Five cats. To his house. To stay for a few weeks. Without asking.

"Some?" he prompted.

"I have some stuff in my car I should take inside."

"We'll get it all later on," he said, again reaching for the gear shift.

"They probably should go in now." She pulled her bottom lip between her teeth.

"They?" he repeated. Then he looked at her car. And huffed out a laugh. "How many did you bring with you?"

Paige felt herself smiling. "Five."

He shook his head, but he was smiling too. He pulled the truck over to the curb in front of his house and shut it off. "We'd better get them in the house then. But hurry."

She scrambled down from the truck and headed for her car.

Five minutes later, they had all five cats and their supplies inside. Kennedy had already left, sans bra, as the dryer was still running, and they knew that meant the clock was ticking.

"We can just shut them in the bathroom or utility room or something," Paige said. "We'll put their food and water and litter box in there, and they'll be fine. Then they won't be roaming all over the house."

He shook his head and opened the door of one of the cat carriers he'd set on his living room floor. Fred and Bernie both shot out. Paige opened the one she'd carried. Eddie crept out more slowly.

"They should explore their new home," Mitch said.

Paige started to correct him with something like "their *temporary* new home," but she couldn't make the words come out. He knew where she stood on everything. And it didn't really matter if he didn't, or if he didn't totally believe her. *She* just had to remember it was temporary, and she wasn't interested in settling down or falling in love or making any promises to anyone.

Especially the promises part. She'd made promises in the past. Promises she'd felt compelled to make. Promises that seemed like the right thing to do.

Those promises had broken a lot of hearts and changed her relationship with her mother permanently. Paige didn't think she and her mom would be totally good again until Paige was married.

She wasn't going to make *any* promises of any kind to anyone unless she was one thousand percent sure she could keep them.

"Are you sure?" she asked as Bernie immediately jumped up

on the coffee table in front of Mitch's long brown couch and reached for a half-full glass of water.

She grabbed it quickly, knowing exactly what was about to happen. Bernie knocked over every glass that he found. Full, half-full, or empty. It was as if upright drinkware personally offended him.

He'd ruined two computer keyboards, and stained at least three shirts doing that at home before *she* had finally been trained to attend to or pick up all glasses.

"I'm sure." Mitch sounded amused as he watched Tiny Tim jump from the floor to the seat of the armchair near the fireplace and then eye the mantel as if trying to figure out how to get up there.

She heard a cupboard door slap shut in the kitchen. She shook her head.

"Fred found a low cupboard with a light door on it," she said.

"He likes cupboards?"

"Yeah. He can hook a paw around the door and pull it open, and then push it open from the inside when he's ready to come out."

"That's kind of impressive."

"He usually only does it when it rains. He hates the rain," she said. "But he's probably kind of freaked out right now. He's really pissed about the long drive."

"He's fine," Mitch said. "There's nothing in those lower cupboards he can hurt. Just small appliances mostly."

"You don't mind cat hair in your toaster?"

"My toaster's on the countertop. But I can wash the blender and food processor and ice cream maker out if I need to use them."

"You have an ice cream maker?"

"I do. Used it once."

"You don't like ice cream?"

"Love it. But Ben and Jerry do a fine job of making it, and it's a lot faster and easier to let them do it."

They stood smiling stupidly at each other for a long moment.

"So the cats are really okay here?" she asked.

"Of course."

Eddie was up on the couch now, sniffing and looking around. Mitch moved, grabbing the blanket that was draped over the back of the couch and spreading it out over half of the cushions. Eddie immediately walked onto the blanket, kneaded it a few times with his paws, then plopped down.

"You're going to have cat hair all over your stuff."

Mitch took the three steps that separated them and looked down at her. "As long as I have *your* stuff all over my house, I don't mind a little cat hair."

"My stuff?"

"Your bras in my dryer. Your shampoo in my shower. Your hummus in my fridge." He gave her a grin and moved in closer, his voice dropping. "Your sweet ass—and the rest of you—in my bed every night."

Her breath caught in her chest. *Dammit.*

"Your roommate doesn't hate cats, does he? He's not allergic?"

She'd almost forgotten that Mitch had a guy living with him, but the fact came back to her suddenly.

"Griff—Griffin Foster. He's a veterinarian."

"What? Really?"

"Yep. Joined Tori in her practice and is taking care of the otters and the rest of the petting zoo."

"So he won't mind the cats."

"Well..." Mitch grinned. "He's a grumpy ass. Kind of pissy about being here in Autre taking care of goats when a few months ago he was the head vet at the National Zoo, leading their propagation program."

Paige's eyes got wide. "What happened?"

"He yelled at a donor at a fundraiser and got fired. So Tori gave him a job."

"Wow. I'll tread carefully."

"No." Mitch shook his head. "I want you comfortable here. He'll be nice and tolerate the cats. Or he can go live with Ellie and Leo. And he does *not* want that."

"You'd kick your roommate out to make room for my cats?" she asked.

Mitch tucked a strand of hair behind her ear. "Yes. Without question."

"Griffin is a jerk?"

"Griffin is great. I like him a lot. His attitude about fainting goats and pot-bellied pigs... which love him, by the way... is hilarious."

"But you'd pick my cats?"

"I pick *you*."

Yeah, reason number seven this was a bad idea... Mitch Landry was pretty damned irresistible.

3

Mitch wanted to take her straight to bed.

And not let her out for two weeks. Or until she promised that she was going to stay in Autre. For six months. He'd say six months anyway. He wanted a hell of a lot more than that, but even six months would be a huge promise for his gorgeous commitment-phobe. He knew this about her. She hadn't kept her allergy to romantic relationships a secret.

It hadn't kept him from falling for her and wanting more though.

And now she was here.

He couldn't believe it. Well, believing that *another* guy had proposed and that it had freaked her out enough that she'd gotten in her car and out of town wasn't that hard to believe.

What the fuck was with the guys in Appleby, Iowa? You didn't just propose to a woman because you found her attractive, you'd known her forever, and you were both single.

Fine, she'd told him that she'd dated the others who had proposed. Not seriously. Not for long. But at least they had a small reason to think that she might say yes. What was with this last guy at her sister's wedding? He hadn't even taken her out to dinner?

Mitch worked on taking a deep breath. There was no need to get riled up about the dumbasses back in Iowa who Paige had turned down. She was here now. With him. In Autre. In his house. And she wasn't leaving at least until after Tori and Josh's wedding. That was three weeks. Three weeks of having her here, with him, showing her what this could be.

Three weeks of having her in his life.

His life that consisted of a huge number of loud, no-filter, nosy-as-hell family members.

They were going to scare her off.

The thought hit him as he stared into her huge blue eyes. The eyes he'd already seen light up with humor and excitement, love—even if it was love for her cats—and passion.

He couldn't let his family spook her. They were exactly like the people she'd traveled a thousand miles to escape. They were involved in everything, around all the time, full of advice and admonishment. They were also, he had to admit, crazier than hers.

Her family was meddlesome.

The Landrys were that... and so much more. They laughed and yelled and couldn't define the word "privacy". But more, they had Cajun customs and traditions and a blue-collar bayou lifestyle that might be a lot for a yoga-practicing, cat-crazy vegetarian from Iowa.

They believed in ghosts, they believed in bayou magic—to varying extents, but they all agreed the bayou was a special place that people didn't fully understand—and they loved fiercely. Which meant taking care of each other and protecting each other, even when the other person didn't want taking care of or protecting.

They also fought like crazy and could hold grudges that sometimes spanned lifetimes.

Paige really couldn't be with him, even temporarily, without being with them all.

That was going to give this woman hives.

He was going to have to work this out somehow. Because he couldn't let her go.

He heard a truck coming down the street and instantly snapped into action.

"We need to go," he told her. "Come on." He grabbed her hand and started for the front door.

The chance that the truck didn't belong to a relative was about point two percent. This wasn't a through street. It dead-ended three houses down from his. The only people driving by were his neighbors. And all three of his neighbors were cousins.

Sure, the truck could be one of those cousins going home with no idea that Paige was here and no intention of stopping at Mitch's.

But the chances that it was a relative coming over to meet Paige were about ninety-nine percent.

They crossed the porch as the truck pulled up behind Paige's car.

Yep, that was Owen. And Maddie. And Kennedy. And Ellie.

He was going to have to have a word with Owen later. He should know better than to enable this.

Then again, Owen would do anything for Maddie.

And then there was Kennedy, who had dirt and secrets on all of them. The brattiest of his Autre cousins, and one of the only girls, Kennedy had always been *around*. They learned when they'd gotten older, and it was too late, that she'd always been paying attention and keeping track of the things they hadn't wanted their parents to find out about.

Maybe the worst of all, though, was Ellie. Their grandmother. The feisty matriarch of the family. *She* could get them all to do just about anything. In part, because they all loved her dearly. And in part, because they were all just a little bit scared of her.

Plus, she cooked for them all every day. You never wanted to piss off the woman who could keep the best gumbo in the state away from you.

"Paige?"

She was staring at the truck full of Landrys. "Yeah?"

"Run."

They sprinted for his truck and scrambled inside as Owen's truck doors opened.

"Hey!"

"Mitch!"

"Dammit!"

That was all he heard as he started the truck and pulled away from the curb.

He only slowed at the stop sign at the end of the street, not coming to a full stop. He looked over at Paige.

She grinned back at him. "That was close."

"You have no idea. Those are just the scouts."

"Just checking me out?"

"That and making sure you don't get away before everyone else showed up."

Her eyes widened. "There were more coming?"

"No doubt. Probably had to load up the food and beer and stuff."

"They were bringing lunch over?"

"Well, there's never *not* a good time for food and beer around here."

She nodded. "Kennedy did tell me that I wasn't going to get any grilled cheese while I'm here."

He glanced over at her. "I'll get you grilled cheese, Paige."

She smiled. "Can I eat it at your house without your whole family?"

He hesitated. "That will be more difficult," he said honestly.

"That's what I figured."

She definitely didn't sound like she thought being included in the big family dinners, grilled cheese or not, was something to look forward to.

He turned the truck out onto a narrow dirt road that cut through the field behind his house. This would take them down to the bayou, a few miles from where the Boys of the Bayou docks were. This was a private road, and the spot where he was taking her was never visited by tourists or really anyone other than the family.

They would be able to get right up to the water's edge, but it was a smaller branch of the bayou that was hard to get to even by boat because of the varying depths of the water. He and Owen and Chase had gotten an airboat stuck out here last summer and had needed Sawyer to come pull them out.

They bumped along the road for a few miles before he slowed. The swamp didn't have specific set boundaries, and it wandered and spread as it liked, so it was a bit of a guessing game as to how far out they could go before the ground got too soft for the truck. High trucks with big tires were fun... and necessary out here.

"Here we go." He turned them down another narrow path, and they drove out from a small cluster of trees. The ground was mushy, but nobody was going to sink.

"Oh, wow," Paige said as the bayou came into view.

"You live by a river," he said as he turned the truck so he could back up, and they could sit in the bed and watch the water meander by.

"Yeah, but the river is different from this," she said.

She was studying the trees. They were mostly big cypress and tupelo. Spanish moss draped the branches creating the stereotypical picture of a swamp.

He shut the truck off. "Let's go sit in back."

She nodded and started to open her door.

"Hang on, Hawkeye," he said, jumping out of the truck. "You're not dressed for this."

She was smiling when he opened her door.

"Hawkeye?" she asked.

"Iowa is the Hawkeye state, right?"

She nodded.

"And Josh calls Tori 'Iowa,' so that can't be your nickname." He held his arms out.

"I need a nickname?" she asked, as she slid to the edge of the seat.

"Well, you'll probably hear a lot of 'darlin' and 'honey' and 'sweetheart,' too," he told her honestly. There was something about her that made him want to use endearments. That was not his norm with the women he dated.

Then again, neither was having them move in with their five cats. He had sleepovers but never more than one night at a time, and he'd never lived with a woman he wasn't related to. And that hadn't happened until his dad got a job that kept him out of town for a few days at a time, and Mitch had moved in with Ellie and Leo.

And he hadn't had a sleepover—or a quickie or even a hot make-out session—with anyone other than Paige in the past six months.

Yeah, there was a lot of "out of the norm" stuff going on here.

"Sweetheart is maybe okay," she told him.

"You don't like darlin' and honey?"

"Darlin' makes me want to take my clothes off, and honey makes me think of lying in bed in the dark, sweaty, and breathing hard after you made me come twice in a row."

He froze with his arms extended to help her out of the truck as his whole body went hard.

"And my grandma calls me sweetheart," she said with a sly smile.

He narrowed his eyes. "Come here... darlin'."

She put her hands on his shoulders as her smile grew. Mitch scooped her up in his arms. She gave a little gasp but then relaxed, letting him carry her to the truck bed. He had boots on, better to handle the marshy ground than the sandals she was wearing, but truthfully, he would have used any excuse to get her into his arms.

He lowered the tailgate with one hand as she clung to him. Then he set her down and climbed up beside her.

"So..." she said.

He prepared for her to say something else flirtatious that would make his cock press even more insistently against his zipper.

"What are those trees?"

He let out a breath and laughed as she pointed to the tupelo trees.

"Those are cypress, right?" she asked, moving her finger to the right. "With Spanish moss."

"Yep. The others are tupelo."

"It's amazing, isn't it?" she asked. "The same river feeds the waterways where we both live, but the swamp is so different from the river in Iowa."

He hadn't really thought about that, but suddenly the idea the water that flowed past her town in Iowa ended up here in his bayou was awesome.

"That is pretty amazing," he agreed after a moment.

"So I read that Spanish moss is harvested and used for a bunch of different things," she said, still looking out at the trees. "They used to stuff mattresses with it and things like that. Now it's more decorative and used for crafts and stuff." She angled him a look. "They put it in voodoo dolls sometimes though."

"You looked up Spanish moss?" For some reason, that touched him.

"I looked up a bunch of stuff about Louisiana in general," she said. "Spanish moss was part of that."

"You were looking into where I live?"

She turned her head and met his gaze. "And where I'm going to be living for a while."

His heart thumped. *Don't overreact. Don't spook her.* "Henry Ford stuffed the first Model T car seats with it," he said, instead of commenting on her living here for the next few months. Or forever.

"Really?"

"Yep. There are dozens of uses."

"And it's not really moss at all," she said. "It's a flowering plant that's actually related to pineapple."

He grinned. "You did do your homework."

She looked pleased. "The Native Americans called it 'tree hair,' and then when the Spanish and French settlers came, they came up with names for it that were supposed to be insulting to the other. Since the French outlasted the Spanish in this area, 'Spanish moss' stuck."

"You've got it," he said. "So do you know about the tupelo tree fruit and honey?"

"No. I didn't read about tupelo trees."

"Well, the Ogeechee tupelos have a fruit we call 'Ogeechee limes.' They're used in drinks and sauces. But what they're *really* known for is the honey. Gets a really high price. Kind of a vanilla flavor. Beekeepers bring their hives down here by boat and float the hives along the water when the trees are blooming in April and May."

"Wow." Paige was looking out at the trees again and seemed genuinely fascinated.

"I'll get you some so you can try it."

"I'd love that." She gave him a sweet smile.

The kind of smile that made him want to declare that she

could have anything she wanted from him for the rest of his days.

He was so screwed here. This woman was going to meet his family and go running.

"We can come down and check out the bees in April, too," he suggested.

Was he pushing his luck asking her to still be here in April? Maybe. Giving her a reason to stick around? Hopefully.

She slid him a look that said it was maybe more pushing his luck. But she nodded. "Maybe."

Well, that wasn't *back the fuck off, buddy.*

"What else do you want to know about the bayou?" he asked.

"I think I want to know what you wanted to get me alone for."

He looked at her. That was a question with many answers. The simplest was that he just wanted to be *with* her. Talk to her, hear her voice, see her face, make her laugh. They'd been apart for a week, and he'd missed her. It had been six months between the first time they met and the second. He'd thought of her constantly, texted her, acknowledged that she was the reason he had no interest in any other women.

But this time… since he'd left Iowa, he'd been nearly aching for her. The texts had still been sweet and fun, but they'd wound him tighter every time one came in. He'd actually talked himself out of getting in his truck and heading back to Appleby twice.

Now she was here. She'd come here, *to him*, of her volition. And now he was wound tight in a new way.

Having her here, in his world, in his life, was going to make it so much harder when she left.

If she left.

No. He couldn't do that. He couldn't think about it like that. He needed to just enjoy the time she was here.

He reached for her hand and threaded his fingers through hers. "I've missed you," he said honestly. "I wanted a chance to find out if you're okay. What you're thinking. What I can do."

She studied their hands, then lifted her eyes to his. "You mean that, don't you?"

"What?"

"That you want to know what you can do for me. How you can make it all better. Without even knowing what 'it' is or what it would take to make it better."

He thought about that. Then lifted a shoulder. "Yeah."

She took a deep breath. "Maybe I should spend the night and then head out."

"Back to Iowa?" His frown was deep and immediate.

"No. Just... maybe I should just road trip. See some sights. I wanted to get away and have alone time. Maybe that's the way to do it. Now that I'm packed up and on the road."

She'd told him last week that she'd been planning a Year of Aloneness—her actual term for it. She felt stifled by her family and frustrated with their expectations and she wanted a chance to do her own thing out from under their watchful eyes. Her plan was pretty specific. She'd been saving up money to go to Colorado Springs. She planned to teach yoga and just live alone, enjoying her space, and the chance to make her own choices without explanation or judgment. For a year. She didn't intend to leave home for good, but she needed a break.

That story had been what prompted him to invite her to Louisiana.

And here she was.

Of course, she'd told him about her Year of Aloneness when he'd told her he was thinking about moving to Iowa to be closer to her to see what could come of this connection they had.

She had pushed back on that immediately. Hard.

He was okay with it, to an extent. She was young. Only twenty-two. She'd been proposed to four... make that now five... times. Her mother wanted nothing more than for her to settle down. Her mom and her older sister and who knew how many other relatives thought her collecting cats instead of having babies was a red flag. They thought her owning a yoga studio instead of doing something "normal" like teaching or running a bakery the way her older sisters did was weird.

Paige just wanted to be left alone.

He did *not* want to leave her alone.

Which meant that he needed to cool it.

"You can't drag those poor cats out on a never-ending road trip," he said, brushing his thumb over the back of her knuckles.

She nodded. "Could I leave them with you?"

He met her eyes. "Leave them here while you travel?"

"Yeah."

He pulled in a breath. If that was what she needed, then yeah, he'd keep her cats. "Yes."

Several seconds passed as they just looked at one another. "Thank you," she said.

"For cat-sitting?" He shrugged. "I've alligator-sat before. Cats move around more, but they won't take off my hand when I feed them, so I'll probably be okay."

Her eyes rounded. "You've *alligator-sat*?"

"Sure."

She shook her head. "Okay. Well, actually, I meant thank you for just agreeing. For being... a friend."

He squeezed her hand. "That's what you need then? A friend?"

"And a roommate."

"You can stay as long as you want to."

She turned on the tailgate to face him. "And the orgasms we talked about."

His body heated. He reached to cup the back of her head

and pulled her in, resting her forehead on his. "Can fucking do."

"Does it *have* to be in your bedroom?" she asked, her breath hot on his lips.

"We'll have to kick Griffin out of the living room some nights."

"I mean..." She was suddenly climbing into his lap on the tailgate. "What about here?"

His hands settled on her hips. She felt so good. Smelled so good. She was gorgeous, and he remembered everything about how she tasted and felt and sounded when they were naked together.

"Whatever you want, darlin'."

She shivered lightly and smiled down at him. "I've been thinking about you non-stop. But my vibrator is a very poor substitute."

He gripped her hips harder. The image of her spread out on her bed in that little apartment in Iowa, naked, using her vibrator while thinking of him, was crystal clear in his mind.

"Did you bring your vibrator to Louisiana with you?"

"I did."

"I'm going to need a replay of some of that."

She gave him a sexy smile. "I think that can be arranged."

"But if you need a good bayou fucking, I can take care of that right now."

Her pupils dilated, and her breath caught. "I do. I do need that."

He skimmed his hand down her side and slipped under the bottom of her t-shirt. His hand slid up to cup one breast, teasing the nipple with his thumb.

She moaned softly. "I've missed you touching me."

More than anything dirty she could have said, those words caused fire to spread through him, making his gut clench and his cock swell.

"Need you, Paige," he said gruffly. He stripped her shirt up and over her head, tossing it behind him into the truck bed.

"Yes." She reached for her bra hooks, but his hands were already there.

The bra joined the t-shirt. He filled his hands with her breasts. He teased both nipples with his fingers, but that wasn't enough for her apparently. She lifted onto her knees, bringing one nipple to his mouth.

"Fuck, yes." He loved when she told and showed him exactly what she needed and wanted. He drew the stiff point into his mouth, sucking softly, then harder when her hand went to the back of his head, urging him closer.

"That makes me so hot." Her voice was breathless.

"Same. You're so fucking delicious," he said, switching sides, licking and sucking and nipping.

She made another moaning sound, and then she was tugging his shirt up. "Need more."

Mitch leaned back just enough to grab the back of his shirt between his shoulder blades and pull it off.

Paige pressed against him, her breasts rubbing over his chest, her soft, silky skin heavenly against his.

"*More,*" she said again.

"Front seat." He grasped her waist and started to lift her.

"No. Here."

"Softer seat up there and the condoms."

"Oh." She gave him a little smile. "Okay, but you need to put some sleeping bags and stuff back here. Soon."

"You asking me to bring you down here regularly?" It was stupid how hot that made him. Making love to Paige along his beloved bayou wasn't a brand, new fantasy but that she was the one suggesting it made it even better.

"Yes. Please." She ran her hands up and down the sides of his neck. "Bring me here and fuck me among the cypress and tupelo trees, Mitch."

His cock hardened even further, and his brain couldn't process anything but *every fucking day*.

He squeezed her ass. "You might regret asking me that."

"Never."

"That makes me want to take you hard and over and over. You might get sore."

She smiled. "Make me sore."

He blew out a breath. "Damn, girl." That was it. He scooped his hands under her ass and slid off the tailgate.

She wrapped her legs and arms around him as he carried her to the front of the truck.

"Take your pants off," he ordered.

She immediately undid the button and zipper of her capris, wiggling on the seat to push them down.

He opened his fly to relieve the pressure of his cock against the zipper but then just watched her.

Capris and a tiny scrap of purple silk were on his truck floor a second later, and Paige Asher was sitting bare-assed naked on his seat. It was a ridiculously erotic picture.

She leaned forward, bracing her hands on the seat between her knees. "Come here, Bayou," she said.

4

He stepped forward. She ran her hands up his sides, over his ribs to his chest.

He loved her touch, but he couldn't keep his hands off of her. He stroked up the outsides of her thighs to her hips then brought his hands together, his thumbs rubbing over her belly and down to her mound.

"Lie back."

She did, propping up on her elbows on the seat. He lifted one of her legs, so her heel was on the seat, the other dangling off the end. He shifted that hanging leg so she was spread open for him.

He took a ragged breath. "Damn, you are so fucking gorgeous. On my truck seat, out here in the wild." He ran a thumb over her clit and down to the wet heat below. He circled, just teasing. Her head fell back, her long blond hair pooling on the seat behind her.

"I'm going to get hard every time I get in this truck from now on." He circled her clit lazily with his thumb.

"Good." The word was breathy.

"Need you to come like this," he told her. "I need you as hot and wet and soft as I can get you because I'm going to fuck you hard and fast."

Her stomach sucked in, and she lifted against his finger. "Yes."

He pressed harder against her clit, rubbing with enough friction to get her climbing. Then he leaned in, replacing his thumb with his mouth as he slid his middle finger into her. She was tight and slick, and the resulting moaned, "*Mitch*," made him push his jeans out of the way and fist his cock to counter some pressure.

He sucked and licked, pumping his finger deep. Her hand gripped the back of the truck seat while her other went to her breast.

The sight of her like this, spread open, her pussy offered up to him, her fingers teasing her own nipple made him growl, low and soft.

"Oh, Mitch, yes."

And then there was the way she said his name like that. As if he was everything she wanted and needed.

At least at this moment, he was. And he intended to keep it that way for the next few minutes.

"I've eaten you like this in my dreams a dozen times," he told her gruffly, stroking his finger deep and then adding a second. "I've made you come, calling my name right here like this."

"I've thought of your dirty mouth every single night," she said, nearly panting.

"While you got yourself off."

"Yes."

"Did you cry out my name, Paige? When you came on your vibrator?"

"Yes."

That fired him up even more. That he was the one she

called out to when she was coming, even when she was alone, made every possessive fiber in him rear its head.

He wasn't typically a dominant, selfish guy. At all. He was easy-going and didn't get worked up about much. It was his best trait. Or so everyone said.

But Paige made him feel like beating his chest and yelling, "*Mine!*" He wanted to take up all her time, all of her thoughts, all of *her.*

He was in so much fucking trouble here.

"Come for me so I can take you," he told her.

She pinched her nipple and lifted closer to his mouth.

He stroked his fingers deep and sucked on her clit harder. His other hand ran up her thigh and over her stomach, stroking back and forth, then around to her ass, lifting her closer.

"Mitch!"

He could feel her inner muscles clamping down, and he picked up the rhythm.

"I could do this all day," he told her honestly. "I love making you sound like that."

She gasped, and then she was coming, her pussy milking his fingers, her thighs shaking.

"That's my girl," he said huskily as she came down slowly, his fingers still deep.

When she'd relaxed into the seat, he withdrew and pulled her hips to the edge of the seat.

Her eyes on him, he pushed his jeans and boxers to his knees. He stroked his cock, the pressure both a relief and a tease.

"I want," she said simply. She pushed herself up to sitting and reached for him.

Her fingers wrapping around his shaft was enough for him to have to grip the open truck door. His fingers dug in as she stroked up and down his length.

"Not sure I've got the stamina for this," he told her, his other hand going to her hair and running through the blond strands. "I've missed you so fucking much."

"Just give me two minutes," she said, her attention on his cock.

He gritted his teeth. Two minutes. Two minutes. He could do two minutes.

She turned on the seat and leaned in so she could lick his head.

"One minute," he said, his jaw tight.

She smiled but didn't even lift her gaze. She took him into her mouth, sliding him over her tongue, then closing her lips and sucking.

She couldn't take him very far, but she kept her hand wrapped around the base of his shaft, squeezing and stroking as she moved her head up and down.

"Paige. Baby. Darlin'," he panted.

"It hasn't been a minute yet," she informed him, moving so she could run her tongue up and down his entire length.

He gripped the truck door harder and curled his fingers into her scalp. "I'm not going to make it."

She lifted her eyes to his. "Do you want to come in my mouth, Mitch?"

Fuck. Yes. And no. He shook his head. "Need your pussy."

"But this is so good." She took him in her mouth again.

He groaned. Then tugged on her hair. "Pussy," he repeated. Firmly.

She lifted her head, a sexy smile on her lips. Then she ran her tongue over her bottom lip.

He reached blindly for the glove box and the condoms he kept there.

He handed it to her. "While you're down there."

Her smile grew. It was full of *I-love-having-power-over-you.* That should probably make him nervous. Her having that power *and* her knowing it. But instead, it made him want to give her everything. For her to know that he was wrapped around her finger and would do anything to make her happy, to make sure she knew how incredible she was, to help her do everything she wanted to do. And that extended so far outside of the bedroom that it actually made his heart squeeze. If she wanted to go, however far away, he would let her. If that's what she wanted and needed.

"We don't need those, remember?" she asked.

He did remember. He definitely remembered. When they'd been together in Iowa, she'd told him she was well protected.

But there were other reasons than not wanting a pregnancy to use them, and that was up to her. "You sure?" he asked.

"So sure."

She lay back on the seat without any urging from him, and all he could do was take her hips, bring her ass just off the edge of the seat, and then thrust.

"Oh, *yes*," Her head fell back, and her eyes closed.

Mitch paused for a moment, taking a deep breath and willing his body to last at least a few minutes before blowing.

When he thought he had control again, he pulled out and thrust forward.

Her body took him as if it had been molded exactly for his cock. Her pussy gripped him, and every time he thrust deep, he hit a spot that caused an "Mmm" sound from her.

This was exactly where he wanted to be. How he wanted to be. Making this woman open up and feel good and love being with him.

If it was only sex for now, so be it. He'd make everything else about her stay on the bayou as amazing as he could too.

He gripped her hips. "What do you want, Paige?"

"More. Harder."

Well, that he could absolutely do. He picked up the pace, thrusting faster and deeper.

"Yes. Yes. Yes." She gasped and moaned.

That was exactly what he was going for. He took her ass in his hands, changing the angle and drove deeper.

"Oh, *yes*," was her response to that.

Then she nearly killed him. She reached for her clit, rubbing and circling as he fucked her harder.

"Baby, yes. Make yourself come on my cock," he told her roughly, gripping her ass tighter.

Her circles got faster, and he felt the result on his shaft. He pumped deep, fast, the sounds of skin on skin and her moaning and his harsh breathing combining with the calls of the bayou birds and the singing of the insects.

This was fucking perfect.

A moment later, she was there, crying out his name, her body clamping down on his, her neck arching.

He let go then, plunging deep, letting his orgasm claim him.

He groaned her name, his body shuddering as he came.

Her legs tightened, around his hips, as if wanting to hold him still, right there, wanting everything he was giving her.

He slumped forward, bracing his hands on the truck seat on either side of her. Her legs around him, held him in place, as the waves of pleasure slowly faded, and his breathing started to even out.

He was sweating, but his body felt more relaxed than it had in…since he'd last been spent from sex with Paige.

"You okay?" he asked her.

Her eyes were still shut. One arm rested over her chest, and the other hung off the seat.

Her lips curved into a smile, but she didn't open her eyes. "I'm so damned good, I never want to move."

That sent a shot of satisfaction through him that was surprising in its intensity.

It was sex. He'd made lots of women feel that way.

But there was something about giving Paige the I-want-to-stay-like-this-forever feeling of pleasure that meant a hell of a lot more.

Maybe because she was difficult. She was anti-staying anywhere for long at the moment. She was here for a short-term fling and getaway. She'd either head back to Iowa or out to Colorado when she was done here.

He wasn't sure what "done" looked like exactly. She'd told him a week ago that she was saving money to live in Colorado for a year. Maybe that's what would determine how long she was here. He'd offered her a free place to stay and a job if she came to Louisiana.

Or maybe she was using Josh and Tori's wedding as her timeline. That was three weeks away. There would be a lot of fun preparations and celebrations leading up to that.

Of course, that would all involve his whole family, which was probably the last thing that would convince her to stay.

He finally pulled back. While he got rezipped and buttoned, Paige reached for her pants and panties. Mitch went to the truck bed to grab their shirts and her bra.

When they were both fully dressed, he leaned back in, bracing his hands on the seat again, caging her in. He kissed her long and slow. Her hands ran up his shoulders, then to the back of his head, as if wanting to hold him in place.

Yeah, he'd love for her to want more of this. All of this. Often.

Forever.

He lifted his head. "You wanna sit in back some more?"

She nodded. "We should talk."

He shifted back. He wasn't so sure he wanted to talk. For fear of the things she'd say. Like reminding him that she wasn't staying, no matter how good the sex was.

With a deep breath, he stepped back and held out his hand. She looked relieved when she took it and let him tug her forward and then sweep her up to carry her to the truck bed again.

He climbed up beside her and was surprised, but pleased, when she scooted close and draped one leg over his thigh. He settled his hand on her knee.

"Okay, tell me what you need."

She met his eyes. "Really?"

"Why the surprise?"

"I don't remember the last time someone asked what I need. Other than you asking me what I'd like you to do to me." Her smile was mischievous and sexy.

He couldn't resist leaning in and giving her a quick kiss. "Really," he said against her lips. "Tell me what you need while you're here in Louisiana."

She took a deep breath, and he leaned back.

"Okay, I think I need some rules."

"Rules?"

"Yeah. For us. For what we're going to do and expect while I'm here. And some structure around how things are going to go."

He nodded, trying very hard not to squeeze her knee and beg her to stay. "Got it. Okay. Well, you told me that you planned to go to Colorado for a year and were saving up money."

"Right." She paused. Then said, "I found a yoga studio that will need another instructor. And there's an apartment that will open up around that same time."

Mitch felt his chest tighten. He might have squeezed her knee too. "When?"

"August."

He was able to take a breath. "That's seven months."

"Yeah." Paige tucked her hair behind her ear. "I was kind of thinking that staying here, getting to know Louisiana, just being away from Appleby and everyone, while I save up money over those seven months might be nice."

He nodded, trying not to slump in obvious relief. Seven months wasn't forever, but it was better than three weeks.

"You can stay as long as you want," he finally said.

She smiled, and his next heartbeat was a little harder.

"Can I help you with the otter enclosure? Or other projects or something?" she asked.

He grinned. "I don't know if you're really the manual-labor-outside-all-day type."

She shrugged. "I'm not. You'll have to teach me."

"Not that I don't want you around, but I have a better idea," he told her.

"Yeah?"

"The Boys of the Bayou is my cousins' business. Swamp boat tours and fishing and hunting expeditions."

She nodded. He'd told her about the business before.

"They need a receptionist in the office. Someone to take reservations and keep the tour schedule and greet the customers when they show up for the tours. Manage the gift shop. Stuff like that."

"No one's doing that now?"

"Kennedy was," he said with a grin. "But she's helping Bennett with his foundation, and she's busy on some boards and committees for the Governor. Oh, and she's going to be Mayor of Autre."

Paige's eyes widened. "She is? Really?"

"Really. There's a special election in May, and everyone loves her. Oh, and no one's running against her." He grinned. "So yeah, she's really busy. And Bennett's loaded, so she doesn't have to work for money anymore."

He was really happy for Kennedy and Bennett. They seemed like total opposites, but they got each other in a way that made

Mitch downright jealous sometimes. They also shared a passion for making people's lives better and for protecting the environment, particularly the bayou, and that made their mission for public service in government, local and bigger, meaningful.

"So. Wow." Paige was still obviously processing that.

"Anyway, she was the receptionist until recently. Now everyone is trying to pitch in and make it work. Maddie is even doing tours with Sawyer, Owen, and Josh because the business has grown, and there just isn't anyone who can do the job full-time."

Paige nodded slowly. "I could do that."

He grinned. This was perfect.

Well, not *perfect*. It would allow her to save up money to go to Colorado. But with this setup, he could help his family with their business *and* Paige with what she wanted.

It might not be what *he* wanted, but what she needed would trump that for him every time.

That was how he knew he was falling for her. Or had already fallen for her.

He would do anything he could for the people around him. The town, Paige's home town, even the visitors who came for swamp boat tours. That was just who he was. He did whatever he could to make things around him better.

But when it came to his family, it was next level. He'd move heaven and earth. Sacrifice anything of his own. Even put himself in danger.

And he felt the same way about Paige.

Already.

"That actually sounds really great," she said. "Will they go for it?"

"They? You mean Sawyer and Maddie and Owen and Josh?"

She nodded.

"No question about it."

They needed the help, but even if they hadn't, if Mitch had come to them with a suggestion that would help someone he cared about, they'd do it. The love and loyalty, and support went both ways in the Landry family.

"Well, then that's great."

She was studying his hand where it rested on her leg and chewing her bottom lip.

"What else?" he prompted.

She sighed and lifted her gaze. "Just... what this is with us."

"This is whatever you want it to be."

He meant that. He wanted more than he knew she was going to give, but he could deal with that. He wasn't going to make this hard on her.

"Wow," she said softly. "You really mean that."

"Of course."

"It's just... I mean, I'm used to my family pushing me to go on dates and settle down and get a real job and get married. I have guys I've known my whole life asking me to marry them after a couple of dinners. Everyone is just always pressuring me. I guess I'm not used to someone actually really caring what I want without thinking they know better. And I'm not used to them being okay with it when what I want isn't what they want."

And all of that was exactly why he was going to do the right thing here and let her call the shots. It was the reason she was here in the first place, and he was damned glad she was. For however long it lasted.

Her hair had fallen forward from behind her ear, and he reached to tuck it back again. "No pushing," he said.

She pressed her lips together and nodded.

"So tell me exactly what you want from me."

"To hang out. Get to know you better. See where and how you live. Laugh." She leaned in. "Kiss. A lot."

He pressed his lips to hers, then released her. "Done. All of that."

"But—" she added.

He sighed. "Lay it on me."

"Maybe separate rooms?"

Shit. He should have seen that coming. He took a breath and let it out. "Okay."

"Really?"

"My house has four bedrooms. Only two are in use. You want your own space you can have it."

Fuck. He hated all of that.

"I want to spend some time in your room though," she said. "Is that terrible? Does that make me a tease? Is that not fair to you?"

Well, he hadn't even thought about touching another woman since he'd met her, so it wasn't as if he'd be having women over if they were just roommates.

"It's fair if we both know upfront that we're roommates with benefits. And friends," he said.

She nodded but didn't say anything for several seconds. Finally, she responded with, "You're a really good guy."

Yeah, he'd been told that all his life. It was what he worked to be. What he prided himself on.

But now he thought that maybe he was just a dumbass.

5

There was no one waiting for them at his house when they got back.

Which was a surprise and a relief. But Mitch needed to talk to his family.

He and Paige went in through the backdoor, stepping into the kitchen.

"Tell you what," he said. "You make yourself a grilled cheese. I need to head up to Ellie's."

"I don't have to go?" She winced. "I mean... should I go?"

He gave a short huff of a laugh. "Not this time. I'll tell them about you wanting the receptionist job and everything, get that ironed out. There will be plenty of time to meet everyone."

That was an understatement. His family was going to be pissed when he showed up without Paige.

"Okay." She hesitated.

"What do you need?"

The look on her face with his question was a combination of surprise and relief and gratitude that was becoming familiar already.

Did no one in this woman's life give a shit how *she* was feeling or what she wanted?

"Maybe you could bring back some bread pudding?" she asked.

That was not what he'd been expecting. He grinned and nodded. "Absolutely. But I'll warn you," he said, moving in close. "One taste, and you might find yourself heading up to Ellie's on your own sometime."

"That good, huh?"

"Yep."

She seemed to be thinking it over. Then she nodded. "Yeah. Bring it. I mean, I'm going to meet and get to know them all when I'm working at the office, right?"

"For sure."

It was going to be like throwing red meat to wild cats, as a matter of fact.

"But Ellie's is right across the road from the office, so at least that's a perk to having to put up with them all."

And he wasn't exaggerating when he said them *all*.

Leo, his grandfather, drove the bus for the tour company that picked tourists up in New Orleans and delivered them back to their hotels after their bayou tours.

Sawyer, Owen, Josh, and Maddie, Owen's fiancée, actually did the tours, taking airboats full of visitors out onto the bayou to see the plant and animal life and to teach them about this unique part of the world.

Kennedy, until recently, had been the receptionist and general wrangler of everyone, from employees to visiting kids to otters and the occasional snake and even a gator a time or two.

Yeah, he was going to have to mention the alligators and snakes to Paige. And how to get rid of them if they showed up.

And he would. Eventually.

Ellie and Cora owned and operated the bar across the

road. They served locals and tourists alike and had everything from gumbo and fried alligator balls to Hurricanes and beer on the menu. They even hosted a crawfish boil every Friday night.

The rest of the family were regulars at the bar and did a lot of "popping in" at the tour company office.

Aunts, uncles, cousins, even Mitch's dad, showed up for food and drink, but more for the gossip and laughter.

His dad, Sean, was a shrimp boat captain. He'd worked for others for a long time but had finally bought his own boat. He worked long hours and didn't make the trip to Autre daily, but he definitely stopped in whenever he could, and Mitch talked to him every day.

Mitch's cousins, Fletcher, Zeke, and Zander, all worked in Autre too.

Fletcher was a teacher. He'd always been into books, and the other guys had called him Einstein even as they begged to copy off his papers and tried to bribe him to do their homework. Which he only ever did once. Incorrectly. After his brothers had failed their English assignments because of him, they'd stopped asking.

Zeke and Zander, his twin brothers, also worked locally.

Zeke owned his own construction company and was an accountant on the side. Which was hilarious. Especially, considering all the shit he'd given Fletcher about being a nerd. Zeke just kept his geek tendencies hidden underneath his long hair, tattoos, and penchant for motorcycles.

Zander was the local cop. He'd been a detective in New Orleans for a couple of years, but as soon as the long-time town cop retired, Zander stepped in. He claimed he'd always wanted to serve and protect his hometown. The truth was, the gig here was a lot easier and gave him more fishing time than his job in New Orleans had.

So, yeah, Paige was going to "get" to meet a lot of people. In fact, the moment they all heard she was in the Boys of the Bayou office, he wasn't going to be able to keep them away.

"I'll be back soon," he said, kissing Paige on top of the head. "Soon-ish," he amended.

She smiled up at him. "I'll eat and unpack and hang with the cats. I'm very good at being alone."

Yeah, and she liked it.

That was definitely going to be a problem around here.

Mitch headed for Ellie's. It was nearing dinner time—the best time to catch as many family members as possible—though he couldn't be sure who would be there.

Josh, Owen, Maddie, and Sawyer often had evening tours—sunset over the bayou was something to see—and even a few night-time tours a week. The swamp was nice and spooky at night, and those tours were popular.

But business was a little slower this time of year. In part because fewer people traveled in January, in part because there were much cooler temperatures, even in Louisiana, and in part because the animals—particularly the gators that so many came to see—were much less active in the cold.

He grinned. Cold was definitely a relative term. After his time in Iowa, he wasn't sure he'd ever call *any* temperatures in Louisiana *cold*. Paige was in a t-shirt and capris today, for fuck's sake. And he'd been able to get her *out* of those clothes outdoors, and neither of them had felt the least bit chilled.

He couldn't wait to show her all of the fun ways their home states were different. And yet, their *hometowns* weren't all that different. They were small, and everyone knew everyone else and helped each other, and there was history and roots. Paige had some mixed feelings about all of that, he knew, but seven months was a nice chunk of time. Plenty of time for her to get to know Autre. And him. And maybe change her mind.

He parked on the side of Ellie's. There wasn't really a parking lot. The bar sat along a dirt road on a lot that was also mostly dirt. And some straggling grass. People often walked to the bar. Autre wasn't very big. A lot of his relatives lived not just walking distance to the bar, but yelling distance from their front porches to one another.

Ellie and Cora lived in the two houses just east of the bar. Sawyer and Juliet, Josh and Tori, and Owen and Maddie were within a three-block radius. Sawyer and Josh's mom and dad lived a street to the north. Mitch had spent a lot of time between that house and Ellie's, permanently moving in with Ellie and Leo when he started junior high.

He headed in through the side door that led into the kitchen.

Cora was at the stove. As always.

"Hey, honey," she greeted with her big, bright smile.

He leaned over and kissed her cheek. "Hey. Everyone here?"

"Yep. Out front."

"Because they think I'm bringing Paige over?"

She looked up. "Of course. Where is she?"

"My house."

Cora studied him. "She's not coming up tonight?"

"Nope."

"Her idea or yours?"

"Mine."

Cora nodded. "Okay."

Cora was the sweeter of the two older ladies who ran this place. His grandmother was a lot of things, but no one described her as sweet.

Not that Cora didn't want Paige up here and spilling her secrets and stories. Cora was as interested in it all as anyone. She was just a little more easy-going about it.

"You want to come out and hear the deal?" he asked her.

"There's a deal?"

He nodded. "There is."

Cora wiped her hands on her apron. "Well, then, of course I do."

Mitch held the swinging door that led to the main part of the bar open for his grandmother's best friend.

Sure enough, everyone was there. Most nights, *most* of them were here. But everyone was accounted for tonight, and that was unusual. He knew it had to do with Paige. They fully expected him and Paige to show up here tonight.

"Mitchell Landry," Ellie scolded the moment he stepped out from the kitchen.

"Hey, Ellie." He continued past her as if he had no idea she was upset with him or why.

He headed for the tables at the back of the restaurant where the family gathered, leaving the front tables for guests. Most of the town felt like family, so it was more a formality than anything, but it was habit that the family used the big ten-top table and the ones around it to gather and eat, talk, bullshit, and even fight. Like any family, they had disagreements and told each other to fuck off from time to time. But when the next meal rolled around, they'd all be there.

It was a sure sign that something was up when he pulled out a chair, and everyone shut up and looked at him.

Getting this group to *all* shut up at the same time took a near miracle.

Or some really juicy piece of news.

Mitch sank into his chair and looked around as if he had no idea what *they* were expecting.

Kennedy swiveled to look around the room behind her, then faced him again. "Hey."

He lifted a brow. "Hey."

"You scare her off already?"

"Nope."

"Did *she* scare *you* off? I didn't think she looked crazy, but

I've been around all of you so long I'm not sure I could spot crazy anymore."

"Nope."

She narrowed her eyes. "Then where is she?"

"I realize that this phrase doesn't have a lot of meaning to you," Mitch said. "But maybe your hotshot lawyer fiancé could explain it." He leaned in. "It's none of your business."

"Mitchell!" Kennedy gasped. "How dare you say such a horrible thing to me."

Mitch looked at Bennett. "No help?"

Bennett held up a hand. "Normally, I'd be on your side, but Kennedy has special powers over me. I can't tell her she can't have things she wants."

"Sex is not a special power," Mitch told him.

"Maybe you're not having the right kind of sex," Owen piped up. "Maddie gets anything she wants from me too."

Maddie nodded. "I do."

"Thing is," Mitch said. "I'm not having sex with *you all*. So I don't have to give you *anything*."

"But you *are* having sex?" Owen clarified. "Kennedy said Paige is gorgeous."

Well, that was kind of like saying the bayou was wet. Mitch looked at his cousin. "Yeah?"

Kennedy nodded. "Oh, yeah. And she was jealous for a minute there when she thought I was a girlfriend."

Mitch had to admit he liked that. He wanted Paige to know —and believe—that he was all into *her* and not interested in anyone else. But knowing that she wanted him to herself was definitely nice.

"Okay, here's the deal," Mitch said, shifting forward and resting his elbows on the table.

"Ellie!" Leo called. "He's starting!"

"Not without me!" Ellie called back. "I will cut you off from fried pickles for a month!"

Mitch did really like fried pickles. All pickles, but especially ones dipped in batter and fried. He waited.

Ellie finished what she was doing behind the bar, and she and Cora headed for the table.

Mitch looked around. Sawyer and Juliet were at the far end of the table. Josh was next to them with Owen on his other side. Maddie was in the chair next to Owen but was snuggled so close they could have shared a seat. Kennedy and Bennett were next to them. Zeke and Zander lounged at the next table with Fletcher.

Everyone was here except Tori and Griffin.

He was definitely going to have to fill Griffin in, since he was going to have a new roommate for a few months.

"Where's Tori?" Mitch asked Josh, assuming the two vets were together.

"Delivering twin calves," Josh said. "She and Griff won't be here for a while. But she and Paige are friends. She's gonna be thrilled Paige is here."

Mitch nodded. That was good. A friend who wasn't a crazy Landry, by blood anyway, would be good for Paige. Tori had come into this family in a similar way. She'd showed up on the docks one day looking for Josh after they'd met the previous year at Mardi Gras. She'd been thrown into this bunch with no warning or prep time. She'd be able to give Paige some tips. Or at least sympathy.

"You'll fill her in?"

Josh shrugged. "Of course."

"Without embellishment?" Mitch added.

"I didn't say that." Josh grinned at him.

Mitch sighed. "Okay, here's the rules about Paige."

"There are *rules*?" Kennedy asked.

"Yes."

"What do you mean by rules?"

"I'm going to tell you."

"But, like, these are *her* rules or your rules?"

"How about you shut up, and I'll explain?" Mitch asked.

Kennedy frowned and crossed her arms. "I don't like rules."

"We're all very aware of that." Bennett pulled Kennedy closer and said something in her ear.

Kennedy rolled her eyes, but she relaxed a little.

Mitch regarded his family. God, he loved these people. They had done so much for him. He'd been the only child of a single father who hadn't expected to ever *be* a father and who had had no idea what he was doing. After Mitch's mom had left them, Sean had admitted he couldn't do it alone and asked for help. The family had stepped up. Big time.

Mitch had never lacked for female influence in his life. Or male, for that matter. He'd never been hungry or alone or scared. He'd always felt loved and secure. He hadn't had a mother of his own, but he'd had five motherly figures in Ellie, Cora, and his aunts Hannah, Callie, and Elizabeth. He'd never needed anything.

He loved them fiercely. He'd do anything for them.

And at least once a week, he wondered what it would be like to be *alone* for a week. Or a month. He was sure he'd like it.

"Well, come on then," Ellie said. "I've got work to do."

Mitch was almost never the center of attention with this group. He was fine with that. It was very easy to blend into the background with this family. They were loud and rowdy and fun and full of energy. He rarely had to say more than a dozen words at dinner time. He didn't have funny and exciting stories, like the guys did about their tours, or that Juliet did about some of the people she met through her legal work, or that Zeke and Zander had about their group of friends.

He also didn't exaggerate like Leo and Owen and Fletcher. They made every story just a tad—okay, often more than a tad —bigger and funnier and more exciting.

He also never had everyone's full attention all at once.

Suddenly he was very glad about that. This group was intense.

"Spill it," Leo told him.

"Yeah, Mitch, tell us *everything*," Owen said.

"No way," Mitch said. He gave his cousin a grin, though, and he knew that Owen knew, just with that, how happy Mitch was to have Paige here.

"Good for you," Owen said with a chuckle.

"Rules," Mitch said. "Paige is here *temporarily*. She's gonna work as the new receptionist at the tour company. No one is gonna talk to her about staying, about how great she's doing and how much you'd love for her to take the job for good, or about any other job. No giving her a job in your office." He directed that at Bennett, then looked at Juliet. "Or yours." He looked over at Zeke and Zander.

"We really could use some help with the phones," Zeke said with a grin.

"Paige isn't available."

"Well, what are we going to do with the receptionist position after she leaves?" Maddie asked.

"Hire someone else," Mitch said.

"Well, maybe we're interested in someone who can give us more of a commitment right now," Sawyer added.

"Too bad," Mitch told him. "You need someone now and she's here now."

He knew they'd give her the job. That wasn't even really a question. They were just giving him shit.

"How long will she be here?" Josh asked.

"'Til August. As long as no one scares her off."

"Scares her off?" Juliet repeated. "How would we do that?"

Mitch snorted. There were a number of ways a family like his—a huge number of people who had settled in one place and *settled* deep—could spook a commitment-phobe like Paige.

"No talking long-term or forever type stuff. No asking her for more of a commitment or any promises," he said.

"What's this girl's problem?" Sawyer asked with a little frown.

"Nothing." Mitch frowned back at him. "She wants to hang out here for a few months, get to know Louisiana, enjoy some bread pudding. Just simple, basic stuff without anyone getting ideas about her putting down roots or doing anything more serious."

"So, she's on vacation," Maddie said.

"Yeah."

"An extended vacation though," Leo pointed out. "August is a long ways off."

Mitch nodded. "But she's heading to Colorado then."

"What's in Colorado?" Ellie asked.

"A job." It was really best to keep this simple.

"What kind of job?" Kennedy asked. "What does she do?"

"She's a yoga instructor."

There was a beat of silence. Then Juliet said, "She could do that here."

Of course, she could. Yoga was something she could do anywhere. And Autre didn't have a yoga studio. Not that people were really *demanding* yoga services here. But she had a free place to stay and wouldn't have many expenses here. She wouldn't have to try to make millions.

Mitch shut that down immediately. See, this is what he was going to have to work on. There weren't a lot of reasons Paige *couldn't* stay.

Except that she didn't want to.

"We can win her over," Cora said. "You know we can. If you want us to."

Mitch looked up at her. Her words made something knot in his gut.

"We definitely can," Juliet said. "I came here with no intention of staying, and it took about ten minutes with you all to make me fall in love."

Ellie looked over at her eldest grandson's fiancée. Her expression was full of happiness and affection. Everyone knew Ellie loved Juliet and Tori, the girls who had come to the bayou for simple, temporary reasons. They were now as much a part of Ellie's family and heart as Maddie, Cora's granddaughter, who she'd known all of Maddie's life, and Kennedy, Ellie's own granddaughter.

"Yeah, but Sawyer had a lot to do with that," Fletcher said from the next table. "Paige has only got Mitch."

There were several head nods at that, and Mitch scowled at them all. "Fuck off."

They all laughed.

"Well, Sawyer *did* have a lot to do with that," Juliet said, squeezing the big man's thigh.

His eyes were full of love and even a little heat when he looked at her.

"But I fell for the rest of you too. And the town and the bayou. And all the craziness." Juliet said.

"You do *not* like the bayou," Maddie told her friend with a grin.

"I like *looking* at it," Juliet said.

Everyone knew that Juliet was not a fan of being in or even on the water. She put on hip-waders and a life jacket when she had to get too close to it, just in case. *Just in case* was Juliet's favorite phrase. But she'd overcome some of her fears of the water in her time in Autre. Still, she was a firm-dry-land kind of girl for the most part.

"Here's the deal," Mitch said.

Again, all eyes were on him. He didn't like it. He wasn't used to it. At all.

And they were terrible listeners anyway.

"Paige is young. She's only twenty-two. And she's... been proposed to five times."

Several pairs of eyes rounded at that.

He nodded. "Yeah."

"Damn," Owen said. "She must really be something."

"She is." Mitch couldn't disagree there.

"And she wants to hang out with *you* when she could have pretty much any guy she meets?" Zeke asked.

Mitch nodded but then said, "Because I promised *not* to propose."

Ellie rolled her eyes. Leo shook his head.

"Never make a promise to a woman you can't keep," Leo said.

"I can keep this one," Mitch told him. "She's said upfront she doesn't want to get married for a *very* long time, if ever."

"So why did she come clear down here from Iowa to hang out with you for seven months?" Maddie asked.

"Because every time she turns down a proposal, her mom gets more worried." Mitch sighed. This wasn't really that hard to understand when Paige explained it. "She was engaged," he told them, backing up in the story Paige had told him in Iowa last week. "She and her mom's best friend's son were dating, and the families were thrilled. He proposed right after graduation, and she said yes. Then she broke things off in the middle of wedding planning. Broke his heart and everyone else's. Disappointed her mother deeply. Now her mom worries that she'll never settle down and have a family."

"Well, getting married and having kids isn't for everyone," Maddie said.

Juliet nodded. "I have girlfriends who are nearing thirty and have no plans to get married. At least not yet. Twenty-two is really young."

Mitch nodded. "Exactly. But where she's from, it's just... expected. Her family is big and all lives in her hometown and is all in everyone else's business." He looked around the table and got several smiles. Yeah, that sounded very familiar to all of them. "So, with all of these expectations and her mother's constant desire to set her up and with this most recent proposal..." He frowned thinking about that. Jesus. He thought she was amazing, of course, but these Appleby guys just pulled engagement rings out left and right, it seemed.

"How recent?" Josh asked.

"Two days ago. At her sister's wedding reception."

Josh's brows shot up. "She was just with *you* at the festival. Well, *me*. Everyone saw us there. We were holding hands and everything."

"*You* were holding Paige's hand?" Kennedy asked her brother. "Where was Tori?

"Pretending to be Mitch's fiancée," Josh said with a grin.

Mitch sighed as the group's attention swung back to him. Yeah, this all *seemed* simple when he thought about it, but explaining it made it seem convoluted.

"I showed up in Appleby to surprise Paige," Mitch said. "Everyone wanted to know why. Paige panicked and told them I was there to repair her furnace. And that I was her friend Tori's fiancé. Then Josh and Tori came over to the festival the next day and, obviously, I had to play that part. That left Josh as the extra cousin who had tagged along and who was then flirting with Paige on the impromptu double date."

Everyone took a second to process that.

"Anyway," Mitch said. "I guess her having a blind date to the Apple Festival didn't faze this guy at the wedding reception."

"Wow, deep and abiding love there," Juliet said dryly.

"For obvious reasons, she's a little skittish about the ideas of proposals and weddings and settling down," Mitch said. "So, I offered her a place to get away to for a while and—" He shrugged. "She took me up on it."

"But *you* have no intention of getting serious?" Kennedy asked.

"Nope."

But only because Paige doesn't want that.

The truth was, proposing to her didn't seem that crazy to him. For *him* to do. Not some Iowa jackass.

"You're just going to be... what then?" Kennedy pressed, "Just friends?"

"Well... yeah."

Sure. They could just be friends.

He was pretty sure.

6

"Uh-huh."

"Sure."

"Okay."

Those were the general reactions around the table to Mitch's claim.

"What?" He scowled at them. "Paige doesn't want anything serious, so I'm not going to get serious."

It's not like he got serious with women anyway. This shouldn't be so hard to believe. He dated very casually. More often than not, he just hooked up. Sometimes more than once with the same woman, of course, but they never made promises.

Finally, Ellie spoke. "So, Paige came here because she needs an emotionally safe place to be until her job in Colorado starts. She trusted Mitch to be a friend and not put expectations or pressures on her. She clearly feels comfortable staying with him, and he's now here asking us to support him and have both of their backs."

Mitch nodded as his grandmother summarized the situation.

"Then that's what we'll do," she said. "We will help you and Paige have exactly what you want—a friendship that is safe and supportive and happy without anyone getting hurt."

Mitch nodded again. He felt everyone's eyes on him, but he focused on Ellie. "That's what I need from you all."

"Then that's what you'll get." She gave him a smile that was full of love. "Whatever you need."

"Thank you."

Ellie looked around the table. "Everyone got that?"

Everyone nodded, though not many looked totally convinced.

"Do you really think she should be living with you then?" Sawyer asked from the end of the table.

Mitch frowned. "Why not?"

"Just seems that living with a woman you're crazy about for seven months isn't the best way to keep things casual."

"I'm not going to push her for more than she wants to give," Mitch said, his frown deepening.

"But it will be hard on *you*," Juliet said. "You are being her friend, giving her a place to go when she needed to get away. That's great. But there's plenty of other places for her to stay."

There were nods around the table.

Of course, there were. There were multiple houses in the family, and none of them were full to the brim.

"What? She's gonna come stay with you and Sawyer?" Mitch asked.

"No," Sawyer said immediately. "Juliet and I need the whole house to ourselves."

Owen snorted. "You can't have sex in one room with the door shut?"

Sawyer, who had been a grumpy asshole a lot of the time before Juliet had shown up, shrugged. "Not for seven months."

Juliet blushed.

"Why not?" Owen countered, his grin huge. "It's kind of what bedrooms are for."

"It's not what my bedroom is for," Cora said. Cora had been widowed for years and didn't date. Her late husband had been the love of her life, and she wasn't interested in being with anyone else.

"And you and Maddie were sure using your kitchen in ways that went beyond cooking the other day when I stopped by," Fletcher said from the next table.

"You ignored the t-shirt on the door handle," Owen said with a shrug. "That's your own fault."

"I wasn't complain' about the view of Maddie's bare ass I got as she ran upstairs," Fletcher said, shooting Maddie a grin. "Just sayin'."

Maddie shook her head. "I'm not sure if I should be blushing right now or saying thank you."

"Thank you," Fletcher assured her. "Nothin' to be embarrassed about."

"Then thank you very much, Fletcher. What a lovely thing to say," Maddie told him, her tone dry.

"What, no compliments for *my* ass?" Owen asked. "You got a pretty good look at that too."

"And a lot more," Fletcher agreed. "But dude, I have a mirror. I mean, it's not really fair to you to compare, I know, but I can't help it."

"You tell yourself that," Owen said. "I don't want to hurt your pretty boy feelings."

Mitch couldn't help but grin. His family shared everything. Which meant they often *over* shared. There were very few filters and very few topics that were considered out of bounds.

"Pretty boy?" Fletcher asked. He stretched tall, making his muscles bunch and ran a hand through his hair. It hung to the top of his collar, and Maddie and Tori both complained that he had better hair than they did.

Zeke and Zander had longer hair too. They wore it pulled back in ponytails a lot of the time or sometimes "man buns." At least that was what Kennedy called the style. They both had tattoos too, and Zeke had a few piercings.

Owen and Josh both had tattoos as well, but nothing like the younger Landrys. They were all just a touch wilder. Owen had done some pretty stupid shit in his time. He loved women and loved a good party and raised hell growing up. He and Maddie had been pretty wild *together*, as a matter of fact.

But Fletch, Zeke, and Zander were just a bit *more*. It was hard to put his finger on it, but Mitch always knew that going out with Owen meant he'd have a really good time. Going out with the others meant he'd have a really good time and possibly need bail. Or stitches.

Okay, Owen had spent some time in the little cell in downtown Autre. And in the hospital. There was an epic story about Owen and Maddie's brother, Tommy, and a plate-glass window. It had always been Owen taking the younger guys to parties with him when they weren't quite old enough.

So, it was all Owen's fault. Yeah, that made sense.

"You are such a pretty boy," Josh agreed. "The hair, the jewelry."

"Jewelry?" Fletcher asked, dropping his arms. "This?" He pointed to the ear that was pierced.

"And that." Josh pointed at his wrist.

"This is a leather band," Fletcher said, holding his arm up.

"It's a bracelet," Josh said.

"It's leather."

"So?"

"So..." Fletcher looked at Zeke and Zander.

They just shrugged.

"Well, the girls don't mind," Fletcher said, reaching for his beer. "I care a lot more about what they think than what you think."

Mitch grinned as he sat, taking this all in. This was how it usually was with his family. He got to sit back, listen to them all, watch them all. And just be. He definitely didn't need to be the center of attention.

There were plenty of attention hogs in the family.

Mitch let the conversation, joking, and laughter go on for another ten minutes, but finally, he pushed his chair back and stood. Thankfully, Zeke was getting up as well.

Mitch didn't even bother to tell them he was heading out. Obviously, he was leaving. The family did keep track of one another, but at the same time, it was pretty easy for them to all guess where he would be. Ellie's, the docks, or his house. Or in his truck traveling in about a thirty-mile radius of Autre. He didn't get too far from home. None of them really did.

It was interesting that all the Landrys who had settled down had done so with people who had come to Autre intending to stay only temporarily but who now called it home. Tori, Juliet, and Bennett were all from elsewhere. Maddie was from here but had lived in California for twelve years. Still, when she'd come back that last time, she hadn't intended to stay. Not for good.

So, it was *possible* that Paige might decide to stay.

Mitch shut that thought down immediately.

Ellie stopped him on his way out the back door.

"Sawyer has a point."

Mitch looked at his grandmother. "About?" But he knew what she was talking about.

"Living with a woman who you'd like to be more serious with but who doesn't want that."

"You think I'm going to get my heart broken?"

She nodded. "I do."

He felt his eyes widen. "Really?"

"You already have feelings for her. I was there when you

called Chase and told him you were thinking about staying in Iowa," she reminded him.

Chase, one of his best buddies and Juliet's younger brother, had been in Autre for Christmas. He was in medical school at Georgetown and so didn't live in Autre, but he had every intention of returning to the bayou to be their small-town doctor. Bailey, the alligator conservationist he'd fallen in love with, had a lot to do with that.

Another example of someone not from here who'd spent a short time in Autre and upended his whole life plan to come back.

"Yeah. And she shot it down right away," Mitch said about the idea of him staying in Iowa.

"And now she's here and staying for a while."

Mitch put a hand on a hip and regarded his grandmother. "You know, you're not usually the one talking people *out* of falling in love."

In fact, his whole family was love and happily-ever-after crazy.

Ellie nodded. "Well, Josh and Owen and Sawyer and Kennedy wanted to fall in love."

Mitch laughed. "I don't remember Sawyer and Kennedy *wanting* to fall for Juliet and Bennett."

Ellie smiled. "Just because they didn't realize it didn't mean it wasn't true."

Ah. "And me? You don't think I'm ready or want to fall in love?"

That made a jab of pain hit him in the chest.

He was ready.

That thought stunned him slightly. He was crazy about Paige, yes. He had an inkling that he could fall in love with her. But he hadn't really thought about it as being *ready* and wanting it. He'd been a very happy bayou bachelor for a long time. When had this ready-for-love thing happened?

Over the back end of an alpaca on a hot, sunny day in July outside of Appleby, Iowa. When he'd met Paige Asher.

Dammit.

"I think you are," Ellie said. "But not with Paige."

Mitch frowned, the pain in his chest felt sharper. "Why not?"

"Because *she's* not ready," Ellie said. "So she's not the one."

"How did you know Juliet and Bennett and Tori were the right ones for them?" He didn't mention Maddie. Everyone had always known that Maddie was the right one for Owen.

"It was obvious," Ellie said. "They didn't *know* they were going to fall in love because they were here for other reasons and temporarily. But they hadn't ruled it out."

Mitch thought back to the first time he'd seen Tori and Josh together. And Juliet and Sawyer. And Bennett and Kennedy. And, of course, Owen and Maddie.

Yeah, it had been obvious.

"And Paige has ruled it out," he said, flatly.

Ellie nodded. "And until she opens herself up to it, she could definitely break your heart."

Yeah. Fuck. She sure could.

He swallowed hard. "Did I fuck up telling her to come here, knowing how she felt?"

Ellie shook her head. "No. You were doing what you always do." She gave him a smile full of love. "You were being exactly what the person in front of you needed you to be. In this case, Paige needed a friend and a haven. So you, of course, gave that to her."

"So, I'm a sucker who doesn't think about what *I* want but just goes along with everyone else." He sometimes felt that way, actually. He didn't have a lot of goals of his own. Everything he did was according to what other people needed or wanted. He often felt like his grandpa's fishing boat on the bayou, just floating along, letting the current—and the people around him —determine where he went.

"Sometimes," Ellie agreed.

Mitch snorted. His grandma wasn't the warm, fuzzy, cuddly type. She was wide open with her thoughts and feelings. They all knew how much Ellie loved them, but they also knew when they'd screwed up and pissed her off. If he wanted an opinion or input from Ellie, he knew it would never be sugarcoated.

"I'm a sucker?"

"Yes. You are so into making everyone else's life easier that you don't worry about yourself."

"That's a bad thing?" It wasn't. Or it better not be. It was how his father had taught him to be.

Be helpful, be grateful, make yourself useful, make them glad to have you around.

Those were the things Sean Landry had told him repeatedly growing up.

"It's not always a bad thing," Ellie said. "But it can, obviously, leave you open to heartbreak. And I don't like that idea. I want you to be happy, Mitch. And helping Paige will make you happy. To an extent. But if you start thinking this is something more than she does, you could end up hurt. I don't want her to make you unwilling to look for love."

"You think that love might come along for me while Paige is here, and I'll blow it off because of her?"

"Maybe. Or after she leaves, and you're nursing a broken heart."

"So you're afraid that Paige being here is going to make me less willing to try a relationship with The One when she comes along?"

Ellie nodded. "Maybe."

Mitch sighed. "What do I do, Ellie?"

They all called Leo and Ellie by their first names. There

were too many grandparents in the area to refer to them as grandma and grandpa, and Leo and Ellie weren't the Maw-Maw or Papa types.

"Move her out of your bedroom, for starters," Ellie said. "Keep your hands and lips to yourself. Think of her as a roommate and a friend, but nothing more."

Mitch had figured that's where this was going. It was strange that this advice was coming from one of the biggest romantics he knew. Ellie was tough and gruff and had a no-nonsense edge, but she was definitely a believer in happily ever after.

"Okay." He'd be a dumbass not to agree. For one, because she was very likely right. She often was. For another, she'd probably smack him upside the back of his head if he didn't agree.

"I love you, Mitch," Ellie said.

"I love you, too."

"Now go home. And take the box of food to Griffin." She pointed at the to-go boxes on the bar.

They were plain brown boxes that looked like shoe boxes. She'd used Styrofoam containers for years. Then Bennett Baxter had come along and convinced her to change to something more environmentally friendly.

She'd rolled her eyes. But she'd done it.

Ellie was stubborn, and she liked things her way and was right ninety-nine percent of the time. But she was also reasonable. Ish. And she respected people who earned it.

Mitch should listen to her about Paige.

He knew that.

"I need some bread pudding, too. For Paige."

Ellie looked approving about that. "You know where it is and how to use a serving spoon."

He chuckled. "Yes, ma'am."

He dished up bread pudding for Paige, added it to the stack of boxes, called goodnight to everyone, and headed for home.

To Paige.

———

Paige came down the stairs with her hair up in a towel. She'd eaten her grilled cheese, fed her cats, and then taken a shower. Everything had been easy to find, and she felt a lot more normal now.

It had been a long day. Between the drive and emotions of seeing Mitch again, she felt like it had been a week since she'd left Iowa rather than just two days.

She'd texted Piper and Whitney before she'd gotten in the shower. Then had relented and texted her mom and two sisters in a group message.

As she went back down the stairs, she read the responses.

Oh, my God! Paige! That's amazing! had been Piper's response. She was the boldest of any of the people Paige had texted. Piper also wasn't a bit worried about Paige's addiction to cats. "Do what makes you happy," had been Piper's response whenever Paige talked about how her mom worried about her life choices.

That's...wow, had been Whitney's reaction. *You're okay though?*

Paige typed, *I'm completely okay. I got here with no trouble, Mitch was really happy to see me, and I can stay as long as I want.*

She thought about her response as she stepped into the living room. Mitch *had been* really happy to see her. She smiled. She'd had nothing to worry about, obviously. Everything she'd thought she'd felt in Iowa for him was still there. And very reciprocal. All the details about her staying had just fallen into place. He had room for her. He was going to get her a job. He was fine with her just being here and them being friends and having some fun until she was ready to go to Colorado.

This was going to be great.

A few months of hanging out in a new place, working at a completely new-to-her job, and hot sex? Why would she turn this down?

Her head still bent over her phone as she reassured her friends, and avoided the messages from her sisters and mom, Paige rounded the end of the couch.

She sensed something and looked up.

And screamed.

The guy sitting on the couch looked over with a frown. "Jesus," was all he said.

Her hand over her pounding heart, Paige worked to take a deep breath. "I didn't know anyone was here."

"Yeah, well, I didn't think I should open the bathroom door and inform you I was home," he said. He lifted a bottle of beer to his mouth and focused on the television again. It was tuned to a basketball game. "Fuckers," he muttered at the TV.

"You must be Griffin." Obviously. The guy was sitting here as if he lived here.

"Yep."

"I'm Paige."

"Hey."

Her eyebrows arched. Then it registered that he had a cat lying next to him, pressed up against his leg, and another on his lap. Eddie looked blissful against Griffin's thigh, and Griffin was lazily stroking a big hand over Bernie's back.

So, her cats liked him.

Well, not Fred. He was probably still in the lower cupboard next to Mitch's stove. He didn't like anyone or anything right now.

"Aren't you concerned about finding a strange woman in

your house?" she asked. She plopped into the chair perpendicular to him and propped a foot on the coffee table.

He looked over at her. "Not really. I figure murderers and robbers don't take showers at the crime scene."

"But you didn't know it wasn't Mitch in the shower," she pointed out. "You weren't expecting him to come downstairs?"

"His truck is gone, and the scent coming from under the bathroom door was *not* Mitch's soap."

"Damn, you're like a detective or something."

"Observant." Griffin lifted his bottle again.

"You're cool with having a new roommate?" she asked. Did he know anything about her? Kennedy had known who she was.

"If you smell like that all the time, sure," he said. "Plus, you come with cats."

He stroked a hand over Bernie again. She could hear the cat purring even from where she sat.

"Mitch said you're a vet and wouldn't have a problem with the cats." He'd actually said Griffin could move out if he did, but she didn't mention that part.

"Animals are far superior to humans," Griffin said.

"They might want to sleep on your bed. With you."

"They will," he said.

"Oh?"

"I'm big, warm, and don't move around much in my sleep."

She grinned. "Good to know."

"And they'll think they're getting away with something. Cats like that."

He wasn't wrong. When she was working and had papers spread all over her coffee table, the cats only wanted to lie on the ones she needed most. When they hid her socks, it was only her favorites. Even if she put another pair on the floor, they'd ignore it for the ones they *knew* they weren't supposed to mess with.

"How long have you been in Autre?" she asked.

"About two months." He didn't say it with any kind of enthusiasm.

"Do you like it?"

He sighed and looked at her again. "No."

"No?" She hadn't been expecting that. Tori *loved* Autre. She'd been smitten with more than Josh when she'd come to Louisiana. And it had taken about a day.

"No." He didn't elaborate.

"Why not?"

"I was living in D.C. before this. Working at the National Zoo. I was working with endangered tigers. Now I'm in a tiny town in Louisiana taking care of goats." He rolled his eyes.

Paige studied him. Okay, that sounded kind of sucky. Autre was probably a step down for a guy who had worked with tigers in Washington D.C.

"What happened?" she asked. She knew there was some issue with a donor but she'd love to know more of the details.

"I yelled at the wife of one of our biggest donors." Griffin's eyes were back on the TV, and he took another drink of beer.

"Why?" Paige asked.

"Because she was being an entitled bitch."

Paige could accept that. Entitled bitches needed to be yelled at.

"And they fired you?"

"I don't know how to braid hair."

Paige blinked at him. "What?"

Griffin looked over. "If you're looking for a best friend, I thought I'd tell you that I don't know how to braid hair or paint toenails."

She arched a brow. "First, that's what you think grown women do with their girlfriends?"

He shrugged. "I don't really care. Just making a point."

"Right. Second, I'm trying to be *friendly*. Since, we're going to be living together for the next few months."

"And will you be wanting to sit around and talk about our feelings every night during those months? Because I'm going to have to adjust my work hours. And buy something stronger than beer."

"You're a real charmer."

"So I've been told."

7

"Good thing you're nice to my cats," Paige told Griffin after a moment.

"Cats are easy. People who aren't nice to them are dicks."

"Even big cats? They're easy too?"

"A hell of a lot easier than people," he said.

Well, that was a no-brainer.

"So what *can* we talk about if not our feelings?" Paige rolled her eyes. They hadn't been talking about feelings, exactly. Plus, she wasn't really a touchy-feely-spill-her-guts girl either. Griffin needed to chill.

"Basketball," Griffin said. He finished off his beer and set the empty bottle on the end table. "Football. Hockey."

"We can't even talk about tigers?" she asked. "Or other cats? I'm a huge fan. I've got eighteen more back in Iowa."

He looked over at her, his eyebrows up now. "*Oh.*"

She knew exactly what he was thinking. "I foster and run an adoption center. And a cat café. That's also a yoga studio."

"Uh-huh."

She frowned. "What's that mean?"

"It means you have a lot of cats."

"You like cats," she protested. "What's wrong with having a lot of them?"

"I like hamburgers too," he said. "But I don't have twenty-three at once."

"Hamburgers and cats are not the same things."

"It's excessive," he said simply.

"But..." It was excessive. She was helping the cats. She got them fixed, so they didn't keep having more kittens, and she found them good homes to go to.

"Well, I prefer animals to people a lot of the time, too."

Griffin just gave her a nod and focused on the TV again.

She studied him. He was very good-looking. Like *really* good-looking. Dark, shaggy hair, dark eyes, scruff on his jaw, muscled arms, one that had a tattoo stretching from under the sleeve of his t-shirt to his elbow. He was in good shape. He wore the t-shirt with a pair of athletic pants. His stomach was flat, and his legs muscled, his bare feet were long.

He had a don't-give-a-shit attitude practically emanating in waves though.

"So what's so fascinating about tigers?"

She did think tigers were fascinating. All big cats. All cats, period. But she wanted him to talk more. Mostly because it bugged her that he didn't want to. She supposed she got that contrariness from hanging out with cats all the time.

"Nothing."

She rolled her eyes. "You just dedicated your professional life to them because you couldn't think of anything else?"

"Yep."

That's how it was going to be, huh? He wasn't going to engage.

"Goats are pretty cute."

He just made a *harrumphing* noise at that.

She grinned. "What about the otters? Mitch told me there are otters. *They're* cute."

"Water weasels," Griffin said.

"Okay, it's official. You're definitely a grump. No one doesn't think otters are cute."

"They're noisy. And little beggars. And have sharp teeth."

Paige laughed. "Tigers have sharp teeth."

He made that *harrumph* sound again.

Paige sat just smiling, watching him pet her cats. Yeah, he might be grumpy, but a guy who liked cats wasn't all bad. She liked him even if he didn't want her to.

"What about lions and panthers and stuff?" she asked after a couple of minutes.

He sighed. He'd probably thought she was done talking.

Her life was full of people who wanted to talk to her all the time. Wanted to know what she was thinking and feeling. She was here in part to get away from that. Why couldn't she just leave Griffin alone?

"What about them?"

"You like them too?"

"Yeah."

One-word answers were going to drive her nuts. "What do you like about them?"

"Everything."

Right. She sighed. And wondered where Mitch was. He liked to talk.

Of course, he liked to talk about feelings and being crazy about her. Which was really nice on the one hand. On the other, it made just hanging out here complicated and made her think maybe she shouldn't stay for seven months.

It also made her kind of want to stay longer than seven months.

She should enjoy her time with Griffin. Her *quiet* time with Griffin. She focused on the game he was watching. Tim jumped up on her lap, and she smiled, rubbing him behind the ears in the way he loved. The cat settled on her lap, and she and

Griffin watched the rest of the first half of the game without a word.

Not one. Not a single word.

Paige spent a lot of time alone in her own apartment and didn't miss human conversation, but it was different when there was a person sitting *right there*. She'd never met anyone who could sit for thirty minutes straight with another person and not say one single thing.

Griffin should be her new favorite person.

But she was pretty sure that as long as Mitch Landry was around, there was no way any other guy was going to even come close.

By the time Mitch did come in through the back door, all five cats had found a new human to adore. Even Fred, who had finally come out of the cupboard. All of them were on or near Griffin.

They apparently preferred the quiet, broody type.

They definitely preferred the type with a bigger lap and hands.

Paige heard the back-kitchen door open and sprang from her seat.

Someone to talk to! One of her favorite people to talk to, in fact.

That thought nearly stopped her steps, but she chalked it up to Mitch being new and interesting to her. In that she didn't know all of his stories and everything about his growing up years and his entire family—the way she did all the guys she'd dated in Appleby. Hell, all the *people* she knew in Appleby.

"Hi!"

Mitch looked up from where he was toeing off his boots back by the back door. He gave her a big grin, and Paige immediately felt a swoop in her stomach.

"Hey."

"How is everything?"

"Everything is... good." He frowned slightly when he said it though.

"They're not mad that I didn't come up for dinner?"

"No. Everything is fine." He grabbed a couple of brown boxes off the counter and started toward her. "Is Griff here?"

"Yep."

Mitch smiled and stepped around her, heading into the living room.

Huh. His grin had said he was happy to see her, but not even a kiss?

You're roommates. He's not your boyfriend. You don't need kisses hello. Or goodbye.

Maybe they were only going to kiss when it was going to lead to the bedroom.

And she'd told him earlier that she thought she should have her own room. So, maybe this was just him adjusting to that.

She followed him into the living room, where he greeted his roommate. His *other* roommate.

"Ellie sent food," Mitch told him. He was grinning at the sight of Griffin covered in cats. "I guess you don't mind our guests."

Griffin looked down at his lap, then at the cat that was tucked under one of his arms. "I've definitely watched basketball with worse friends."

Mitch chuckled. "Want me to put the food in the kitchen?"

"Nah, just take a cat."

Paige lifted a brow, but Mitch stepped forward and scooped Eddie and Bernie up. Tim, Fred, and Calvin all lifted their heads—one from the cushion next to Griffin and two from the back of the couch—but they didn't jump down or scurry off.

Paige shook her head. Her cats were pretty laid-back. If they weren't trapped in a car going God-knew-where. They were around the yoga classes every day and loved the attention and human touch they got there. But she was surprised that they'd adjusted to these two men so quickly.

Griffin got to his feet and took the chair Paige had been sitting in. He pulled the coffee table closer and opened the boxes of food.

The spices were fragrant, and Griffin took a deep breath and actually smiled.

He freaking smiled.

At some mix of shrimp and rice. While she'd been unable to even get many words out of it.

And damn, the guy was gorgeous. The broody thing didn't make him *less* attractive, but the smile definitely amped it up.

Mitch took Griffin's vacated seat on the couch with the two cats he held. The others didn't so much as shift. So now Mitch was the one surrounded by and covered in cats.

Paige couldn't help but feel a little swoop in her stomach at the sight.

Any guy who liked animals was automatically hotter. But it was a sure sign she had deeper feelings for Mitch because, in spite of the smile and everything, Griffin sitting there with her cats hadn't done as much for her as Mitch sinking into those cushions and stroking a hand over Bernie from head to tail.

She wanted to be the one on his lap.

And not necessarily for anything sexual. She would be happy just cuddling with him the way the cats were.

"There's bread pudding in one of those boxes for you," Mitch said, inclining his head toward the coffee table. "Don't let Griffin eat everything."

"Really?" She leaned to grab the box Griffin hadn't opened.

Bread pudding. She wasn't sure she'd ever had it, but dang, it looked and smelled amazing. The cinnamony smell made her mouth water, and she took the second spoon Mitch had set on the table as well.

Paige joined Mitch on the couch, getting as close to him as

she could—Tim was in the way and didn't seem the least bit inclined to move—and tucked her feet under her. She angled her body so she could prop an elbow on the back of the couch and face Mitch.

But as Griffin dug into his food, Mitch just sat watching the game and petting cats.

She studied him. Huh. This didn't seem like him. He was *so* into her that she always felt like she was the center of his attention when they were together.

Not that she needed his constant focus. In fact, she wasn't sure how she'd handle that long-term. As in the seven months she was staying here, of course.

It was better that he not be incessantly in her space.

Probably.

She took a bite of the bread pudding. And gave a little moan. Oh, wow, that was good. Full of carbs and sugar, of course, but dang.

She opened her eyes—not realizing they'd drifted shut—to find Mitch's hot gaze locked on her face. She licked her bottom lip. His eyes followed. She felt a swirl of warmth in her belly.

He quickly snapped his attention back to the television.

Huh. What was that about? "So your family is fine?" she asked.

He nodded but kept his eyes on the game. "Yeah. They're great."

"Did you see Tori?"

"Oh, no." He glanced at Griffin. "She and Griffin were at some cow birth."

Griffin nodded as he chewed. He swallowed. "Finished about an hour ago. She wasn't feeling great, so probably headed home."

Mitch frowned at that. "She was sick?"

"Kind of. She just seemed a little off," Griffin said. "It was a long day though."

Mitch pulled his phone from his pocket. "I don't think Josh knows she's not feeling good." He tried to shift Eddie off his other arm so he could text, but Eddie wasn't moving.

Paige reached for the cat, lifting her food box into the air and bringing the tabby into her own lap.

Mitch gave her a little smile, then focused on his phone. He typed out a quick text—she assumed to Josh—and then set the phone on the arm of the couch.

"She wasn't *sick*," Griffin said. He lifted what looked like a muffin from the other box. "She was just tired. I wouldn't just blow her off if she was sick, you know."

He seemed genuinely insulted that Mitch would think he didn't care that Tori wasn't feeling well.

"I know, man. But Josh was up at Ellie's, and I'm sure he'd want to know if Tori was home."

"Okay." Griffin glanced at Paige. "Wouldn't want our other *roommate* to think I'm a dick." He bit into the muffin

Paige lifted a brow. "I don't think you're a dick. I don't know you well enough to know that yet. But I don't find you to be a charming conversationalist."

Griffin snorted, and Paige felt herself smile.

"I'm not a charming anything," Griffin said, popping the rest of the muffin in his mouth. "If you're looking for charming, definitely stick with that guy." He inclined his head toward Mitch.

Paige looked at Mitch again. She slowly nodded. "Yeah, I think I will."

Mitch's gaze met hers, and she felt a little jolt of awareness. And emotion.

The emotion she was going to ignore. But the awareness— i.e., the strongest attraction she'd ever felt for anyone—she liked. She was going to wallow in it, in fact.

She reached out and put a hand on his shoulder, stroking her thumb over the end of his collarbone.

Mitch stood swiftly.

He had a good hold on Bernie, or the cat would have tumbled to the floor. The other cats looked at him with a *what the hell, man?* look.

Paige felt the same. She frowned at him. "You okay?"

Considering where they'd each had their hands and mouths, on each other—even just a couple of hours ago—she hadn't expected touching his shoulder to repulse him.

"We... need to talk."

Oh. Great. He didn't want her to stay.

What had happened when he'd gone to talk to his family?

She sighed and put Eddie down on the cushion Mitch had just left. It would be nice and warm for the cat, at least. Then reluctantly set the bread pudding on the coffee table.

"Okay." She got to her feet.

Mitch put Bernie down with Eddie, grabbed his phone from the arm of the sofa, and started for the stairs.

Paige glanced at Griffin. He was watching Mitch go.

"You can have the rest of my bread pudding." She cast a regretful look at the box. "It's probably for the best."

Griffin looked up at Paige. "Okay. And just let me know if I need to put headphones on."

"To drown out our yelling or my crying?"

"Sure, that's what I meant."

"Does he really look in the mood to do anything but yell or make me cry?" she asked.

"Uh." Griffin glanced at Mitch, who had already started up the steps. "Yeah."

"You think?"

"The guy's wound up about something. Mitch never gets wound up. About anything."

"That doesn't mean he doesn't want to yell."

Griffin chuckled. "Maybe 'yelling' means something

different in Iowa. But that guy isn't going to yell at you the way I know yelling."

Paige felt her stomach flip. Mitch was wound up, huh? And he wasn't going to yell? Well, then maybe she definitely wanted to get upstairs.

"So you *do* know how to talk," she commented, stepping around the end of the couch.

"I know how to amputate a leg and unclog a toilet too. Just because I know *how* doesn't mean I like to."

Paige's eyes rounded. "Right. Got it."

Griffin smiled, but he turned his attention back to the game.

Paige took a deep breath and headed upstairs.

The old house had eight steps up to a landing, then a ninety-degree turn to the remaining ten steps. At the top was a wide area that had a door straight ahead and then two on either side. The door straight ahead was the bathroom. The others were bedrooms.

Mitch was pacing the area outside of the rooms. He stopped when she stepped up the top step.

"You're not okay," she told him.

"I'm... fine."

"What's going on?"

"I just—" He huffed out a breath. "I realized you were right about separate bedrooms. And in that vein... I think we should try to keep our hands to ourselves."

She had definitely not been expecting that.

She frowned at the stairs. Griffin had not gotten this right either. He thought he was so smart.

"So no sex?" she asked.

"Right."

"Why?"

"Because you need a friend. You need a place where you can relax and not worry about expectations others are putting on you."

Paige folded her arms, but she nodded. "Right."

"Well, if we keep sleeping together and living together and playing house for seven months, my expectations might get out of control."

Ah. She pulled in a breath. "Oh."

He ran a hand through his hair and tucked his hands into his back pockets. "Yeah."

"And your family helped you figure this out," she guessed.

"I told them why you're here, and they think it's great that you thought to come here. But they're thinking that it might be best for both of us if we just..." He just looked at her for a few seconds without finishing the thought.

"If we just what?"

He shook his head. "I swear it made sense back there when they said it."

"But now?"

"Looking at you, standing there, just outside my bedroom door, it doesn't make sense at all."

That caused heat to curl through her belly. She glanced at the door to her left. The first one at the top of the steps. His bedroom.

"So, what do we do?" she asked. She honestly didn't know.

She wanted him. She'd wanted him since the first time their eyes had met. And she'd had him. It had been hot and fun and dirty. The best sex of her life.

But... she liked this guy. He was a good man. He helped strangers. His family meant the world to him. He made her feel smart and funny and interesting and he thought she was the most beautiful thing in the world. He worked hard. He laughed and loved hard.

She did not want to break his heart. She did not want to make promises to him, even implied ones, that she couldn't keep.

"I guess we try to just be friends. No physical stuff."

That sounded like a really good idea.

She hated it.

But she nodded. "Okay."

"So, you can take that room." He pointed at the door furthest from his.

She had to smile at that. "Okay."

"I moved your suitcase in there."

She'd pulled it up the stairs and left it in the bathroom after she'd showered. She hadn't known which room was his for sure.

"Thanks."

"And... I'm going to head to bed."

She nodded. "Okay. I think I will too." It wasn't like the man downstairs was going to entertain her or engage in a deep conversation with her. Or even a not-deep conversation. And if Mitch didn't want to hang out, then yeah, she might as well go to bed and read or something.

He stood just looking at her.

She looked back.

"This is going to be the hardest thing I've ever done," he finally said.

Well, at least there was that. She smiled. "Glad to hear it."

He gave a short laugh and ran his hand through his hair again. "If you change your mind on the getting married thing, I want to be the first to know."

Her eyes went wide. But it was more just surprise that he'd said it. She didn't actually feel the stab of dread that she would have expected. "Uh. I thought you said you wouldn't propose."

"That wasn't a proposal."

"You sure?"

"Pretty sure." He frowned. "Was it?"

"I'm going to give you a pass on it this time because you didn't actually *ask,* but watch yourself, Landry," she said.

It was the strangest thing to be fighting a smile. Proposals had always sent a wave of panic through her. Even when Garrett had asked her. He'd actually been her boyfriend for over a year at that point. She'd been expecting it, more or less. And still, the question had made her catch her breath. Not in a good way. She'd forced a smile and said yes.

Now she was trying to keep from smiling at the man who was *not* supposed to be talking about marrying her.

"Goodnight, Paige," he finally said.

"Goodnight, Mitch."

They still just stood looking at each other.

"You need to go to your room," he said, his voice a little tight.

"I will. You too."

"Yeah, but—" He sighed. "You're right by my door."

She looked at the closed bedroom door again. And smiled. "I guess I am."

She didn't want to torture the guy. He was trying to be noble. Or something. But she wouldn't deny that she liked that resisting her would be difficult.

"You need to move *away* from my bedroom door, Paige." His voice was a little gruffer.

"You're in my way of getting to my bedroom too," she pointed out.

"But are you tempted to throw me over your shoulder and say to hell with all of your good intentions? Already? Within twenty minutes of deciding you even have good intentions?"

She laughed even as warmth filled her. Not just heat. Not lusty heat anyway. But a feel-good warmth that she didn't quite understand. But she liked it. "Kind of."

He swallowed hard. Then said, "Go to bed, Paige."

She moved to the right, away from his door. As he came forward, she playfully pressed her back against the far wall.

He smiled, in spite of himself, and went to his bedroom door. He twisted the knob but paused and looked over at her.

She inched her way toward her bedroom, still against the wall. When she got to her door she reached for the knob and shot him a smile. "Goodnight, Mitch."

"'Night."

"And I'm just right here if you have any nighttime needs. Bad dreams." She paused. "Good dreams."

"Stop it."

"Stop what? Just being a good friend." She grinned.

"My dreams might include white dresses and tuxes," he warned.

Again, no sense of *oh shit*. Instead, she tipped her head. "You're pretty good at bringing all of that up without asking the four-word question."

He didn't comment on that. "See you in the morning."

"Okay." She gave him another smile, then slipped into her room, feeling his eyes still on her until the door shut.

She slumped against it, pressing her hand to her stomach.

Dammit. She really liked him.

It was *really* too bad they weren't going to kiss anymore.

Maybe she should just head to Colorado now. She didn't have as much money as she'd intended to have when she showed up in Steamboat Springs in August, but she could figure something out.

If she was here for a fun, flirty fling, and now Mitch had decided not to fling with her, then maybe she didn't want to stay here.

This town was full of Landrys. According to both Mitch and Tori, the Landrys believed in romance on a very grand scale. When you fell for one Landry, you got them all. Tori had told her all about how they'd accepted her and brought her into the family without question and how she couldn't help but love them.

Just the kind of thing Paige wanted to avoid.

But those people who made strangers part of their family so

easily had apparently talked Mitch *out* of the fling idea. And they hadn't all descended on the house when he'd showed up without her. And now she was in her own bedroom.

Well, damn. Maybe she wasn't going to have to avoid them. Maybe they were going to avoid her.

That was good.

Right?

It was. Probably. Mostly. She didn't want to deal with his family wanting to know when they were going to get hitched.

It looked like they had decided that not only was that not going to happen, but it *shouldn't* happen.

She frowned and pushed away from the door. Huh. They *didn't* want her and Mitch to be together forever?

She definitely wasn't used to that.

But this was good. She could stay here, work the job Mitch had set up for her, save up the rest of the money she wanted to, and avoid the whole topic of marriage. To anyone in Appleby and, evidently, to Mitch Landry.

Yeah, that was good.

The niggling what-the-hell feeling that accompanied her to bed and kept her from concentrating on her book was just her being ridiculous.

She was getting exactly what she wanted.

It just didn't feel that way.

8

That night was hell.

Mitch tossed and turned and second-guessed his decisions and wondered what Paige was doing. And what she'd do if he walked down the hallway and joined her in... whatever it was.

The next morning was even worse.

He came down the stairs to find Paige doing yoga in his living room.

Which was bad enough, but she was also wearing the half sweatshirt that fell off one shoulder and showed teasing peeks of her bare stomach and back as she moved. She'd worn that shirt the first time he'd spent the night with her at her apartment in Appleby. She'd been wearing it when he'd showed up to surprise her a week ago at her yoga studio.

He loved that shirt.

He also fucking hated it.

He gritted his teeth, averted his eyes from her ass as she bent to stretch, and headed for the kitchen.

But he didn't get far.

"Morning."

He turned back. "Morning."

She looked so good. Sexy. Sweet. *Right*. Waking up to her in his house was an exquisite torture that he'd never experienced before.

"Griffin made coffee," she said, seeming lost about what to say.

"He makes good coffee." Yeah, he had no idea what to say either. Then he frowned. "You saw Griffin this morning?"

"Yeah. He came down as I was starting."

Starting yoga. Dressed like that. Mitch felt a very stupid rush of jealousy.

Griffin was a good guy. They'd been living together for two months, and Mitch hadn't had a single problem with him. He was a fucking grouch, but that didn't faze Mitch. It had nothing to do with Mitch. He didn't love the way Griffin clearly felt that being in Autre and working with Tori was a step-down, and he wanted more. But who was Mitch to judge?

Griffin had messed up at his last job. Mitch thought he'd done the right thing from what he knew about the situation. Some big donor to the zoo had been at a fundraiser with his wife. They'd been on an exclusive behind-the-scenes tour. They'd been shown the new baby tiger that had been born. A huge boon to the zoo because the species was endangered. It had been Griffin's project and the main reason he'd gotten the job.

Then the donor's wife had touched the baby tiger. Which was a huge no-no. The baby could have been rejected by its mother if handled by humans.

Griffin had informed the woman that she needed to get away from the cub and reminded her that she'd said she understood the rules laid out ahead of the tour.

Of course, he hadn't said it quite like that.

Or in any kind of normal tone of voice or volume.

He'd been fired that same night.

Griffin was now here because his friend from vet school, Tori, had been appalled that he'd been fired and had offered him a job as her partner in her vet practice, which had been growing steadily since she'd come to Autre.

Everyone loved Tori.

She was sweet and loving and patient and smart and went above and beyond for every one of her patients.

Griffin was... smart. And fiercely dedicated to animals.

But he was not sweet or patient.

And he thought goats and otters were a waste of his talents. Evidently.

In spite of the fact that the otters loved him. Like *loved* him. Followed him around, squeaked, and talked to him as if he was some kind of otter celebrity, begged for his attention.

It was hilarious.

To Mitch. And everyone else. Except Griffin.

But no, he didn't need to worry about Griffin hitting on Paige. He wouldn't do that to Mitch. Even if he was inclined to try to be flirtatious or charming or even friendly. Which Mitch couldn't imagine, frankly.

"I'm... going to make breakfast," Mitch finally said. He was going to ignore the thought that if *he* and Paige weren't involved, then it wasn't really an issue if another man flirted with her anyway. "Do you want anything?"

She shook her head. "I brought my shake mixes. I'll just make one after I'm done." Then she frowned. "Oh, but you probably don't have almond milk."

"I don't."

"How about spinach or kale?"

"Uh, no." He actually grinned at that. "But we can go to the store later."

"You can just tell me how to get there. I can go."

"I'll take you."

"You don't have to."

He blew out a breath. "I know. But you're new to town and my roommate, and I should take you to the store the first time. I took Griffin."

She finally nodded. "Okay."

"And I can see if Cora has spinach. I'm sure there's no kale." No one in Autre ate kale. He'd put money on it. "But she might have spinach or, at least, vegetables."

Paige smiled at that. "You don't have vegetables here?"

"No."

"Fruit?"

He shrugged. "No."

"What do you eat?"

"I eat at Ellie's almost every meal but breakfast. And sometimes that too. If I'm here, I'll make a sandwich or eggs or cereal."

"And Cora is?"

"My grandma's best friend, and the main cook at Ellie's."

Paige nodded. "Got it. Well, don't bother her. I'll be okay until we go to the store."

"You sure?"

"What will her reaction be to someone asking for spinach for a protein shake for breakfast?" she asked.

He thought about that. Then nodded. "She would probably be okay with it. But she'd want to add grits on the side."

Paige grinned. "Right."

"And probably put cheese and lots of butter in them."

Her smile grew. "Yeah, I might skip the grits."

Mitch felt himself relax a little. He wanted her. With an intensity that still surprised him. But he also liked her. And having her here, taking care of her, felt good.

"How about eggs? I'll scramble them and put nothing on them."

"Egg whites?" she asked.

He sighed as if put upon. "I guess."

"Thanks." She just looked at him for a long moment. "I appreciate it. Everything."

He was glad she felt like coming here was a good thing. But he wasn't sure if "everything" included *not* getting more involved and spending every night in bed together.

Because he didn't want her to feel like that was a good idea. Exactly.

"I'll let you know when they're done," he said.

"Thanks." She pivoted on her back foot and went back to stretching.

Her sweet ass *right there* in those yoga pants that concealed nothing. Including the fact, she was not wearing underwear.

With a muttered curse, Mitch headed into the kitchen.

It was just seven months.

It was going to be the longest seven months of his life.

H e made it through breakfast and her showering. They were alone in the house. They'd already had sex. Several times.

It was *his* idea to keep the physical stuff out of their relationship.

Twenty-four hours ago, he would have headed upstairs and joined her, putting her up on the counter and making her come with his mouth before fucking her in the shower as the water rained down on them.

Now he was sitting in his kitchen, nursing another cup of coffee, and reading the newspaper.

As if news about a four-alarm fire or a big jazz festival in New Orleans could keep his attention away from the naked woman upstairs.

He did wonder if his friends Caleb and James, firefighters stationed at the house just on the edge of the French Quarter, had been at the fire. But jazz festivals in NOLA were as common as food festivals. Two things that city loved were its music and its food.

Finally, he heard Paige coming back down the stairs.

He folded the paper and crossed to the sink with his cup.

"Is this okay to wear in the Boys of the Bayou office?" she asked.

He turned to face her.

She was dressed in denim shorts and a bright pink t-shirt with a light gray zippered sweatshirt over it. Her long bare legs ended in gray tennis shoes. Her hair was loose and falling in waves around her shoulders.

She looked so damned gorgeous. She looked like a classic All-American girl. The guys coming into the office today, tourists and delivery guys alike, were going to love this new addition.

He leaned back on the counter and gripped the edge to keep from reaching for her.

"You're going to freeze in those shorts."

She looked at the window. "What's the temp today?"

"In the low 50s."

She smiled. "It's negative two at home. *Negative* two. I think I'll be okay in fifty-something."

He couldn't help his answering smile. "Did you bring jeans? Full jeans? Or did you just pack your summer wardrobe?"

Paige looked down at herself. "Mostly summer wardrobe."

"It gets colder at night."

She looked up. "I thought I'd have someone to keep me warm at night."

He swallowed and curled his fingers into the counter. "You don't want me to propose."

Her eyes widened. "No. I don't."

Just saying the word "propose" didn't count as a proposal. He assumed.

"Then it's probably best if we sleep separately."

She took a deep breath. "So no sex? Really? Not at all?"

He loved that she looked disappointed by that idea.

He was a good guy. He was. By everyone's account. Well, maybe not a couple of girls that had wanted the proposal from him that Paige was so averse to. But *most* people thought he was great.

But he wasn't a saint.

"I didn't say not at all."

"You kind of did."

"I said we shouldn't *sleep* in the same bed together every night."

"So like Monday, Wednesday, Friday?" she asked, her tone and expression making it clear that sounded dumb.

He blew out a breath. He knew his idea might be a little crazy, but they needed some guidelines.

"I want to date you," he said. "I definitely want to have sex with you. I also want to give you a place to stay. So we just need some rules."

She narrowed her eyes slightly, but she nodded. "I'm listening."

"Because I said I want to have sex with you?" he teased.

"Yes."

He laughed. Having this gorgeous woman that had him twisted in knots want him so much and be so open about it was a turn-on like nothing he'd experienced before.

"Okay, so Tuesday, Friday, Saturday are date nights. Tuesdays we stay in. Watch a movie or sit on the porch—"

"Can we lie in the hammock together?" Paige interrupted.

He nodded. "Sure."

"I'm in."

Well, that had been easy. "You like my hammock?" he asked.

"That—" She pointed at him. "You can't do that if we're not sleeping together."

"Do what?"

"Say things in that sexy, flirty tone of voice."

"Did I use a sexy, flirty tone of voice?"

Her eyes narrowed again. "You did."

"Huh."

"You don't even know when you're doing it?"

"I guess not all the time."

She rolled her eyes. "What happens on the other nights? The non-date nights?"

"Well, Friday is always the crawfish boil at Ellie's. We'll go to that together and... other stuff."

She gave him a *watch it* look.

His voice must have sounded sexy and flirty then too. He grinned. "Saturday nights are, of course, a traditional date night. I'll show you the area. We can go up to New Orleans. That kind of stuff."

She nodded. "But what about the *other* nights?"

He laughed. He couldn't help it. Her wanting him this much was nice. "Monday, Wednesday, Thursday, Sunday we're friends, co-workers, roommates."

"And that's it?"

"Yep. No meals together. No kissing or touching."

"No sexy, flirty stuff," she said.

"I'll try."

"You *better*. If I jump you on a Monday, it will be your own fault."

He smirked. "You're going to have to have some self-control, Ms. Asher. *You're* the one who doesn't want a diamond ring."

She narrowed her eyes again and nodded. "Right."

"So, when we're home together, we can't sit on the couch together. You can't walk around in only a towel after your shower. You need a robe. And—" He paused. "This is a big one."

"Okay."

"No yoga in the living room. And definitely, no wearing that sweatshirt."

He knew that she knew which sweatshirt. He'd been very open about what that half sweatshirt did to him.

"But there's not enough room in my bedroom to do yoga," she said.

"What about front porch yoga?" he asked.

She glanced toward the front of the house as if thinking. "That could work. Or..."

"Or?"

"What about the otter yoga you'd mentioned in Iowa?"

He had mentioned otter yoga. She did cat yoga in her studio in Appleby. The cats hung out in the studio and joined her classes. The animals mostly just laid around, stretching and purring and getting attention from the participants. He'd tried to entice her to Autre with the idea of otter yoga.

He grinned. "Yes. Otter yoga. Definitely otter yoga."

She smiled. "That might work."

"The otters won't be laid back like the cats. They'll run around and squeak, but they're pretty cute."

"It will make it interesting," she said. "Is there space there for yoga mats?"

"Yep. It's behind Leo's old trailer. There's a lot of space. Until, we get the new enclosure finished. Then we'll move them there. But there will definitely be space there too." He could actually add a little more space around it.

Of course, adjusting the plans for the enclosure to include an area for otter yoga led by a woman who would be gone in August was ridiculous.

He was going to do it anyway.

She tipped her head. "Okay. Well, there needs to be some rules for you, too, then."

"Like what?"

"No walking around without a shirt on if it's not Tuesday, Friday, or Saturday."

That seemed fair. "Okay."

"And no walking around in just a towel after your shower either."

"Okay."

"And no honey or darlin' stuff."

He nodded but couldn't help the grin.

She noticed. She frowned. "And *no* dirty talk or flirting or innuendos."

"I'll try."

She studied him. Then sighed. "This all seems like a very fine line to walk."

"It will be," he agreed.

"Think we can do it?"

"I hope so. Because I'd really like to take you out. I'd really like to keep having the hottest sex of my life. But I'd also really like for neither of us to end up with a broken heart."

Something flickered in her eyes with that. She swallowed and nodded. "I'd really like that too."

"Good then."

"I promise to keep this agreement going."

There was something odd in her tone when she said that. As if she was making a solemn vow.

"Well, there is some good news about the agreement," he said.

"What's that?"

"Today is Tuesday."

I t was her first date night with Mitch.

That seemed so weird. They'd already had sex. They'd even had a date.

Except they really hadn't.

He'd been in Appleby for the winter Apple Festival, and they'd attended, walking among the booths and trying the different treats and games and checking out the crafts.

But he'd been pretending to be Tori's fiancé, and Paige and Josh had been pretending to be on a date.

That was a long story.

But it did mean that she and Mitch hadn't really *dated* yet.

And now she was living with him. And still wanted him in a way she'd never expected to want a guy.

Okay, so maybe they should date. And should have some rules around their situation.

She did *not* want to break his heart. She did not want to break his family's hearts. She wasn't sure that would or could happen. Maybe none of them would want her and Mitch together, and they'd be thrilled when she left in August. But there was the potential for her to get to know them and like them and...

Her heart could get broken.

She hadn't felt broken-hearted over ending her engagement to Garrett exactly. She'd felt relieved and had been absolutely certain it had been the right thing to do. But she'd been broken-hearted over how it hurt everyone else. Over the way it had changed her relationship with her mom. And Garrett's mom.

She'd always really loved Garrett's mom. As her mom's best friend, Shelly had been a part of her life for as long as she could remember. To know she'd hurt Shelly, had disappointed her, and ruined all of her dreams for their families being connected and her sharing holidays and grandchildren with her best friend forever, had been a blow.

Shelly's pain and her mom's clear disappointment, and her distrust of every decision Paige made from there on, had made Paige *very* leery of relationships and making promises in general.

She didn't like disappointing people. She might sometimes annoy them or even piss them off when she *wouldn't* make a promise or commit to something, but she'd rather be upfront about it and not have them depending on her to do something she wasn't certain she could do.

So laying everything out with how things were going to proceed with her and Mitch was good. She appreciated it. It seemed like walking a tightrope, but it was the best solution. She knew what he expected from her, and she just needed to stay true to that. She wouldn't wear that sweatshirt anymore. She wouldn't sit next to him on the couch. She wouldn't kiss him on any day but Tuesday, Friday, or Saturday.

She could do that.

She liked it a lot, she'd decided by the time they got to the Boys of the Bayou office. She was determined to adhere to all of the rules.

"Kennedy is going to show you everything you need in here today," Mitch said as he shut the truck off.

"Okay." She'd at least already met Kennedy. Though she definitely got the impression not much was going to get past Mitch's cousin.

"I've got a bunch of stuff to do with the enclosure today and have to pick up a couple of busloads of tourists," he said. "But I'll be around if you need anything."

"Okay." She was studying the front of the tour company office.

The office was a simple wooden building that sat upon the slight hill above a few wooden docks. She could just see the end of a couple of boats. There was a tiny gravel parking lot a few yards to the north with a walkway leading to the deck that surrounded the building. There were three small buses parked in the lot at the moment. They were white with large windows and looked to seat about forty people or so. The side sported the Boys of the Bayou logo. A large bright green cartoon alligator that was walking upright and grinning with BOYS OF THE BAYOU in black lettering across his stomach.

"Hey."

She looked over at Mitch.

He seemed about to say something. Instead, he leaned over, cupped the back of her head, and pulled her into a kiss. It was sweet. No tongue. No moaning or wandering hands. It was just a kiss. But it made her feel warm.

She was smiling when he pulled back. "What was that for?"

"I'm glad you're here. I love the idea of you working here. Which is stupid, I know. But just having you around feels good. And—" He gave her a grin that made her feel more than warm. "It's Tuesday. I'm going to take advantage."

For just a second, she felt her throat tighten. He liked having her around. That was the kind of stuff that felt like an expectation without it actually *being* an expectation.

"I haven't even started the job," she said. "I might really suck at it and get fired, and then I won't really be around."

She felt a flicker of panic that was *very* unusual. She was laid back and calm. Dammit. But she also didn't work for other people. She'd been a waitress at the café in Appleby for a short time in high school. She'd babysat for a few kids here and there. But her only *real* job had been working for herself.

It was those stupid expectations and letting-people-down thing again.

And she'd just now realized it. Sitting in Mitch Landry's truck, about to go into her new job for his family, she'd just realized a huge reason she hadn't wanted to work for other people.

Besides being able to set her own schedule. And the cats, of course.

She was going to be working for Mitch's family. They were going to expect her to help them. To answer the phones and not screw up the schedule and not upset their customers.

Ugh. Why had she agreed to this?

She knew she was being a little ridiculous. Working for other people wasn't the same thing as saying yes to spending the rest of her life as someone's wife. And daughter-in-law. And sister-in-law. And mom. Yeah, Garrett had wanted kids. Their moms had talked about their shared grandchildren all the time. That had absolutely added to the pressure.

But this was a job. Answering phones. Booking tours.

The worst thing that would happen would be she'd put someone on a tour that was already full, and they'd have to refund their tickets.

It wasn't like agreeing to spend the rest of her life with someone and then backing out. And costing two families thousands of dollars. And making it so that a really great guy wouldn't even go on a date for two solid years after.

"Hey."

Mitch was frowning when she focused on his face again.

"You okay?" he asked.

Damn, she'd gotten lost in those thoughts for a second. And the regrets. She typically just avoided thinking about all of that.

She forced a smile. "Yeah. Fine."

"Are you nervous about today?"

She wasn't *not* nervous, she supposed. And that sounded better than *I'm really hoping that you and your family don't regret having me here and investing in me.*

It was just a part-time job. They knew it was temporary. She was helping *them* out.

This wasn't them making a long-term commitment to her any more than it was her making one to them.

But yeah, she couldn't shake the memory of Garrett telling her she'd stolen two years of his life that he could have been with someone else. Someone *good* for him.

Mitch still looked concerned, so she nodded. "Yeah. I'm a little nervous."

Nervous that me being here is a huge fucking mistake.

She was being selfish. She didn't want to deal with her mom and family... and town... for a little while, so she'd run away and was now here complicating things for Mitch.

"It's going to be great. My family is the best."

Yep. Exactly what she was afraid of.

But she followed him out of the truck and up to the office.

"Mornin', Ken," Mitch greeted.

Kennedy looked over from where she was perched behind the tall counter that clearly served as the front desk. There was a computer monitor to one side. A phone, a big schedule book, and several piles of papers were set along the top. Kennedy sat on a tall stool. She was wearing jeans and a dark green polo with the Boys of the Bayou logo on the left side.

"Did you bring coffee?" she asked.

"Nope." He glanced to where there was a refreshment station set up.

There was a single-serve coffee pot with a whole display of coffee pods, tea bags, and packets of hot cocoa. There was also a pitcher of water and some alligator-shaped cookies.

"You've got coffee," he said, gesturing at the station.

"That's tourist coffee," Kennedy said. "I need real coffee."

Mitch looked at Paige. "She means strong and with some chicory in it."

"I've never had chicory coffee," Paige told him. She'd read about it in her Louisiana research.

"You gotta try it," he said. "Some people love it and some hate it. But you eat some weird stuff, so you might think it's great."

She laughed. He wasn't wrong.

"So go get us some," Kennedy said with a frown. As if Mitch should already be on his way to fetch coffee.

"I thought I'd get Paige settled here first," Mitch said.

"What do you do if there are two seats left on a tour but a family of four calls and can only do that tour time?" Kennedy asked.

"Uh," was Mitch's reply.

"And what happens when the boat gets all the way out, and a little kid starts puking?"

"I, um..." Mitch answered.

"And what do we do if we take out a bachelor party and they're horribly obnoxious, and the other members on the tour complain when they get back?"

"I... don't know."

"So why don't you just go get the coffee, Mitchell?" Kennedy asked. "I think I can handle 'settling' Paige in."

He shot Paige a look. Paige was fighting a smile. She liked Kennedy. She was no-nonsense, and Paige got the feeling that she'd always know where she stood with the other woman.

She liked that. A lot.

If she pissed Kennedy off or went against expectations, Kennedy would tell her. That's what Paige needed. Wanted even. She knew she'd screw some things up but as long as people felt comfortable telling her that and how to fix it, she'd be fine.

And if she told Kennedy this was just a temporary job, and she wasn't interested in anything long-term with Mitch either, she thought Kennedy would take her at her word and wouldn't expect anything more.

"Yeah, okay." Mitch still looked a little hesitant to leave.

Paige felt a little thump in her chest. He was feeling protective. That was so nice.

And bad. Really bad. He couldn't feel responsible for her.

"I'm fine," she told him. She was independent and smart and capable and didn't need to be protected.

"You're sure?"

"Yep. I'm good. And I'll tell you all about it while we cuddle in the hammock later."

His eyes flickered with heat, and that did the trick of making him relax and grin. "If I don't keep your mouth busy with other things."

That made her lower stomach flip, and heat spread. Yeah, *that* he couldn't do on non-date days. She liked it way too much. But this was Tuesday. Thank God.

"Ahem." Kennedy cleared her throat. "If she's dirty daydreaming about you today and doesn't get any work done, I'm coming for you," she told Mitch. "I have to be in New Orleans all day tomorrow and Baton Rouge on Thursday, so she's gotta catch on quick."

Paige smiled at him. "Yeah, Mitch. You better go get the coffee, and then get to work and keep those comments to yourself. Until later."

"Oh, I'll be texting you those comments and more," he promised. Then he leaned in and kissed her quickly. "But don't come up to the otter enclosure during your break later."

"Why not?"

"I might be working with my shirt off."

She grinned. She did really love teasing and flirting with this guy. It was good that it was only allowed three days a week. "But... it's Tuesday."

For that, she got another sexy grin and another kiss. This one was a little longer and deeper.

They only broke apart when Kennedy threw a pencil and hit him in the shoulder.

"Get out of here. Don't come back. Even with coffee," she told him. "I'll have Leo bring us some."

Laughing, Mitch winked at Paige and waved at his cousin. "Have a good day, ladies."

Grinning, and maybe even a little flushed in the cheeks, Paige joined Kennedy at the counter.

"I'm ready to learn it all," she told her.

Kennedy nodded, but she was studying Paige thoughtfully.

"What?" Paige finally asked.

"I was just thinking that of all my brothers and cousins... and I have a shit-ton... Mitch is the only one I would consider lecturing a girl about."

Paige froze. She wet her lips. "You want to lecture me?"

Kennedy sighed. "I really don't. I'm not really into lecturing people. Or telling people *not* to mess with my cousins or brothers. In fact, I *love* it when people mess with them."

"But not Mitch?"

"Mitch is... awesome. He will do anything for anyone anytime," Kennedy said.

Paige nodded. "I've already seen that in action."

"So, yeah." Kennedy frowned as if puzzled. "I guess I feel like I need to say something like 'if you hurt him, I'll feed you to the gators'."

Paige felt her eyes widen. "But?"

"I'm just not used to feeling that way," Kennedy said. "Most of the guys need someone to shake them up a little."

"Mitch doesn't?" Paige felt a little squeeze in her heart, and she wasn't even sure why.

"No." Kennedy still seemed a little confused by what she was feeling. "No. Mitch is so... great. He's just always there. For everyone. I mean, he's a smart ass and teases and jokes and all of that, but he is genuinely *good* and generous and so unassuming. I have never asked Mitch for something that he didn't do and do one-thousand percent for me. He's..." She trailed off. "He's just a really, really good guy. So yeah, if you mess with him, I'll have to put bugs in your bed or otter poop in your shoes or something."

Paige just nodded slowly. Kennedy was feeling protective of Mitch. But clearly, that was new for her. Still, Paige got the impression for some reason that she didn't want to be on Kennedy's bad side.

"It's not serious between us. And he knows that. We're definitely on the same page, and no one's going to get hurt. No need for bugs or poop."

Kennedy nodded. "Okay. I mean, I have *plenty* of otter poop but... gross."

"Agreed."

"Okay, so let's go over the computer system first."

Just like that, Kennedy turned to the computer and started opening windows.

Paige blew out a little breath and then took the stool next to Kennedy, determined to concentrate and learn this job so she could do it with the one-thousand percent dedication that Mitch gave to everything.

And she wasn't going to think about how Mitch made her want to be a better person.

Much.

9

They worked for four hours.

Paige felt pretty good about everything at the end of that time.

She'd taken a few calls with Kennedy there to coach her. She'd scheduled two tours. She'd issued one refund. And she'd refused to issue one refund.

"Okay, I'm going to head home for a little bit. I need to make a couple of calls for Bennett," Kennedy said. "You can take your lunch break."

"Oh, okay," Paige said.

Dammit. It was too far to walk to Mitch's. That meant she was going to have to find something closer.

And she knew what was closer.

Ellie's.

Mitch had mentioned that it was right across the road from the tour company, but she'd also noticed it when they'd driven up this morning as well.

Fuck, fuck, fuck.

She was going to meet his family because she didn't want to starve? This was very unfair.

Would it be too much to ask Kennedy to stop over there and assure everyone that she'd already taken care of threatening Paige and that everything was cool?

Kennedy was at the door when she swung around. "You know what it is?" she asked.

"What what is?"

"The reason I'm feeling protective of Mitch."

Oh, that.

"I've been thinking about it all morning. It's so weird. But here's why." She crossed back to the counter. "Mitch was raised by just his dad."

Paige nodded. She'd known that, actually.

"His mom left when he was a baby, and his dad needed help. He came to the family, of course. My mom, my aunts and uncles, my grandma and grandpa, Cora, everyone pitched in and helped raise him. He's more like a brother to all of us than a cousin."

Paige pressed her lips together.

"But he's not like a brother in that he never seemed... or seems... to take anything for granted. Like he knows we all love him and are there for him, but he's always just grateful. My mom used to say that she wished he'd understand that they all took care of him out of love. It wasn't a favor or an obligation. But he lives his life grateful for all of that."

"Grateful," Paige repeated. "Like he doesn't think he deserves it?"

"I remember my mom arguing with his dad. His dad would always tell him to not be any trouble and to be helpful and to be sure that everyone was glad he was around."

"Oh." Paige's heart squeezed.

Kennedy nodded. "I know. I don't think my uncle Sean meant to make Mitch feel bad. *He* was grateful for their help, and he didn't want Mitch to be any trouble. But, obviously, that kind of rubbed off. That's why Mitch will always go above and beyond. Now it's just a habit, just who he is. But it comes from growing up feeling like he had to pay people back for the things they did for him."

Paige didn't know what to say. She had the urge to go to Mitch and wrap him up in a huge hug and assure him that he was wonderful and she loved having him around and that he didn't *owe* her, or anyone, anything.

"Anyway," Kennedy said. "That's why I'm feeling protective." She grinned. "Thank God I figured that out because wow, that's weird."

Paige actually laughed at that.

Kennedy was still grinning when she said, "So don't fuck with him. He's sweet. And I do *not* use that term lightly when it comes to Landrys."

Paige swallowed and nodded. "Promise."

"Great." Kennedy turned on her heel and left.

And all Paige could think was *dammit*.

She'd used the P-word.

She'd *promised* to be good to Mitch. She'd promised one of the scariest of the Landrys that she wouldn't hurt Mitch.

She blew out a breath.

She should go home. She should pack up and go back to Appleby before she messed more things up here.

But you've already agreed to do this job for at least a little bit.

Yeah. She hadn't *promised* to stay for any period of time, but of course, they expected her to help out at least for a little bit.

Expected.

That E-word wasn't much better.

And, she'd also made the date-night and non-date-night agreement with Mitch.

Again, no specific commitment to a period of time, but he was certainly *expecting* them to hang out tonight and go to the crawfish boil on Friday.

And she wanted to. She wanted to date Mitch.

Ugh.

On impulse, Paige pulled out her phone and sent off a text to her sister Josie.

Did you talk to Mom?

Josie responded right away. *I did. She's relieved you're okay. Mad you didn't call her. Curious about Louisiana.*

Yeah, that all seemed about right. Paige had called Josie last night to check in and assure her sister that things were fine. She knew that Piper and Whitney had already talked to Josie the day Paige left and convinced her that Paige was safe and happy and had a plan. Josie had then, by default, been the one to tell their mom and rest of the family where Paige was and what she was doing.

Last night, she'd talked to Josie personally.

Her sister wasn't as adventurous as Paige, or at least that was how it seemed to everyone, but Josie did have the travel bug and understood wanting to get out and see some of the world.

She was also a hopeless romantic. No doubt Josie thought Paige and Mitch were going to fall madly in love and live happily ever after. That was truly what Josie wanted for everyone she knew. So, she was far more supportive of this trip than their mother or other sister would be.

She'd be a great middle man—woman—for Paige.

Paige: *I started my new job, and everyone is so nice, and I'm staying with a friend in a nice house. It's fifty-six degrees today and I'm good.*

Those were all the things her mom would wonder about.

Josie: *I'm glad. And Mitch? You've seen him? He was glad to see you?*

Paige: *Yes, I've already seen him, and he was thrilled to see me.*

She thought about that answer. He really had been happy to see her. That was so nice. Sure, she'd had a few minutes of doubts and nerves, but she hadn't honestly *doubted* Mitch. Not for long.

He really was a good guy. She totally understood why Kennedy felt protective of him. *She* felt a little protective of him. His mom had left, and his dad had made him feel like he had to work to not be a burden on his family.

Josie: *I miss you already, but I hope you're having fun, and I have to admit, I'm jealous of the spontaneity.*

Paige smiled at that. Josie was awesome. Sure, in Josie's mind, the ultimate happiness was marriage and family and a job she loved in their hometown. And there was nothing wrong with that. But if Paige told her that she was honestly, fully happy working at a swamp boat tour company and doing otter yoga, Josie would be happy *for* her.

Her mom would be too. Mostly. Dee would be less thrilled about the distance between Appleby and Autre. She'd want to know what was going on with Mitch. She'd look up facts about Louisiana and send Paige tips on what to do if she ran into an alligator and probably mail a care package of mosquito repellent and sunscreen because she'd know Paige was making her own. They would never be as good at the really strong store-bought stuff.

But, at the moment, anyway, that made Paige smile. She and her mom were very different people. But Paige knew Dee loved her. Paige knew she gave Dee headaches and kept her awake at night sometimes with worry, but never had Dee said or given the impression that Paige was any kind of burden. Dee had happily sent Paige, Josie, and Amanda to relatives' houses for dinners, to spend the night, for help on homework, and so on. She'd asked for help at times, like Mitch's dad, but she'd never told the girls to not be a problem. Dee had, in return, helped out with nieces and nephews as well. It was what family did. Paige had grown up knowing that she could depend on not just her mom and dad and grandparents, but all of her aunts and uncles and even friends of the family. Of course, all of those people were also ready to scold her if she got into trouble or misbehaved. But even that, she knew now, was out of love. And she'd never felt indebted.

Thinking about it now, she realized it really was nice to have so many people looking out for her.

She kind of hated that Mitch felt they'd been doing him a favor by taking care of him.

Paige: *I love you. Thanks for having my back. Always. I promise I'm really good, and I will keep in touch.*

That was a promise she felt completely fine making.

Josie: *I love you too, and I'll always have your back.*

Paige smiled at her sister's text, feeling better than she had in a while about her relationship with her family.

The door to the office opened just then, and Paige looked up.

When she saw the older woman coming in, she had to admit that she'd been hoping it would be Mitch.

A second later, she felt a flash of nerves.

An older woman. Was this Ellie?

Paige sat up straighter on her stool and pasted on a smile. "Hi."

"Hello." The other woman's smile was sweet. She crossed to the desk, and Paige noticed she was carrying a box like the ones Mitch had brought home for Griffin last night. "I'm Cora."

Paige relaxed a little for some reason. Cora was the cook at Ellie's and Ellie Landry's best friend. She was as much a part of Mitch's life as his grandmother from the sounds of it. But she *wasn't* Mitch's grandmother.

"It's so nice to meet you. I'm Paige."

Cora smiled and set the box on the counter. "It's lovely to meet you too. I brought you some lunch."

Paige loved the woman already. "Wow, that was so nice of you."

"Mitch said that you might be a bit intimidated coming over to the restaurant on your own today, and he wasn't able to get away." Cora smiled and leaned in. "I think he just wants to be there the first time to be sure we all behave."

And Paige loved Mitch.

Well, she didn't *love* love Mitch, of course. That would be ridiculous. But it was so sweet of him to think about what she'd do for lunch and know that going to Ellie's alone would have been a lot.

"He's such a sweetheart," Paige said, almost without thinking. She wasn't sure she'd ever called a guy a sweetheart before.

"Oh, he is." Cora said it with sincerity and a soft smile.

Paige smiled in return. Mitch was well-loved. It was obvious already. She'd thought of him for months as the hot, confident, charming Louisiana boy who'd gotten her out of her panties in under an hour of meeting him. She'd assumed he was a playboy who had any woman he wanted and a different one every weekend. That had been in July.

When he'd shown up again last week, they'd had more time together. She'd definitely found him fun and funny and his competence and willingness to jump in to help her hometown out sexy as hell. During his entire time in Appleby, he'd twisted her up emotionally in a way no guy had before.

But seeing him here now, around the people who knew him best and loved him, was adding a layer. Clearly nothing he'd demonstrated in Appleby had been fake. He was a genuinely good guy.

Paige's stomach rumbled, and she opened the box.

It was shrimp and rice and some vegetables.

Oh.

"Oh, no."

She looked up. Cora seemed concerned. Oops, she clearly hadn't hidden her reaction well.

"It's great," she assured the woman. She could pick around the shrimp.

"Are you allergic to shellfish?" Cora asked. "We run into that sometimes, but I never ask. Ellie or the girls take the orders."

"Oh, no, I'm not allergic."

"You just don't like shrimp?" Cora laughed. "I know that's possible too, but I don't understand it."

Paige smiled. She liked Cora. "No. The times I've had it, I liked it fine. I'm just... I'm a vegetarian."

Cora frowned. "Yes. Mitch told me. That's why I didn't bring sausage."

Paige laughed lightly. "Some vegetarians do eat fish and seafood. I just don't." She winced. "I'm sorry."

Cora waved her hand. "Don't be sorry. Come on." She took the box from Paige and closed it up.

"Come on?"

"I'll take you up to the kitchen. You have free reign over anything in there. You can teach me some new things."

Oh. Paige hadn't expected that. "You don't need to do that. I'm fine with cheese or eggs or—"

But Cora was already at the door. She pulled it open and looked back. "Come on now. We'll go in the side door. No one will even know you're there."

Paige didn't really feel she had a choice, so she followed Cora out, locking the office door behind her with the key Kennedy had given her.

Fifteen minutes later, she'd made rice and vegetables, and Cora had insisted on adding vegetable broth, tofu, and yes, even kale to her shopping list. She waved off all of Paige's attempts to insist she didn't need anything special.

"What are you going to eat while you're here?" Cora asked.

"I can... make do. Or buy my own ingredients."

"We're already buying everything," Cora said as if that was a ridiculous suggestion.

"But... no one pays you for food here?" Paige asked.

"Well, not family." Cora gave her a look that suggested *that* was the most ridiculous thing she'd ever heard.

"How do you afford to feed them all?" Paige asked with a laugh.

"Oh, honey, we haven't bought a shingle, or a single screw, or paid for any labor or a delivery fee or gas for our vehicles or anything in years and years," Cora said. "It all works out. We all take care of each other."

That made Paige feel warm. And she realized she could relate. That was how her family was. How Appleby was, for the most part.

"Well, I'm not family, so I will pay you for my groceries," Paige said. "But it would be great if you can get everything."

"You're family," Cora said simply. "You'll do no such thing."

Paige's heart did a little flip. She wasn't sure if it was a good flip or an *oh shit* flip though. She swallowed. "I can't do anything with shingles."

Cora smiled. "We've got shingles covered."

Paige shook her head. "But I don't know what I could contribute to make it even."

"There will be something." Cora didn't seem a bit concerned as she stirred a big spoon through one of the huge pots she had bubbling on the stove. Whatever it was smelled divine.

"I don't have many talents," Paige told her. That was actually true. She knew a little about bookkeeping for her business. She knew yoga. She knew cats. She knew vegetarian cooking. She knew... nope, that was about it.

"Everyone has talents." Cora bent and pulled the oven door open, checking on two different pans she had inside.

"I don't know if I have *valuable* talents," Paige amended.

Cora gave her a sweet smile. "Value is relative. A gold watch to someone who already has one isn't worth as much as a hot meal is to someone who hasn't had one in a week."

Paige blinked at her. Well, that was... very wise.

"Maybe I can help in here."

She looked around. She'd been cooking for herself for years. She'd told her family she wanted to be a vegetarian at age ten. Her mother had said that she would make her a meatless lasagna on lasagna night, but if it was meatloaf night, she wasn't making a second meal. She didn't have time for that. They'd agreed Paige would make peanut butter and jelly on those nights and that she'd have to slowly learn to cook for herself.

She knew her way around a kitchen and lots of herbs and spices and ways to modify recipes. Surely that could be helpful in a restaurant. Okay, *maybe* it could be helpful in a restaurant.

"I cook with a lot of meat," Cora warned.

Paige nodded. "I understand. I won't lecture the customers." She smiled. "Much. Maybe family. People who haven't eaten meatless dishes don't realize how good they can be. Maybe I can convince them to try a few things."

Cora laughed. "I will enjoy watching you try."

Paige grinned as she took her empty plate to the sink to wash. "Well, maybe I can help with dishes at least or something." She dunked her plate into the soapy water. And immediately felt a sharp sting. "Ouch!" She jerked her hand back.

Blood was already running from the cut on her index finger.

"Oh, fuck." Cora hurried to her side. "I have knives in there. I'm sorry."

Paige shook her head. "It's not your fault."

Cora took her hand and headed to another sink. It was a sink that you'd find in a home bathroom rather than the huge stainless-steel restaurant kitchen sink. Cora ran her finger under the water and soaped it. Then she handed Paige a clean towel. "Here, press on it. I'll be right back."

Paige grimaced as she pressed against the cut.

Cora crossed the kitchen to a tall free-standing pantry with glass doors. It had several shelves that were full of little bottles and jars. She looked them over and selected one from a higher shelf, then also grabbed a box of bandages. She came back to Paige, unscrewing the top of the jar.

The salve inside was yellow. Cora dipped some out on her finger. "Let me see it."

Paige peeled the towel back. The cut was only lightly oozing now. It was about two inches long and ran down the outside of her index finger.

Cora made a little clucking noise and then touched the salve to the wound. It smelled lemony. "Rub that in.

Paige did as Cora unwrapped a bandage.

"What's the salve?" Paige asked.

"Oh, one of my homemade concoctions." Cora held the jar up.

The label read SHIT, THAT HURTS!

Paige grinned. "You made it?"

Cora nodded as she applied the bandage. "Calendula flower infused oil with beeswax and lemon essential oil. The mixture acts as a—"

"Natural antiseptic and will keep the skin soft as it heals," Paige filled in with a smile. "I love it."

Cora then surprised Paige by kissing the tip of her finger and pressing it to the top of the bandage too. Paige smiled. That was something her own grandmother would have done.

Things weren't that different here in Autre after all.

"You know essential oils?" Cora asked, returning to her cabinet to store the jar and bandages.

"I do. And calendulas. I make a similar salve. I use helichrysum oil though."

Cora now looked impressed. "I've used that as well."

"Where do you get your calendula flowers?" Paige asked. If there was a place nearby that sold flowers and herbs that could be used in some of her favorite "concoctions," as Cora called them, she'd have to check it out. Maybe she and Mitch could make it one of their Saturday dates.

But Cora grinned and crossed to another door off the kitchen, motioning Paige with her. She opened the door at the back of the restaurant. It opened into a little greenhouse.

Actually, it wasn't all that little. It was the size of the kitchen and was filled with plants. They sat on shelves made of concrete blocks and wooden planks and hung in planters overhead.

"You grow all your own stuff?" Paige asked.

"Most of it."

"Wow." Paige stepped out into the greenhouse. "This is..." She just paused and took a deep breath, drawing in the multiple scents and *feelings*. Yes, she got feelings from being amongst the plants and herbs.

"Mitch helps me take care of it all."

Paige turned back. "Really?"

"He's got a wonderful green thumb."

"I noticed a lot of plants on his porch."

Cora nodded. "He's always loved plants. He's really enjoying the landscaping around the new enclosure for the otters."

Paige gave a soft laugh. "There's no shortage of interesting things going on around here."

Cora chuckled. "That is a very nice—and accurate—way to put it. Never a dull day."

Paige lifted her finger and wiggled it. "Thank you for this."

"My pleasure. And please, feel free to come in here and help yourself to anything. I'd love to compare notes and share recipes. I'd love to have someone I can talk natural healing with."

"I've never really had anyone who appreciated it the way I do. They love my salves and lotions, of course," she said with a smile. "But no one really gets into it."

Cora nodded. "I'm here. Let's play."

Paige felt that swell of warmth in her chest again. This was already turning out to be a really great day. In spite of some of her earlier realizations about her approach to work and relationships.

Then her day got even better.

"Paige? Are you in here?"

She knew that voice instantly. She stepped back into the kitchen, already

smiling. "Hey!" She met Tori Kramer-soon-to-be-Landry in the middle of the kitchen in a big hug. "How did you know I was in here?"

"I went down to the office to find you, and Sawyer said he saw you heading up here with Cora."

Paige hadn't met any of the Boys of the Bayou yet. They only had late afternoon tours today, so Sawyer had been out checking some fishing lines, Owen had been in New Orleans picking up some supplies, and Josh had been helping Tori with some things on their farm that morning.

"Yeah, Cora got me lunch." Paige shot the older woman a grin.

Cora was already back to stirring and mixing, but she was smiling.

"I can't believe you're here!" Tori said. "This is so great!"

"Yeah, I just... got in the car," Paige said. "Needed some warmer weather."

Tori gave her an *uh-huh* look. "I'm thrilled to see you, of course."

"Thanks." Paige believed her. Tori was one of the sweetest, most genuine people Paige had ever met. But she knew that her friend must think this was odd. "I—"

"Got proposed to again," Tori filled in. "At least, that's the story I heard."

Paige sighed and nodded. "Yeah. What the hell is that?"

Tori laughed. "I can't talk. I knew I wanted to marry Josh in about a week. But you're a catch."

Paige shook her head, but she was smiling. Tori had never seemed like the love-at-first-sight type to Paige, but her and Josh's love story was pretty charming.

But she wasn't really anti-romance. She wasn't completely against falling in love. She was against getting married because it was the next "obvious" step. And she was against marrying a guy who didn't *know* her.

She wasn't so sure about the "you're a catch" part. That wasn't self-deprecating. It was just that half of the men who'd proposed didn't really *know* her. They were basing her "catch" status on things like finding her attractive and her being single. Those really shouldn't be the only two checkboxes on the list of Things I'm Looking For In A Life Partner.

"I just needed a break," Paige said. "And Mitch had offered me a place to hang out and..." She shrugged. "Here I am."

"I'm so glad. We haven't hung out in a long time, and being in Appleby last week reminded me of how much fun we have. Now we can do it here."

Tori turned toward the swinging doors that Paige assumed led to the front of the restaurant. And a bunch of other people.

"Oh, I already ate."

Tori glanced back. "Me too. Come on."

Paige sighed. Tori was so nice. It was absolutely impossible to say no to her. Especially, when all she wanted was to spend time with you.

"I have to get back to work in a little bit."

"We all do," Tori nodded. "Come *on.*"

Paige glanced at Cora. The older woman smiled and nodded. Well, shit.

Paige followed Tori through the door.

It did, indeed, lead out into the restaurant. It actually opened just behind the bar. If she turned to the right, she could step through an opening and out among the tables and booths that filled the building. If she turned to the left, she would be behind the long wooden bar that had, clearly, been there for a long time. It was thick, dark wood, and was nicked and scarred.

There was a short, thin woman with salt and pepper hair that hung to her butt in a long braid behind the bar at the moment. She looked over. Her smile was bright, and she shut off the tap she'd had running into the mug she held.

But then she shook her head and kept the tap running. "Hey," she greeted simply.

Paige looked at Tori. It seemed her friend was fighting a smile.

"Paige, this is Ellie Landry. Mitch and Josh's grandma. Ellie, this is Paige. My friend from Iowa."

This was Ellie.

Paige had assumed, but hearing it verified made her heart thump. She swallowed and smiled. "Hi. It's nice to meet you."

"You too," Ellie said, her eyes on the beer mug she set up on the bar. "Can I get you anything?"

A couple of shots of whiskey might help. "No, I'm fine, thanks," Paige said.

"Okay, just let me know."

Paige stood staring for a second. That was it? She'd really expected... more. Like to be surrounded by Landrys and interrogated. That's what she'd pictured. Her on a chair in the middle of a circle of Cajuns who wanted to know why she'd broken off her engagement, when she was planning to marry Mitch, why the hell she didn't eat meat, and what was up with all the cats anyway.

"Thanks," she finally said to Ellie.

"Over here," Tori said.

Paige turned, relieved to see Tori heading for a table at the back of the restaurant.

So, maybe the Landrys didn't really care who she was and what her intentions with Mitch were. That was... great. Exactly what she wanted.

10

Tori led her to a table where two other women sat. They both had glasses of tea in front of them. They stopped talking and looked up with smiles.

"This is Maddie," Tori said to Paige, gesturing to a gorgeous blond. "She's Owen's fiancée and Cora's granddaughter."

Paige gave Maddie a sincere smile. "Your grandmother is great."

Maddie grinned, her affection clear. "She really is. But she'll lecture a year off your life, without even raising her voice, if you give her reason, so don't let that sweet demeanor fool you."

Paige nodded. "Got it."

"Sit." Maddie pointed to the chair next to the beautiful brunette that, by process of elimination, Paige assumed was Sawyer's fiancée.

Paige didn't even think about arguing. She didn't think she'd get far, for one thing. For another, she was curious about these women. No, she didn't want to be the center of attention, and she didn't want a bunch of new people up in her business and wanting every detail of her life and explanations for every one of her decisions, but she kind of wanted to know *their* business.

No, she didn't miss that irony.

But these people were interesting. They had a very different lifestyle from hers, and yet, there were similarities she was already starting to see.

They got up and went to work. They took care of one another. Cora grew and used Calendula flowers. That alone was interesting and cool. And these women gathering here like this, reminded Paige of her sister, Josie, and the way she got together with her best girlfriends, Jane and Zoe. Paige had been envious of their girls' nights and had really enjoyed the times she and Piper and Whitney had gone out together recently. The thought brought on a twinge of homesickness suddenly.

"This is Juliet," Tori said, smiling at the brunette. "She's engaged to Sawyer, and her brother, Chase, is one of Mitch's best friends."

Paige nodded. "I've heard about Chase." She paused. "Well, I've heard about everyone."

Juliet smiled. "It's really nice to meet you, Paige."

"Thanks."

"Sawyer is so relieved you're going to be helping out in the office."

"Relieved? Really? I haven't even met him yet."

"We all are," Maddie said. "We're so happy with how successful the business is now, but we're..." She glanced around. "Swamped."

Tori groaned and Juliet giggled. Maddie was clearly proud of her joke as she grinned and continued, "Kennedy's been feeling guilty and trying to do two jobs at once. And that makes her extra grumpy. So, we're *all* glad you're here to help."

"Well, you're working horribly long hours with the tours and then working on the books after hours," Juliet said to

Maddie. "And Tori's trying to help out along with her practice and the farm."

Tori shook her head. "But I've got Griffin at least. You're helping out by cleaning up the boats and the office after you get home from New Orleans. And you *hate* being down by the water."

"She's a lawyer," Maddie explained to Paige. "So she's working long hours in the city before coming home and pitching in. And she's got a little... phobia... about the water."

"I'm fine if I've got my life jacket on." Juliet waved that away.

"And your hip waders and hard hat?" Maddie asked, her tone and smile affectionate.

Juliet nodded, smiling too. "Right."

"And Sawyer," Tori said. "He'll keep you safe from... whatever."

"I don't know," Maddie said. "She ended up drenched the other day when she was down cleaning off the dock because *he* startled her, and she dropped the hose, and in some weird domino effect I can't even explain, they both ended up soaking wet."

Juliet rolled her eyes. "You'd think he'd know better than to sneak up on me after all this time."

Tori and Maddie were laughing out loud by now.

"Plus," Juliet went on. "I'm not doing anything extra that no one else is doing. Griffin's helping, but you still have all your clients that won't let anyone touch their animals but you." She looked at Paige. "Tori has a clinic attached to the barn behind their house, but she ends up making more house calls than anything."

Paige nodded. "She always did that for me."

Tori laughed. "Well, it would have been very difficult to get all of those cats to the clinic at once."

"How many cats?" Juliet asked.

"Um... more than ten," Paige hedged. She knew she was a borderline crazy cat lady.

Tori shared a smile with her. Tori knew how many there were, but she wasn't telling. And this was the kind of thing that made Tori so damned likable.

The other woman was older by a few years and had grown up in the next town over, but Paige hadn't known her until Tori had called about an orphaned litter of kittens and had then become Paige's vet.

They'd spent the house calls talking and playing with cats, and the time had extended long beyond the appointment and had included opening a bottle of wine at least twice.

Having another woman about her age who was animal crazy had made Paige feel a little less odd. She suspected Tori felt the same way about their relationship. Paige had been sad when Tori had told her she was moving to Louisiana.

"So the petting zoo is made up of all of your farm animals?" Paige asked Tori.

"Yep."

Maddie grinned. "The cow and the pigs and the goats and the llamas are all here."

"Actually, they're alpacas," Tori and Paige said in unison. Then grinned at each other.

Maddie laughed. "Right. Well, anyway, they're all adorable, and one night when we were all sitting here talking about the otter encounter and how we should call the whole thing Boys of the Bayou Gone Wild as a joke, Josh brought up how much her cow and the pig and the goats would love the attention too, and the idea was born."

Paige had to admit that was funny. Boys of the Bayou Gone Wild definitely brought to mind images of alligators. Maybe even a wild cat or a bear or something. Not pot-bellied pigs, alpacas, and otters.

"I love it," she said. "How long until it's open?"

"Probably a month or so," Tori said. "We're just building the enclosure—well, Mitch and Zeke are building the enclosure with Zane and Fletcher's help. Then we need some new fences and pathways for people to walk."

"And a concession stand," Maddie said. "And a gift shop. And an office." She shook her head. "We actually have a lot of work to do. But it's not *that* different, business-wise, from what we do with the tour boat business, so it shouldn't be too long."

"Mitch can build all of that?" Paige asked. She definitely found his handyman side sexy, but she hadn't known how far it extended.

"For sure," Maddie said. "And Zeke is in construction for a living. He owns his own contracting company. And Zander is his main right-hand guy."

"They're twins, right?" Paige remembered Mitch mentioning them last week in Appleby.

"Yep. Ezekiel and Alexander Landry," Maddie said with a grin. "Their mother hates that we shorten their very noble names, but they've been Zeke and Zander as long as I've known them. She's the only one who calls them by their full names. Unless Ellie's pissed at them. Which does happen pretty regularly now that I think about it."

Paige lifted a brow. "Trouble makers?"

"For *sure*," Maddie said. She lifted a shoulder. "Makes Zander being a cop extra hilarious."

"But they're Landrys," Maddie went on. "I mean, Owen has plenty of great stories too. So does Fletch. And Mitch." She gave Paige a wink.

"From what I understand, a lot of Owen's stories involved a feisty blond who liked to set stuff on fire," Tori mused.

"I did not *like* setting stuff on fire. That just kind of happened," Maddie clarified. But she didn't look abashed by the fact.

Tori and Juliet laughed, and Paige made a mental note to ask Mitch about that story.

The history here between all of these people was a warm, almost tangible presence. They had secrets and jokes and stories and clearly loved and supported each other even during the crazy times.

"Well, anyway," Juliet said with a grin. "Everyone's working hard to keep things going and to expand the Gone Wild business. So it's great that you're here to help out in the office."

Paige realized she admired these people. They were all invested in the tour business to the point of helping out on top of their own work. She guessed that if Juliet needed extra hands stuffing envelopes or answering phones at her office, or Tori needed people at the farm, they'd all be there for that too.

It was just a feeling in the air around these people, and Paige found it very appealing. She wanted to be a part of it. She was glad she was going to be able to help out by being here and make it so *they* didn't have to work at the tour company office.

She shook that off. She'd think about it later. Or she'd ignore that all later.

It wasn't a brand-new concept. She'd helped out at the bakery where her sister worked when they needed extra hands. Her friend Piper had plans to start a summer camp for kids in Appleby and, if she were there, Paige would be happy to help with that too. She knew what it was like to pitch in. Of course. People in Appleby did it all the time.

But she knew those people. These people, the Landrys, were strangers. Yet, she felt compelled to jump in and be a part of the group and a part of what made everything run here.

That was so weird.

She hadn't even wanted to meet them all. She'd hoped to lay low.

Now here she was on day two, not just in the midst of the group of women, but already doing something important. Not just because it was assisting their customers and keeping the business running smoothly but because her being here helped each of them individually.

That felt good.

And weird.

She shot a glance at Ellie, who was still behind the bar, chatting with the people—older men mostly—who occupied the stools on the other side, and filling orders.

Ellie was clearly not as enthusiastic about her being here. But Tori was happy, and Cora had been welcoming, and once they'd gotten past the don't-you-dare-hurt-him stuff, Kennedy had been great. And now Paige was going to be able to help Juliet and Maddie out.

This was good.

And, yep, weird.

"Yeah, I guess our after-hours stuff will be with the animals now instead of at the docks," Maddie said with a sigh.

"The guys are doing a great job though," Tori assured her. "I even caught Griffin over there helping them the other night after he'd made a couple of house calls for me."

"You let Griffin make house calls for you?" Juliet asked. "Since when?"

Tori shrugged. "There's no reason he can't do that."

"Agreed," Juliet said. "But you've never let him before. You're very protective of your patients."

Tori nodded. "Yeah, but Griffin is great."

"Of course, he is," Juliet said. "We've been telling you that for two months."

"I know." Tori suddenly blinked quickly. Then she sniffed.

Maddie frowned. "Tor? What's wrong?"

"Nothing."

Maddie and Juliet exchanged concerned expressions. Juliet sat forward. "Tori?"

"The..." She sniffed again. Then blurted out. "I hate the

plantation, and I don't care about the flowers *at all*! I have a dog that's undergoing chemotherapy, and a pregnant alpaca and a horse that might need to be put down, and I *can't* care about flowers!"

Maddie's eyes were wide, and Juliet opened her mouth and shut it again without making a sound. Twice.

Finally, Maddie asked, "Which of your dogs has cancer?"

"Not *my* dog. One of my patients."

Maddie nodded. "Right, because you don't have a horse either."

"No." Tori wiped at the tears that had spilled over her lower lashes.

"And the pregnant alpaca?" Juliet asked.

"That *is* mine," Tori said.

"Oh, well... that's good. Right?"

"I don't know!" Tori truly seemed miserable.

Maddie shot Juliet another look and then Paige.

Paige shrugged. All of this was new to her. Including Tori crying. She'd *never* seen Tori cry before. They were friends, for sure, but they weren't crying-close. Or Tori wasn't a crier. That seemed more likely, actually. Paige wasn't really a crier either.

Maddie reached for Tori's hand. "Okay, so you hate the plantation."

Tori nodded miserably and wiped her cheek again with the hand Maddie wasn't holding. "But it's sweet that Josh wants to get married there. That's where we spent time together at my friend's wedding. When we fell for each other and everything."

Paige nodded. Tori had told her the story of her best friend, Andrew's, Mardi Gras wedding.

"But I don't want to get married at the plantation. It's too big. Too fancy for us. It has memories, but we're just more... outside-in-the-backyard people."

"Where your goats and dogs can be there," Maddie said with an affectionate smile.

Tori nodded. "Yes."

"Then move it," Juliet said simply.

Tori shook her head. "It's too late. It's three weeks away."

"So?"

"So, I barely have time to see my patients and help out with... everything... and plan the wedding and..." She trailed off. Then sighed heavily. "Everything."

"I get it," Juliet said. "I feel overwhelmed too. I'm representing a couple adopting a little girl with some major health issues, and it's so amazing and beautiful, and I find myself planning a party for *them* and totally blowing off choosing a cake for *our wedding*. I honestly don't care what cake we have. I just want to marry Sawyer. Any cake is fine as long as at the end of the day I get to call him my husband. But the cake for this adoption party?" She laughed. "*That,* I want to be perfect."

Maddie grinned. "That's because it's for someone else. You worry more about others than you do yourself. All the time. And you know we're not picky about cake down here."

"Thanks." Juliet gave her a sincere smile. "And you're right. Even not-great cake is still cake."

"And I haven't told you—or Owen—what's going on with *our* wedding," Maddie said.

"What happened with you?" Tori asked.

"We need a new photographer. And I keep thinking I have time to find one, but I don't know if that's true. I keep putting off calling."

"Why do you need a new photographer?" Juliet asked.

"Because I went to high school with the one we hired, and I... kind of called him a prick the other day."

Juliet sighed. "Why did you call him a prick?"

"Because he was being a prick."

"Ah."

Maddie rolled her eyes. "He's always been a prick. But he said something about upping his insurance to cover whatever might happen at our wedding. I told him that the best way to make sure nothing happened to his pussy-ass at our wedding was for him to not be there, and he said fine, but he wasn't giving us our deposit back, and that's when I told him he was a prick."

Juliet pressed her lips together, but Tori lost her fight with her grin.

"You have to stop being so sensitive when people joke about you setting things on fire and breaking stuff," Tori said.

"The fire was an *accident,* and the car I took apart was totally on purpose. So, it's not like I set things on fire on purpose or break things accidentally." She frowned. "That sounds weird."

Juliet snorted.

"It was a long time ago anyway," Maddie said. "People need to move on."

"But now you don't have a photographer," Tori pointed out. Her eyes welled with tears again. "Everything is falling apart." She looked at Juliet. "You should *not* get married on the dock. If there aren't snakes or something down there, then Chase and Bailey will end up falling off the end or something."

Juliet got a little pale.

"Chase's girlfriend, Bailey, is a little... accident-prone," Maddie told Paige.

"Well, only when she's with Chase," Tori added. "But yeah, when they're together, we're all just waiting for stuff to fall apart or someone to end up bleeding."

"And I hate that he can only be here for *my* wedding," Juliet said. "He's in medical school and can't get away three different times. He's a groomsman for us, but he's really disappointed to be missing the other weddings."

"He's family now," Maddie said with a nod. "It will be weird."

"When are your weddings?" Paige asked.

"Tori and Josh are in February, ours is March, and Sawyer

and Juliet are in April," Maddie said. "We had to get them scheduled before tourist season really picks up. We can't take weekends off then."

"I'm surprised you're not all just having a big triple wedding," Paige said.

The three women's eyes widened, then they looked at one another, and their smiles spread in unison.

"That would be great," Tori agreed. "Juliet would be so much better at flowers and decorating than me."

"I've helped," Juliet said.

"Of course. I just mean, we could just do one big bunch of flowers then."

Juliet smiled at Tori. "You *really* don't like the flower thing, do you?"

Tori sighed and shook her head. "I really don't. The ones you've picked out for me are great, but I would like anything."

Juliet laughed. "Well, I didn't want to butt in. I mean, you and Josh were together before Sawyer and I met, and—" She looked at Maddie. "You and Owen have a ton of history. You don't need to share your day."

"Owen and I do have a ton of history, and we've had lots of days—really good ones and some not so good ones," Maddie said, waving her hand. "Which means we don't need this one day dedicated all to us. Our wedding day is about *everyone*."

"You mean we really could be doing this all together? We could have one big wedding day? Why didn't we talk about this before? I'd love to share it all with you two, and I know the guys would love that too," Tori said, her tears starting up again.

Paige's eyes widened. Wow, she'd never taken Tori for a sap. Over animals? Yes, for sure. But over people? Not really.

"You could all just jump on a plane and head to Vegas and elope," Paige suggested.

"Oh, we couldn't do that to Ellie and everyone," Juliet said.

"Nope," Maddie said.

"Of course not," Tori said, wiping her eyes.

"Ellie would be that mad?" Paige asked. Her mother would be livid, so she got it.

"Oh, I don't know if she'd be *mad* exactly," Juliet said. "It's just...we want them *all* to be a part of it. And the town and the docks and just everything that makes up our lives here."

"But you're just as married if you do it somewhere else," Paige pointed out.

"Yeah." Maddie nodded. "It's not that. It's like... honoring them. Or something. It's like 'hey, look what you helped create. Thank you.'"

"You feel like they helped create your wedding?" Paige asked.

"They all helped create *Sawyer*." Juliet smiled. "He's the man he is, the man I love, the man who loves me, because of these people. And I definitely thank them for that. Obviously, he's his own person but they are a part of him. And I want to say thank you and promise them that I'll love him and be there for him as I promise *him* those things."

"Oh my God."

They all looked at Tori. Who was now crying even harder.

"That's so beautiful," she blubbered. "And so true. I feel the same way. They are a part of Josh too. And they made me a part of this family immediately. And I want to *celebrate* this day with them. I know I'm part of the family anyway, no matter what, but this makes it official, and I want a party, with them all, to commemorate that."

Maddie seemed taken aback by Tori's tears, but she nodded and patted her friend's hand. "It's true. And I want to witness it all. I want to see Josh and Tori make those promises to each other so much. So I know Ellie feels the same way. It's just about loving them so damn much."

Paige just took it all in. It felt like a lot. It really did.

Thinking about standing up in front of so many people making such a big promise made her throat feel tight.

But then she thought about her sister's wedding. She remembered how Josie had looked, gazing up at Grant. And how her own heart had thumped when she'd heard Grant vow to forever love someone Paige loved so much. It felt so good to know that there was someone making Josie incredibly happy and taking care of her and making her feel like the amazing, special person she was.

Yeah, Paige understood all of this to some extent.

It was big. It was important. It mattered to a lot of people.

Which was why it wasn't something to be done lightly or until both people were sure to their *bones* that it was the right choice.

"Well, if we did have just one big wedding, we'd have to move our date," Tori said.

"Yeah, you couldn't do that," Juliet said.

Tori frowned. "Of course we could."

"But you and Josh met on Mardi Gras. You have to get married on Mardi Gras."

Tori shook her head. "I was thinking about that the other day when I was realizing that the plantation is such a bad fit." She sighed. "We met on Mardi Gras, but when we tried to reconnect the next year, it didn't work. What really mattered was the next day when I came down here to find him. When I put myself out there again, for the first time in *years*, for someone. And then when I came after him after Andrew's wedding. Each time I made the big gesture was on the dock. The dock was the place where it really started."

Maddie and Juliet both nodded.

"I guess that's true," Juliet said.

"So you'd move your date? Really?" Maddie asked.

"I would." Tori nodded. "I love you girls so much." Tori sniffed and gave them all a wobbly smile. "And the guys would love to share their day the way they've shared every other big thing in their lives."

"We love you too," Juliet said.

"We do," Maddie agreed. "But are you sure your dress will still fit if we bump your wedding date back a month or two?"

"Why wouldn't it?" Juliet asked.

"Well, she'll be further along in the pregnancy by then," Maddie said.

Tori gasped.

Paige felt her eyes go wide.

Juliet sat up straighter. "What?" she demanded.

"Right?" Maddie asked Tori.

"How...how did you know?" Tori asked.

Now both Juliet and Paige gasped.

"You're *pregnant*?" Juliet asked.

"Shhh!" Tori cast a look to where Ellie and Cora were both working behind the bar.

"So no one knows?" Maddie asked.

Tori shook her head. "We *just* found out."

"How did *you* know?" Paige asked Maddie.

Maddie smiled. "Tori isn't usually a weeping mess. And she hasn't been into the wedding planning thing from the beginning, but she's been handling it."

It wasn't hard for Paige to imagine that Tori wasn't that interested in wedding details like flowers and cakes and bridesmaid dress colors. She was a large animal vet. She spent her days with her hands in places that a lot of people didn't even want to think about, not to mention *touch*. She was an animal-crazy sweetheart, but Paige was sure she'd spent more time as a kid playing outside in the dirt with kittens and ducks and cows than she had with dressing up dolls or having pretend weddings.

Tori took a deep breath. "It was, obviously, not a planned thing."

"But you're happy?" Paige asked.

Tori's face brightened immediately, and her smile was huge. "Yes. I mean, now that it's sinking in. I'd never thought that much about being a mom, but yeah, Josh and I had talked about starting a family, and now..." She sighed, but this was a happy sound. "Yeah, I'm happy. And Josh is over the moon."

Paige felt the crazy urge to grab her friend into a big hug. Tori seemed a little dazed, but also genuinely happy, and Paige had seen her caring for enough animals to know that she was going to be an amazing mom.

"How are you feeling?" Juliet asked. "Other than emotional?" She gave Tori an affectionate smile.

"Good. Mostly. I'm a little nauseous at times, and I get *tired* at the end of the day," Tori said. "But mostly good. I'm only about seven weeks along. So, I'm sure that could all change. And Griffin is going to be mad."

Paige frowned. "Why is Griffin going to be mad?" The guy was clearly a grump, but what did Josh and Tori having a baby have to do with him?

"He'll have to take over more of the practice," Tori said. "At least, for a while after I have the baby. And I might want to be home more. I'll miss the animals, so I won't ever not practice, but the beauty of what I do is that I can do it part-time on a flexible schedule. And I have *lots* of babysitters around here." She grinned at the other two women. "But he'll have to pick up more of the schedule."

"Oh, Griffin would love to do more."

Tori, Maddie, and Juliet all looked at Paige with surprise.

She shrugged. "Griffin and I have talked a little. He likes animals. I think as long as the things he's spending time with have four legs, he'll be okay. Or," she added, "get him a zebra or something, and he'll be golden."

Tori looked interested. "Did he say he wants a zebra?"

Paige lifted both brows. "Would you get him one if he did?"

Tori seemed contemplative. "I mean...we could look into it. He was in Africa, in Zambia, working with a conservationist group, before he had to come home after his parents died. Then he worked at a couple of zoos. I mean, he does love those animals."

He'd been in Africa? He'd lost both his parents? Huh, Dr. Griffin Foster was more interesting—and maybe had more reason to be a grump—than she'd thought.

Paige watched Tori's wheels turn. They would just get Griffin a zebra if that would make him happier? Who were these people? But she couldn't help but grin. She loved that they didn't let things like "normal" and "crazy" dictate their thoughts and actions.

"The otters really love him," Maddie said with a nod.

"Do they?" Paige asked.

"Oh yeah. They follow him around and squeak at him."

"And he's nice to them, right?" Paige asked. He'd been sweet with her cats, but he didn't come off as a softie.

"Oh, for sure. I mean, he rolls his eyes and tells them to calm down and they've had enough treats and that they're attention hogs," Maddie says. "Of course, he only talks to them when he doesn't know there are other people around."

Paige laughed. She liked that. Maybe Griffin *was* a softie underneath.

"He just thinks people suck," Tori said.

"Well, I mean, there's lots of evidence to support that," Paige said with a shrug.

Tori shook her head. "People are mostly good. They just need to be understood and accepted."

Suddenly Juliet pushed her chair back and rounded the table, grabbing Tori in the hug Paige wanted to give her.

"You're wonderful. You and Josh are going to be amazing parents," Juliet said.

Tori started crying again.

Maddie sniffed and wiped at her eye.

Paige felt her throat tighten.

"What is going on over here?"

They all froze. Then Maddie and Juliet pivoted slowly while Paige and Tori looked up.

Ellie was standing at the table looking at them all suspiciously.

Tori quickly wiped her cheeks. "Nothing. Just a... dog. That's got cancer."

Juliet nodded. "I was just comforting her. You know how soft-hearted she is."

Ellie propped a hand on her hip. "I'm used to my boys trying to pull one over on me, but you girls haven't been practicing long enough to have a single hope. Spill it."

Maddie snorted.

"Even you, Miss Maddie," Ellie said, her eyes narrowed. "Though you've been at it longer than these girls."

"You'll notice I didn't even try," Maddie said.

"Smart." Ellie nodded. Then she focused on Tori. "So, what's going on?"

"I don't want to have the wedding at the plantation."

Paige thought that was a good way to go. It was true. But she watched Ellie carefully. Could Ellie tell which truth was *the* truth?

"So don't," Ellie said simply.

Tori nodded. "That's what we were talking about."

"Is that why you haven't had spicy gumbo in a couple of weeks? And why you've been eating a lot more fried pickles? And banana pudding?"

Paige glanced at Tori. Her mouth was hanging open.

"You've noticed what she's been eating?" Paige asked Ellie. That was impressive, considering how many people ate at this place.

"I notice everything," Ellie told her, one eyebrow up. "But especially when it's about food."

"I love fried pickles and banana pudding," Tori said, a little weakly.

"I had heartburn with all of my pregnancies," Ellie said.

Paige was entertained by all of the women's mouths falling open at the same time.

Damn, Ellie was good.

Maddie was the first to recover. "I don't know why we should be surprised you figured it out."

"That's what I was thinking," Ellie said.

"How did we give it away?" Juliet asked. "The crying and hugging?"

"I figured it out a week ago," Ellie informed her.

"Because of the gumbo?" Tori asked.

"Because of Josh," Ellie said, her face softening and a smile curling her mouth.

"Josh told you?" Tori asked.

"He didn't have to. He's like one of those lights with a dimmer switch," Ellie said. "He started glowing brighter after he met you, then even brighter when you fell in love, brighter again when you said yes to marrying him. Only one thing could turn that up even higher."

And Tori started crying again.

And dammit, Paige felt her eyes stinging a little too.

11

"I think we got it," Fletcher said, stepping back from where they'd just finished digging one of the swimming pools in the otter enclosure.

Mitch went to stand by him. "Looks good."

"Griffin's gonna wonder why it's deeper." Fletcher grinned.

"He'll figure out that Tori overrode his plan in about two minutes," Mitch said with his own grin.

"Well, Tori's the one paying for it," Fletcher said. "Or she's the one who convinced Josh, Sawyer, Owen, Maddie, and Bennett to pay for it."

The Boys of the Bayou owners were also the owners of Boys of the Bayou Gone Wild, so they were the ones ultimately buying the supplies and paying for Mitch, Fletcher, and Zeke's time building the enclosure.

"I don't think Tori has trouble convincing Josh of anything," Zeke said, coming to join them on the slight hill that looked down on the first, and larger, of the two swimming pools for the otters.

No, she did not. But she didn't have much trouble with the rest of them either.

It helped that Bennett was a millionaire, of course. And that Kennedy also loved the otters. And that Kennedy could also convince Bennett of nearly anything.

The sketches Griffin had done of the enclosure looked like an otter version of a water park. There were slides and ramps and various levels for the otters to climb on. Of course, they were all disguised as rocks and logs and trees and natural formations. The whole thing looked like a chunk of the river bank had been relocated a bit inland and their river —that even had a built-in current—connected two swimming pools.

Otters had never had it so good.

The whole thing was ridiculous.

And very cool.

"This is huge for just a few otters, isn't it?" Zeke asked.

It was. "I have a suspicion Tori has some plans to expand the otter family size," Mitch said.

Zeke grinned. "And maybe to more than otters."

Mitch wouldn't be surprised.

They discussed a few more of the plans, consulted the sketches, and did some measuring, deciding they could get part of the river dug out and a section of the bank reinforced before dinner.

Mitch, of course, wondered what Paige was doing. When he'd texted her, asking, she'd told him she was fine.

But he was a guy. Who'd heard "fine" from a number of women over the years. Grandmothers, cousins, girlfriends. "Fine" could mean a lot of things.

He'd pressed, and she'd said not to worry. He'd apologized for not being able to get away for lunch, and she'd said it was okay. He'd said he was looking forward to their date-night, and she'd said she was too.

Mitch blew out a breath thinking about it all, even now. Paige wasn't a texter. He knew that. He'd spent six months frustrated about that. Why did he think that would change now that she was here?

He was far more frustrated that she was only about a mile away, and he still couldn't see her and didn't know what she was thinking or feeling.

He'd sensed she was a little nervous this morning about the new job and meeting his family, and... she'd had a right to be. The Landrys were really best dealt with like a shot of home-made moonshine—don't think about it too hard, take it all in at once to get it over with, and chase it with a beer.

He needed to get the girl a beer. STAT.

"So, you're really not going to tell us anything about the hot blond?"

Mitch looked at Zeke. His cousin had his long hair tied in a ponytail and a bandana wrapped around his head. His t-shirt was lying somewhere on the hill behind them, and the tattoos that crossed from his chest, to his left arm, then down the left side of his torso, and over his back moved as his muscles bunched.

Mitch and Fletcher gave him and Zander shit about their hair, but Kennedy, Maddie, and the other girls assured them that, while not all guys could pull off the long hair, Zeke and Zander definitely did. The notches in their bedposts absolutely attested to that.

Mitch decided not to pretend to not know what he was talking about. "No, I'm really not going to tell you anything about the hot blond."

"Been a *really* long time since a girl slept at your house," Fletcher said from where he was digging.

It had been never. At least, not in the house he was in now.

He'd inherited the house from his Aunt Sylvie when she'd passed. Most of his family lived in Autre, and most of the family houses had been passed down from older relatives. The Landrys were a founding family and so had been some of the first to build here. There were lots of Landry family houses. He was happy he'd gotten Sylvie's. It was away from town a bit with lots of space out behind. The land behind his house and the three to the east was Landry land too. But no one was going to ever build on the land. It was going to remain wide open and natural. It was why they'd decided to make it the site of the Boys of the Bayou Gone Wild.

There was plenty of room for the petting zoo animals to roam and for them to put up barns and buildings. Along with a crazy big otter enclosure.

He could see his house from where they were digging right now, in fact.

He couldn't imagine bringing a one-night stand to that house. It was probably stupid, but that house was... a home. It wasn't just a place where he was crashing until he settled down. He was settling down *there,* and that meant... hell, he wasn't sure what it meant when it came to women exactly. It just hadn't felt right to bring someone over who wasn't going to last.

Then, of course, there was the fact that since he'd met Paige, he also hadn't had any sleepovers with anyone at all.

"I don't bring women to Sylvie's house," he said simply, returning to the dig.

"It's *your* house now, man," Zeke said.

Yeah, it was. He knew that. He just kept digging.

"Why's this girl different?" Fletcher asked.

At least they were still working while they pried into his personal life.

Which was another indication that Paige was different. These guys were the ones, besides Chase, that Mitch was most likely to talk about women with. The fact that he wasn't giving them much here probably meant a lot.

"Because I like her outside the bedroom too. She needs me to be a friend. And a place to stay. She just needs a break. I want to give her a place where she can just... be." That was all true.

"She's a friend who drives all the way from Iowa to just... be?" Fletcher asked.

Mitch stopped and leaned on his shovel. He pinned Fletcher with a look. "If Jordan just showed up on your doorstep, you wouldn't let her in and let her just be?"

"'Course I would."

"Same thing."

Jordan Benoit was Fletcher's best friend. She was also a hot blond.

Jordan had been taking care of Fletcher for the past nineteen years. They all loved Jordan. She was part of the family. She was also currently on tour with her rising-country-music-star boyfriend, Jason Young.

"But Jordan would *actually* just be a friend," Fletcher added.

"Paige is actually a friend."

"Paige is single. And you've had sex. That makes her different from Jordan in a couple of pretty important ways."

"It's your own fucking fault Jordan isn't single and you haven't had sex with her," Zeke said with a snort.

Fletcher sighed. This was not the first time they'd all had *this* conversation.

"Hell, if you'd had sex with her, you could have made her single pretty easily," Zeke said. "Jason would have dumped her, and then you'd be together."

Yep. Exactly this conversation.

"She's been with Jason since we were fifteen. They're practically engaged," Fletcher said. For what had to be the hundredth time in his life.

"That's because you're stupid," Zeke said.

"She's taken," Fletcher said. "She's *been* taken."

That's what he'd been saying since they were seventeen, and he'd realized what every other guy in the parish had realized about a year before—Jordan Benoit was gorgeous.

She'd always been cute. But that summer between fifteen

and sixteen she'd developed curves. Though she hadn't seemed to realize it. Or she hadn't realized it was a big deal. She'd stayed the same tomboy she'd always been, hanging out in short shorts and tanks, coming down to the swimming hole in swimming suits without cover-ups, wearing short sundresses, because it was fucking hot in Louisiana in summer. She'd dressed the way she always had. But she'd filled all of those clothes out far differently than she had the summer before.

And every guy in the area noticed.

Except Fletcher.

"Yeah, okay," Mitch said, letting Fletcher off the hook. "It's a little different. Paige and I have chemistry, and we're acting on it. But we're friends first."

"You're acting on it, huh?" Fletcher said.

"Yeah. I mean, if we have an itch, we'll scratch it." Mitch shrugged, wishing he felt as nonchalant as he sounded. "But she's here temporarily, and I know it. This is just 'til she's ready to move on."

Zeke nodded his approval. "Cool."

It probably did sound cool to Zeke. He was very into itch-scratching. And temporary.

Mitch needed to talk to Zeke about it more often. He seemed pretty willing to accept this at face value. That's what Mitch needed. Someone who thought this all made great sense.

"Well," Fletcher said. "Don't go falling in love with her."

Yep, that was really good advice.

"I'm fine," Mitch said.

Zeke nodded, obviously convinced.

Fletcher lifted a brow in an uh-huh-sure expression.

Mitch *definitely* needed to spend more time with Zeke.

M itch pulled up behind his house three hours later. He didn't keep set hours. He worked until the work was done or until he ran out of daylight or supplies or patience.

Today, they'd knocked off when they'd found a stopping point. Which meant the river portion of the enclosure was mostly dug out, and they'd reinforced it enough that any pending rain wouldn't undo a whole day's work. It would just be him tomorrow. Fletcher had only had one day off from school, and Zeke was working on a house renovation on the other side of town.

Griffin's truck wasn't at the house when he pulled in.

That meant he and Paige were alone. At least for a little while.

He'd stopped at the office to pick her up, but according to Sawyer, Kennedy had already taken Paige back to his place.

Mitch ignored the way his heart was suddenly hammering. He couldn't wait to see Paige and hear how her day had been. That was new.

He didn't come home to women. He met up with them or picked them up at their places for dates. But he'd come home to Paige at her place in Appleby, and he'd liked it far more than he should have. And now, kicking his boots off on the back porch and stepping into the kitchen, knowing she was somewhere inside, felt really fucking good.

The kitchen was empty though. As was the living room.

"Paige?" he called.

He hadn't really thought about how the date night was going to go beyond them being together and being able to kiss her.

And he wanted to start right now.

"Out here!"

He followed her voice out to the front porch.

Where she was in his hammock.

And she looked so damn right there that he stopped for a moment and just gripped the door frame between the house and the porch.

She looked over at him with a soft, contented smile.

Soft and contented after a day with the Landrys. That was something.

"Hey," she greeted.

"Hey." He gripped the edge of the doorframe a little harder.

She shifted a little to look at him more directly, the hammock swaying gently. "You okay?"

His heart was pounding hard, and he could hear Fletcher's voice in his head. *She is not just a friend no matter what you say, dumbass.* "Yeah. Do I not look okay?"

"You don't look okay," she said.

"What do I look like?" He wondered if she could see him trying not to fall in love with her as he stood there half on and half off his own porch.

"You look wound-up," she said after studying him for a moment. Her eyes tracked over him. "And hot."

He felt the corner of his mouth tick up. The wound-up part was probably as accurate as anything.

"Hot? As in 'damn, it's hot out there'?" he asked.

She nodded. "But also, damn, you look good all sweaty and dirty."

He looked down at himself. This was how he came home most nights. His t-shirt and jeans were streaked with dirt. As were his hands and probably face. He was sticky with sweat. His hair was probably sticking up.

"You didn't get all sweaty and dirty in Appleby," she said. "You did all that save-the-whole-town manual labor thing, but it was too cold for you to get all messy."

He relaxed his grip on the doorjamb as his grin grew. "You did mention picturing me in a tool belt though."

She nodded, her gaze again tracking over him from head to toe. "I did do that."

"I used tools today too," he said.

This woman's eyes on him did things to him that no other woman had ever done even with her hands, or hell her mouth, on him.

"Big tools?" she asked, her tone flirty and her smile I-know-what-I-do-to-you.

He liked that she knew how to push his buttons. The fact that she wasn't staying—was intent on leaving actually—should make him want to pull back and not let her have a lot of leverage over his emotions.

But he wanted her to know how he felt about her. Even if it hurt in the end.

And hell, it was too late anyway. He didn't know how to hide this.

"Really big," he said, stepping onto the porch.

She licked her bottom lip. "And it was hot and dirty?"

"So dirty," he agreed.

He felt safe crossing the porch to her now. He wasn't going to scoop her up out of the hammock and fuck her right here on the porch.

And he wasn't going to drop to one knee and ask her to stay in Autre with him forever.

At least, not at the moment.

He pulled a chair over next to the hammock and sat.

"You can get in here with me," she said.

"I will. But I need a shower first."

He noticed she had a notebook and pen in hand. She was in different clothes too. She was wearing a tank and shorts. Her hair was in a messy bun, and her feet were bare. She looked so relaxed and like she'd been lying in that hammock after work every day for years.

He wanted that. He laced his fingers together and squeezed.

Maybe he wasn't completely safe from scooping her up and stripping her naked.

Or proposing.

"How was your day?" he asked, trying to get his mind on something else.

"Good, actually." She even said it with a smile.

"Yeah?" He knew he shouldn't sound skeptical, but his family was a lot. "I didn't mean to throw you to the wolves. I mean..." He dipped his head and rubbed a hand over the back of his neck. "I guess I knew that's how it would turn out. As soon as I thought of you working in the office, it was inevitable that you'd meet them all. And probably all at once. And they'd give you the third degree. But I really did intend to get over there for lunch. I should've known not to make a plan like that though."

"It turned out fine," she assured him. "Great, actually. And I didn't really get the third degree."

He looked up. "No?"

"I mean, after Kennedy threatened me."

"Kennedy threatened you?"

"You're her favorite." Paige gave him a grin. "Did you know that?"

He started to shake his head but thought about it. Then he shrugged. "Actually yeah, I guess I did. Not that she's ever said that, but yeah, I'm sure I'm her favorite."

"The guys in your family are a handful," Paige said.

"*Kennedy* is even more so—don't let her fool you."

Paige laughed. "Definitely figured that out. But anyway, after that, I met Cora."

Mitch couldn't help the soft smile he felt stretch his lips. "Cora is the best."

"She really is," Paige said. She lifted her hand and tucked a strand of hair behind her ear.

Mitch noticed the bandage on her finger immediately. He

felt his brows slam together. "What happened?"

She stopped and frowned at the sharpness in his tone, then followed his gaze to her hand. "Oh. Small cut. No big deal. Cora took care of it."

Mitch took a breath. He had definitely over-reacted to that even if Cora hadn't been involved. But knowing Cora had doctored the injury did make him feel better. "You let her put some strange cream on your finger?" he asked.

Paige nodded. "I'm into strange creams."

"Yeah?" That should have sounded weird, but he found it endearing.

He loved Cora. He'd been almost eight before he'd understood that Cora wasn't his grandma by blood. Not that something like blood and DNA had ever mattered to the Landrys when it came to considering someone family. Or not.

"Yeah. And it was a salve, actually. I make mine a little differently, but hers is great."

He leaned in. "You make your own salves and creams?"

"And lotions and scrubs and antiseptics and cleaning solutions and teas," she said with a nod.

Yep, definitely endearing. His yoga-doing-crazy-cat-lady-vegetarian also made home remedies. That tracked.

"She gave me a calendula."

Paige pointed, and Mitch looked over to where a bright yellow pot full of orange flowers had joined the other plants along one of the porch windows.

"That was sweet."

Paige nodded. She was now doodling on the notebook page on her lap. "She told me how to make the salve and said I could take the calendula home with me. I'm supposed to send her some of my salve then."

Mitch felt his chest tighten, but he made himself nod. "You'll be able to email back and forth. I can even show her how to Facetime. Again."

Paige smiled slightly at that. But she didn't say anything.

He focused on the notebook page. It was full of writing. But he noticed there were also sketches. One looked a lot like the Boys of the Bayou dock.

"So your day at the office was okay?"

"Yeah. Kind of busy but nothing crazy. Booked tours, greeted people. No big deal. Kennedy was there most of the day, and when she had to leave, Sawyer helped me out. Josh and Owen are hilarious."

"Good. I'm glad they were all good to you."

Mitch wasn't in the habit of telling his older cousins to mind their manners. Mostly because he never needed to.

Sawyer, Josh, and Owen generally did mind their manners. At least, well enough to have what they said and did chalked up to playfulness and flirting.

And Mitch had never had a woman he'd felt protective of enough to care if she was comfortable around his family.

"And I..." Paige started.

He waited for a few seconds before nudging the hammock and making it sway. "You what?"

"I had lunch with Tori."

"Oh. Good." He should have known that Tori would seek Paige out. That made him feel better. Tori was a friendly face and was one of the sweetest people he knew.

"And Juliet and Maddie."

"Oh."

He loved Juliet and Maddie. They were awesome. But they, like any of the other Landrys—and they were Landrys even if the official ceremony hadn't happened yet—could be a lot in larger doses.

"It was great," Paige said, meeting his gaze with a smile. "I really like them."

He didn't hide the little breath he blew out. "Good. I really like them too."

"We talked about their weddings."

Well, shit.

Wedding talk was the exact topic he would have told the women to avoid at all costs with Paige around.

Of course, all three were brides-to-be. The family was going to have a wedding a month for the next three months, starting in just a few weeks. He imagined those girls talked wedding stuff a lot when they were together.

He reached out and took one of Paige's arms, lifting it and inspecting it from all sides.

"What are you doing?" she asked, bemused.

"Looking for hives."

She laughed. "I lived through it. Didn't even break out in a cold sweat."

He kept hold of her hand when he lowered her arm. He met her gaze. "You're still here, so I guess they didn't scare you off completely."

"Them talking about *their* weddings is okay, I suppose," she said. "I won't get itchy unless *you* ask me about swatches."

He nodded. "I don't really know what swatches are, so I think we're safe there."

She smiled. "But I was hoping I could ask *you* about something without *you* getting any images of boutonnieres or tuxedos running through your mind."

He lifted her hand to his lips simply because now that he was touching her, he couldn't *not* kiss some part of her. "Also, not entirely sure what a boutonniere is, and you will never see me in a tuxedo, so I think we're okay."

He wasn't sure why his heart was suddenly drumming. It wasn't the same feeling he'd had stepping into the house. That had been more of an *I fucking love this* feeling.

This was more of a hopeful feel. And he didn't really understand that. She was *telling* him not to read anything into this. Even if he didn't know what a boutonniere was, he knew she was warning him not to think whatever she was about to say was more than it was.

"Well, I've been thinking about a couple of things and I was wondering if you would take me on a swamp boat ride."

That was not at all what he'd been expecting. "Of course," he said easily. "But now I'm *certain* I don't know what a boutonniere is, and I'm even questioning if I know what a tuxedo is. What do those have to do with swamp boats?"

She laughed. "The girls were talking about all the stuff they have to do for their weddings and everything that's going wrong and they're worried about. They don't seem that into all of the planning. They're all so busy and have been helping keep the tour company going and are planning to help with the petting zoo too. And it's pretty amazing how they're all coming together. I was just thinking that the wedding stuff could be *a lot* easier."

Mitch just blinked. She'd been thinking about the other couples' wedding plans?

She watched him blinking at her for a few seconds. Then she frowned. "Weddings often turn out to be a lot more work than they need to be."

"Okay."

"I've got several friends and two sisters who have planned weddings, and I've been in on a lot of it."

"Right."

Her eyes narrowed. "And I planned one for myself."

His eyes narrowed. "Yeah. Don't remind me."

He didn't need details. He hated the idea that she'd been so close to marrying someone else. And that the whole situation had soured her on relationships and the idea of getting married again.

Yes, she was young. Yes, her mother was pushing her to settle down. Yes, she had plenty of time and should be free to have her relationships on her own terms, whatever those were.

He still wanted her to want to get married.

And that was going to be a problem.

She'd been here for about twenty-four hours with the clear understanding that this was temporary and casual, and he was already thinking about how he wished she'd want to get married.

Fuck.

"Anyway, I think I could help the girls with some stuff. But I want to go on a swamp boat tour before I know for sure that my idea could work."

He straightened on the chair, surprised. "The boat tour is to figure something out for the girls' weddings?"

"Yeah."

"Paige?"

"What?"

"You hate the idea of weddings and getting married and all of that."

She focused on the paper in front of her and colored in a loop on one of her doodles. "Not for other people."

"Paige?"

She sighed. "What?"

He waited for her to look over at him. "Have you become the *wedding planner* for my family?"

12

Paige's cheeks got a little pink, and she pressed her lips together, shaking her head.

Mitch felt his grin stretch wider. "I think you have."

"I..." She wrinkled her nose. "I didn't mean to."

He laughed.

"And I'm not officially. I haven't told them any of my ideas. They didn't *ask* me to help. I haven't done anything."

"Yet."

"I just was thinking about it after we all talked. I couldn't help it." Her voice dropped to almost a mutter on the last four words.

"And you came up with a bunch of ideas to help them out."

"They're just so busy. Helping each other out and helping the family out, and keeping everything going. That's really admirable. And I can't really help with Juliet's law practice or Bennett's foundation stuff or operating on a cow or anything. But—" She blew out a breath that seemed resigned. "I do know a lot about weddings. Even if I don't want to."

Mitch was torn between laughing and wanting to bend her over right here on his porch.

But, while his road was quiet, his neighbors were Fletcher, Zeke, and Zander, who had also inherited family homes. Well, Zeke had built his own a little way down. But they shared this road that jutted out at the end of Autre and butted up against the wide-open land that ran from their back porches to the bayou.

The family and several of the locals affectionately called it Bachelor Row.

It meant he always had three of his best friends nearby.

It also meant he had three of the most obnoxious members of his family nearby.

Driving right past his front porch.

"Okay, come on."

Mitch leaned over, scooping Paige up out of the hammock as he stood.

She gave a little gasp, then a giggle as her arm went around his neck. "Come on where?"

"The bayou. But first, I need a shower."

She ran her hand up the side of his neck to his face. She wiped his cheek. "You are dirty."

"I am."

"I like you dirty."

"I know." He gave her a naughty grin as he headed into the house with her.

"Am I helping with this shower?"

"You are. I really did intend to snuggle with you on the couch and be sweet and romantic tonight, but you blew it."

"I did, huh?"

He started up the steps. She was totally comfortable in his arms and with the idea of being in his shower, and he loved that.

Yes, loved.

He knew that was dangerous, but it was true.

"You did."

"By helping out with the weddings?"

"Yep."

"Because you know that's kind of not my thing?"

"Yep."

"And because it only took your family a few hours to get to me."

He kicked open the door to the bathroom and swung her feet to the floor. He immediately stripped his shirt off. "Yep."

"And because I'm still here even after being with them and talking about weddings all day?"

"Yep."

Paige's eyes ran over his naked torso. There was immediate hunger there that made Mitch's body heat and tighten. The way she wanted him was as much an aphrodisiac as seeing *her* naked. This woman could have any man. Hell, she could have literally been married to five or ten guys just in her own hometown. But she wanted *him*. Maybe she didn't want to get married, but she'd come to him when she needed a place to go. He couldn't let go of that.

And his family hadn't scared her off. Yet.

She hadn't had a full dose, but she was already ass-deep in wedding plans, and if that didn't do it, there was a decent chance she'd stick around.

He reached for her tank top, stripping it up and over her head.

She hadn't put a bra on when she'd changed clothes.

They might have to talk about her going braless and wearing these cock-hardening clothes with Griffin sharing the house. At some point. Right now, Mitch needed to get his hands on his favorite pair of breasts in the world.

He stepped close, backing her up against the wall between the towel rack and the shower. He cupped her breasts, and her head fell back against the wall.

"You make me feel so good." Her hands covered his as he kneaded and teased the hard tips.

"I've been thinking about you all day."

"Me too." Her eyes met his, and she reached out, running her hands over his body too. "But not just the sex."

He crowded closer, sandwiching their hands between their bodies. "What else?"

"Your life. The people in your life. How the people I hung out with today are a part of your every day. A part of who you are. They know things about you, have stories about you that I don't know... but I want to."

Mitch's heart slammed hard against his ribs. He ran his hands down her sides to her hips. "I'm sure they'll tell you." He tried to keep his tone light.

She smiled. "I'm sure they will. And I want to hear them."

He wasn't sure what to do with that. What to say or think or how to feel.

But this felt like *something*. Like she was realizing this was something.

"I want to hear stories about you too," he said. He meant that with all his heart. He wanted to know everything about her. "Even the stories about Garrett."

"Really?"

"Yeah. I mean, I hate him. I will probably always hate him." He said it with a teasing tone. But seriously, the guy had almost gotten Paige down the aisle. Mitch did *not* like him. Even if that was completely irrational. "But he's a part of your story. He's part of who you are right now, and I really fucking like who you are, and I'd like to know all the things that made you."

Something flickered in her eyes, and her lips opened, almost as if she was surprised or touched. Then she nodded. "Okay. Let's tell some stories. On the boat. But right now..." She ran her hands down his abs to the button on his jeans. "I'm feeling pretty dirty too."

Lust licked along his nerve endings. He liked her. He wanted her stories. He wanted *her*. He fucking loved that she wanted to help with the weddings. He had definitely not been expecting that.

But right now? He needed her naked and wrapped around him and gasping his name.

Maybe even screaming it.

He felt the button and zipper on his jeans open as he reached over and locked the bathroom door. Then he pivoted and leaned to turn on the water in the shower as Paige pushed her shorts to the floor.

He froze as he took in the fact that she hadn't put panties on either.

"You can't walk around the house like this when Griffin is here," he said, running a hand up the outside of her thigh.

"He said he was going to be late tonight," she said. "I wouldn't have otherwise."

"You were going to sit on the couch with me like this?" he asked, taking in every inch of her body.

"Yep."

"We were never going to make it through a whole movie."

"That's what I figured."

He shook his head with a half-grin. "You gotta keep your clothes on at the crawfish boil on Friday, girl."

"Well, just while we're with other people, right?" she asked, reaching for his jeans and pushing them down his legs.

He kicked them off as she slid her hand into his boxers, taking his already aching cock in hand.

Mitch braced a hand on the wall over her head as his knees got a little weak from the rush of pleasure. This woman touching him was the best thing he'd ever felt.

"Yeah. Just while we're with other people. And that won't be long, I have a feeling."

She smiled up at him as she stroked him. "And I won't be eating any crawfish so it will be a short dinner for me."

"Well, the drinking and bullshitting and dancing is what really takes the time."

"We can't skip that stuff?" She tightened her grip and moved her fist along his shaft.

His eyes nearly crossed. "We…" He swallowed. "We'll be missed."

"Are you better at the drinking, the bullshitting, or the dancing?"

"Yes," he answered, honestly and with a grin, in spite of the urge to thrust into her fist.

"Then I'll have to be *very* persuasive when I try to talk you into leaving, I guess."

Before he could answer, she sank to her knees in front of him.

"Pa—"

She licked him before he could even say her full name.

Her hot tongue against his cock forced his eyes shut, and he had to just focus on breathing for a moment. She licked his length, slowly and thoroughly, then circled his tip before sucking him into her mouth.

"Fuck," he muttered, his hand going to her head. One hand was still on the wall, essentially holding him up, but the other held the bun on the back of her head.

She followed his urging and took him deeper.

The air around them started to fill with steam, and he groaned as she sucked and licked.

He didn't even feel a niggle of guilt about her doing this for him when he'd barely touched her. He fully intended to repay her for every single stroke.

Paige added her hand to the action, and Mitch felt his climax building. "Darlin'," he said gruffly.

She didn't stop.

He tugged on her hair. "Paige. Baby."

She let him go for only a moment. "Let me do this. Please."

Well, damn, if wedding planning got her going, who was he to argue? He dragged in a lungful of air and eased his grip on her hair. She took him deep, stroking him with her hand at the same time. Her pace picked up as she sensed him getting closer. Mitch locked his knees, his gut tightening.

He watched her taking him, feeling the heat of her mouth, watching the sway of her tits as she moved, knowing that she *wanted* to do this. The lust built quickly, a hot ball gaining in intensity and pressure. Finally, she sucked again, and he let go, spilling into her throat.

She swallowed, still stroking up and down his shaft as he felt the pleasure rush over him. When she pulled back and looked up at him with a very satisfied grin, he was torn between the urge to laugh, kiss the hell out of her, and spank her.

She was clearly pretty damn proud of herself.

And she should be.

But he was going to be proud too. Very, very proud.

He bent and caught her under the arms, turning and putting her on the bathroom counter without a word.

She gasped as her ass hit the cold granite countertop.

But he immediately knelt, spread her knees, and licked her.

"Mitch!" Her hand went to his head, clutching his hair.

Damn right she was going to call his name.

She was hot and wet and *ready*. "Sucking my cock makes you really wet, darlin'," he said between licks with his whole tongue.

Before she could reply to that, he sucked her clit into his mouth.

"Yes!" she cried.

He slid two fingers deep. He knew this woman's body and loved that truth. He knew how to touch her, how to make her wiggle, and clench, and gasp, and cry out, and come. Hard.

"Mitch!"

"Louder, Paige. Fucking say it louder." He stroked deep, sucked hard, pumped in and out of her until she called his name loud enough that Griffin would have definitely heard it in the living room if he'd been home.

Mitch hoped his roommate was home.

Paige's pussy clenched around his fingers as she came hard and fast, and before she'd even caught her breath, he'd scooped her up, stepped into the shower, and pressed her against the tile wall.

He loved this shower. The house had been old enough that they'd needed to redo the entire bathroom when he'd moved in. Zeke and Zander had, of course, done the work with Mitch and Fletcher lending an extra four hands when needed.

The shower had a rainfall showerhead that was amazing. The enclosure had two full glass sides and two marble walls. There was also a built-in bench. It worked to hold bottles of shampoo and soap, of course. The guys had said it would work like a bench in a sauna. But Mitch was pretty sure that they'd all figured it would also be great for sex. He hadn't used it for that. Until now. But it was a *very* good reason to have added that feature.

He kissed her deeply as she wrapped her body around him. The water coursed over them, making their bodies hot and slick, but they clung to one another, kissing with tongues stroking, moans mingling.

"You still okay without a condom?" he asked against her neck, breathing in the scent of her, released from her hot skin by the water and steam.

"Yes. Definitely."

He'd just come in her mouth, but it wasn't enough. He needed her body. All of her. He could go all night, he swore.

If the girl didn't want an airboat ride, he'd keep her right here and fuck her a dozen times before sunrise.

But her wanting that airboat ride made him want her even more.

And hell, he could get her naked—at least naked enough—out on the bayou. That would be sweet. And hot.

He'd never had sex on an airboat, but he knew several of his cousins had.

Two of whom Paige was planning weddings for.

Yeah, that idea made his cock pulse, and he shifted her against the tile, then sank into her.

They moaned together.

He thrust deep and hard. She tightened around him. And with the edge taken off, they drove each other crazy for several delicious minutes.

"This is my favorite way to shower," he told her, buried deep.

She kissed up the side of his neck. "We'll both be late for work every morning if this is a regular thing."

Damn, he wanted this to be a regular thing. He wanted a lot of things with her to be a regular thing.

"Good thing we both have jobs with no set hours." He dragged his hand up and down her side, just loving the feel of her skin.

"I do. I have to be there by the time the tours start."

He thrust again, deep and slow. "Maybe you need a new job."

"I just got this one."

"We need a yoga studio in this town."

She laughed and tightened around him again. She did have *really* good core muscle control, something she'd teased him about—and with—in Iowa too. He *loved* yoga.

"But what about the tour company?" she asked.

"What tour company?" He thrust again, a little harder this time.

She made a noise that was part moan, part gasp, and he did

it again, just to hear that sound. He reached between them, rubbing the pad of his thumb over her clit.

Her head fell back against the wall of the shower. "I don't know about any tour companies. I don't care about any other job. I can't even remember how to do yoga," she said, her voice breathless even as she teased. "I want my job to be having sex with you in this shower."

"That's illegal in Louisiana," he said with a grin, even as he thrust again while circling her clit.

"I think it's illegal everywhere," she said.

"Guess you'll have to give it to me for free."

She tightened around him again, and he groaned.

"You're giving me plenty in return."

For a second, his heart stopped. He wanted that to be true. Not just sexually, though he would gladly give her anything and everything she wanted in that department over and over again. He wanted to give her everything outside of the bedroom —or shower—too.

Paige didn't need him.

She was one of the most independent women he'd ever met. And he knew *a lot* of them. He'd been raised by and around strong women. None of the females he knew needed their men. They *wanted* them. They were with them because they chose to be, not because they needed to be.

That just made it all sweeter. Having a woman choose a man rather than need him was so much more meaningful. He wanted that with Paige. For her to stay here, to be with him, would absolutely be a choice. She wasn't from here. She didn't have roots here. Hell, she didn't even have a job here. To make a life here would take effort. She'd have to meet new people, find a way to make a living, adjust to new everything from weather to traditions. If she stayed, it would purely because she *wanted* to.

And if she left, it would be because she didn't want to stay *enough*.

Suddenly hit by a desire to make her need *something* badly, he gripped her ass with one hand and picked up his pace.

"*Mitch*," she gasped.

With his thumb rubbing her clit, he pumped into her. "Just giving you plenty," he said, his voice gruff.

She gripped his shoulders. "Thank you," she started to tease. "Oh!" she cried as he hit a deep spot.

He needed to be even deeper. The slippery wall wasn't giving him enough leverage. He pivoted and somehow managed to lift a foot to kick all the bottles off the bench. Then he sat, with her straddling his lap. They both moaned as she sank down on him.

This was perfect. He was going to thank Zeke for insisting on adding the bench.

Not only did it make it easier to hold onto her, but it made it a hell of a lot easier to lean in and take a slippery, hard nipple into his mouth. He sucked and felt the tightening around his cock.

It also made Paige start moving. She lifted and lowered herself on him, taking him deep. He reached for her clit again, but her fingers were already there.

Her head thrown back, her long, wet hair falling down her back, her finger circling her clit, she looked like every fantasy he was going to have from here on out.

Mitch just leaned back and watched.

She moved faster, her moans getting louder, her breasts bouncing, and he held her hip, trying to hang on until she was there with him.

"Mitch! Yes!"

Then she clamped down, coming hard, and he thrust up, deep, four times, then gripped her body, holding her tight, filling her as the hot waves pounded through him like the streams of water from overhead.

She sagged against him, and he pressed her against his chest.

After they'd caught their breath and she'd given him a huge smile and slid off his lap, they soaped each other from head to toe. The water was starting to run colder by the time they finally climbed out wrapped in towels.

They were also both grinning like idiots.

"Well, I really like date night so far," Paige said.

"Same. I really should have tried this dating thing before."

She swatted his arm. "Uh, you know how you hate talking about my proposals? I kind of hate hearing about your girls too."

He ran a towel over his hair and thought about that. "Well, mine is born purely of intense jealousy of any man ever having so much as a minute of your attention, not to mention anything like that—" He glanced at the shower. "So, if that's how you're feeling, we're more on the same page than I thought."

She looked at him with narrowed eyes and a hand on one hip.

Fucking adorable. That's what she was.

"You want me to confess being jealous of all your previous women? And you think if I do, it means I have some kind of deeper feelings for you than friendship or wanting to fuck your brains out?"

"Um, yes, Paige, that's exactly what I want and what I think."

"Huh."

"Plus, you want to hear stories about me from my family. Like cute stories about me as a kid and stuff. That means more too." He was feeling very damn happy about that now that he thought about it more.

"I take that back."

"No take-backs."

"You can't call no take-backs *now*."

"I just did. I heard you say that you like me. A lot. Like you *like*, like me," he teased.

"It's the cock." Her gaze went over him. "And the abs. And the ass."

He grinned and tossed his towel toward the hamper, starting for the door naked. "I mean, sure. I get all of that," he said, with plenty of attitude. "But you *like* me, too."

"I'm not going to marry you, though."

He glanced over his shoulder. "Didn't ask."

"Okay. Keep it that way."

"Sure thing... darlin'."

He went to his bedroom to get dressed, feeling pretty damn good about... everything.

He met her back in the middle of the hallway a few minutes later.

She was in shorts, but these were more reasonable than the loose ones that barely covered her ass. These were just denim shorts. With a pale green t-shirt. And white canvas tennis shoes without socks.

And he wanted to rip it all off of her and kiss her from head to toe and make her scream his name again.

He sucked in a breath. Dammit. She was going to break his heart when she left.

13

The bayou was actually quite beautiful.

She'd seen photos online. And she'd had an impression of it. From books or movies or TV, she supposed. She'd seen the trees and Spanish moss and water yesterday from the back of Mitch's truck, but being *on* the bayou was different.

In among the trees, it felt different.

They were now floating in an area that dead-ended where the water was more still.

"It's so pretty here," she said, softly, almost not wanting to disturb the peace. "Quiet."

The airboat had been too loud to talk over when they'd initially pulled away from the dock and headed down the deeper channel to the actual bayou waters. They'd both had ear protection on, and Mitch had sat up behind her on the tall seat where he could manage the boat. She'd sat on the first long bench in front of him with her feet propped on the bench in front of her.

They'd taken one of the smaller boats. This one could hold up to ten people and was reserved for the smaller groups that booked for longer and more intimate tours. They took these boats deeper into the bayou into places where people could get really up close and personal with the wildlife and were willing to pay for more time with the guides who would tell them stories and more facts and trivia as well as answering questions.

Once they got down to the bayou, Mitch had cut the engine, and they'd coasted along the quieter waters. They'd removed their headsets, and he'd been able to tell her about what she was seeing. And yes, stories about growing up on the bayou.

He'd swum and fished and hunted here. He and his cousins had goofed around, played jokes on one another, even had actual fights. They'd drunk beer and moonshine down here. Camped out. Partied. Made out with girls in their trucks.

This was his home. This place was a part of who he was, a place where he had tons of memories. Like Appleby was for her.

And yeah, she liked being here, seeing all of this, hearing his stories, more than she would have expected. More than she should.

Maybe it was because she'd already known most of the stories of the guys she'd dated before, but this felt more intimate than she'd been with any other guy before.

Dating before, even Garrett—maybe especially Garrett—hadn't involved sharing stories. She'd known Garrett's stories as well as her own. Their moms were best friends. They'd grown up almost identically. They'd gone to school together since kindergarten. They hadn't dated until much later, but they'd had teachers and friends and summer activities in common forever.

"This is one of my dad's favorite spots. He first taught me to fish right here."

She looked around. "So, you've been here a lot?"

"A lot. With him. With the guys. Sometimes by myself."

She took in the scenery with a new eye knowing that Mitch had seen this same view, these trees, the slight rise to the north, so many times. And he'd brought her here, specifically, on her first trip down the bayou. That touched her.

Hearing Mitch tell his own stories was a totally new experience. Not just because the stories involved things like alligators and rougarou—definitely not things that made regular appearances in stories from Iowa—but because listening to him tell the stories told her what was important and meaningful to him.

Mitch was sitting next to her on the bench, now that they weren't moving much. He had his arm draped over the back of the bench seat behind her. He leaned in and pointed.

Paige followed his finger, squinting.

"See him?"

"No."

He put his cheek against hers, tipping her chin slightly with his finger, then he pointed again. "There's a big ol' log, then just to the left..."

"Oh!" There was an alligator on the bank next to the log. He blended into the vegetation perfectly. She would never have noticed him on her own. "Wow."

"I can maybe get him to come over. Or a friend of his. Or two."

Paige felt her eyes widen, and she looked at him. "Uh. That's okay."

"You don't want to see him up close?" Mitch gave her a grin.

"Nope." She most certainly did not. "But... how would you get him to come over? You just call him over?"

He chuckled. "Actually, Owen and Sawyer can do that. Josh sometimes."

"No way."

"In certain areas, they can," Mitch said with a nod. "Gators are very territorial, so they stay in their areas. Then those guys go to the same spots over and over to give the tourists a show. The gators know the boats mean they're gonna get fed. So, they start associating the guys' voices with food, and they'll swim over when they hear them."

"You've got to be kidding." Paige looked back at the alligator.

"Nope. I mean, I'd have to try just chucking marshmallows in the water and hope one was swimming close and came over. But those guys have pretty good luck."

"They like marshmallows? No way."

"Nope. They think they're turtle eggs."

"What?"

Mitch chuckled again. "They look like turtle eggs floating in the water. They just swallow them. They don't taste them."

"Those can't be good for them," Paige said, wrinkling her nose.

"I mean, they're basically dinosaurs." Mitch shrugged. "As Bailey says, you don't get to be eight million years old by not being adaptable. I'd think if something like marshmallows could kill them, they wouldn't still be walking around millions of years later."

"Bailey?" Paige asked. "She's Chase's girlfriend, right?"

"Yeah. You'll get to meet her at the wedding, if not before. She sometimes stops down to say hi even when Chase isn't here."

"And she's really into alligators?"

"It's her job. She works for the Louisiana Department of Wildlife and Fisheries and specifically studies alligators and frogs."

"And she's fine with the marshmallows?"

"Nope. She wants us to stop doing that. But she admits that it would take more than a blob of sugar to really hurt these guys."

Paige laughed lightly. "Got it. Well, let's not get the blobs of sugar out today. I don't need the dinosaurs coming over here."

He just hugged her closer to his side.

"How many people can fit on one of the bigger airboats?" she asked after a moment.

"About twenty or twenty-five."

"Do you have any idea how many people Maddie and Owen are inviting to their wedding?"

"No idea."

"Huh." Paige chewed her bottom lip, studying the cove they were floating in.

"But we could get about sixty-five people on one of the pontoon boats."

Paige pivoted quickly on her seat to face him. "What? Really? You have pontoons?"

"Yep. They're covered too."

Her eyes widened. "So, we could hang things from the cover? Decorations?"

"Sure. Probably."

"Is there a sound system?"

"There is. We use them for sunset cruises and bachelor or bachelorette parties, birthday parties, that kind of stuff."

"That would be perfect."

"We can't take them down every waterway. Some are too narrow, but if you just want to get a boatload of people out on the bayou, that would be a way to do it."

"Yes!" She pivoted back to look around. "Could you get it down to the place where Maddie almost shot the alligator?"

She felt Mitch shift, and when she glanced at him again, he was looking at her with a mix of amusement and puzzlement. "Who told you that story?"

"Sawyer."

"Really?" Mitch looked sincerely surprised.

"Yeah. He came into the office before one of his tours. I asked him how he met Juliet, and he told me about how he found her literally hanging off the dock one morning. And how she and her brother came down here to rebuild the dock after

Chase and his buddies crashed an airboat into it." Paige narrowed her eyes, studying Mitch. "Why do you look totally amazed by this?"

"Because Sawyer just isn't... chatty. He's not the one I would have expected to be telling you stories."

Paige gave him a little smile. "Maybe I'm very charming."

His smile was a lot more wicked. "Oh, I find you *very* charming. I'll tell you any story you want me to tell."

"I'm going to keep that in mind." She wanted to hear all of his stories. She shouldn't. That would make it so much harder to keep him in the *casual-fling* category. But looking into his eyes right now, she could admit, to herself only of course, that he'd already jumped over to the *oh-shit-I'm-in-trouble* category.

"And then Sawyer told you about Maddie and Owen?" he asked, clearly intrigued by Sawyer's talkativeness.

That made Paige feel good. She wasn't one to sit around and gossip and trade stories for fun. At least not before now. But today, she'd been asking for a purpose. Still, it did make her feel good to think Sawyer had been comfortable talking to her after only knowing her for a few hours. And she'd enjoyed the stories. Even if they hadn't been fuel for her ideas about the weddings, it had been fun hearing someone talk about how they'd met their true love.

Paige almost rolled her eyes at herself. She wasn't into love stories. She'd heard dozens over the years. Her family was love-crazy. Every single couple had a story that had been told over and over again.

But now that she thought about it, she really did like the story of how her grandparents had eloped. And how her dad had first developed a crush on her mom in third grade when she brought a caterpillar to school for Show and Tell.

She realized that she couldn't remember the details of how her other grandparents had gotten engaged. She knew they'd met at a dance but didn't remember how her grandfather had proposed. She should ask about that story.

"Paige?" Mitch nudged her. "Sawyer told you about Maddie and Owen?"

"Oh, yeah." Paige shook herself and focused. "I asked him how Maddie and Owen met, and he told me they grew up together and had been together until she went to live with her grandparents in California and got back together when she came home after her brother died."

"He even told you about Tommy dying?"

Paige frowned slightly at the concerned look on Mitch's face. "Yeah. Why?"

"That's..." Mitch shook his head. "That's pretty big. Tommy was Sawyer's best friend. His death was terrible and really hard on Sawyer in particular."

That had been easy to read in Sawyer's face. "That was obvious," she agreed. "But yes, he told me."

"Wow." Mitch gave her a little smile. "It's a big deal he felt comfortable telling you that."

Paige felt a little flutter in her chest. "He also told me about how Tori came down here to find Josh when she came back to Louisiana for Mardi Gras last year. I knew about their story mostly—how they met on Mardi Gras and then agreed to find each other again the next year if they were still interested—but I didn't know she caught a ride on one of your tour buses and came down here to find him when they didn't reconnect in New Orleans."

That had sounded so out of character for her friend, and prior to seeing Tori and Josh together, Paige wasn't sure she would have believed that story, but now she had no trouble imagining Tori doing anything to get to Josh. And vice versa.

Mitch grinned. "Yep, the Boys of the Bayou dock has seen a lot of romance."

Paige nodded. "Exactly. So, shouldn't they all be saying their vows on the site where it all began?"

"You mean have the weddings on the dock?"

"Well, I think Josh and Tori should have theirs on the main dock. Juliet and Sawyer should have theirs on the dock they built together. And Maddie and Owen should get married on an airboat in the cove, where Maddie almost shot an alligator for him."

Mitch just stared at her. Paige bit her lip.

What did she know about all of this? These people weren't her friends. She'd been in town for a day. *One day.* What the hell was she doing? She was planning their weddings? The minute they'd started talking about bouquets she should have come up with an excuse and high-tailed it out of Ellie's. Instead, she'd sat there listening to it all, suggesting the girls should be sharing their big day, putting *that* idea in their heads. Then she'd been thinking about the weddings all day. She'd asked Sawyer about their love stories, for fuck's sake.

"Say something," she finally told Mitch.

"That's sexy as hell."

She blinked at him. "What is?"

"You getting involved. Wanting to help the girls. Having these ideas. These *romantic* ideas."

She sighed. "They are romantic, aren't they?"

Dammit.

He grinned. "They are."

"Well, you came to my town and saved the day."

"You're doing this for *me*? That's even hotter."

She laughed. "I don't know who I'm doing it for. I'm just..." She shrugged. "Doing it."

His smile softened. "Now *that,* might be the hottest thing of all."

She shook her head, but she couldn't help but notice the

flip in her chest in the general vicinity of her heart. "You find weird things sexy."

He slid an inch closer. "Nah. You get it. You found it sexy when I rewired the town square in Appleby."

She had. She'd even admitted that to him. "So being helpful is an aphrodisiac?"

"I think it's the caring about other people." He lifted a hand to tuck a strand of hair behind her ear.

"But the people in Appleby were strangers to you. And all of these people are strangers to me except Tori. Why do I care that Maddie and Owen should get married on an airboat?" She shook her head, then sighed. "But they really should."

She could see it clearly in her mind. Even just hearing the story from Sawyer, she could picture how it had all happened, and it seemed that even if *that* wasn't the moment they'd fallen in love—or realized they were in love—that moment showed them what being in love meant.

"Well, this is going to sound conceited," Mitch said. "But me caring about Appleby, and you caring about these weddings, isn't about who they are to us. It's about who *we* are. We see something we can help with, so we do." He lifted a shoulder as if it was all really that simple. "We have that in common. And it's a good thing."

Paige frowned. "I don't see myself that way."

She really didn't. She helped at the bakery, and she helped her girlfriends with advice and loaning them dresses and things like that, but people didn't come to her for *help*. That wasn't a role she filled. For anyone.

"You don't see yourself as someone who wants to help?"

"Well, cats, sure."

He laughed. "You know why you help all those cats, right?"

"Because cats are awesome." But she felt a little niggle in her mind that said there was more to it. And that Mitch really might know.

"Everyone in Appleby thinks that you take care of cats to fill a gap in your life where you should be taking care of people, right? A husband and kids?"

She nodded. When he'd been in Appleby, one of the chattier women in the community had filled him in on a few commonly-held beliefs about Paige's "situation"— i.e., her being unmarried and childless and very happy with that status. It was weird in Appleby to not want marriage and family. Even at age twenty-two with plenty of time for all of that.

"I think they're not totally wrong."

"Hey." She frowned at him. "I thought you were on my side about me being young and it being okay to have a few adventures and some time to do whatever I want before I settle down. *If* I settle down."

She'd actually really appreciated the way Mitch had been an ally when she'd told him about her plans for a Year of Aloneness and not wanting to get married for a *long* time.

"I am. I just think that they're on to something. I think you *do* care. A lot. And you want to take care of something... someone. More than one someone. The thing is, everyone in your life is so busy worrying about *you* and taking care of you that there's not really room or time for you to take care of them."

"They all take care of each other," she muttered. "They don't really want my help."

Maybe it was because she was the youngest of her sisters and of all the grandkids, so they didn't think of her as capable of really being *helpful*. Or maybe she just didn't have any true skills that were useful to anyone else. That one she knew was partly true.

And maybe, she just never really offered. Because when her mom or oldest sister asked her to babysit or help with her niece and nephew's school projects, she assumed they were trying to jump-start her biological clock. That wasn't entirely *untrue*. But maybe that wasn't the only reason they reached out to her.

Man, that all made her sound kind of shitty when she really thought about it.

Mitch nodded. "Right. They don't really give you a chance to take care of them, so you take care of cats."

Except that maybe they did sometimes reach out, and she assumed they had ulterior motives, and she said no. Suddenly she was feeling like she needed to call her mom.

She swallowed. "And now that I'm here, I'll have people to take care of?" she asked. Then she laughed lightly. "There's so damn many of you. There's no way you're not all being taken care of."

He lifted a brow. "You heard all the wedding drama first hand. No one's taking care of that."

Well, he had a point.

"We all have a place," Mitch told her. "We're all pieces in a big puzzle. Sure you get the general idea of the big picture, even if something is missing, but it's not *complete* without each piece."

Paige felt a warmth in her chest. "That's really nice that you all just find a way to fit."

"Well, we *make* ourselves fit."

"What do you mean?"

He shrugged. "Zeke became a contractor so he could help out with repairs and remodeling around here as well as putting up new houses and buildings for the town. He's also an accountant, though he mostly does the books for family businesses. It's why Zander became a cop, too."

"Really?"

"He always wanted to do something like that. Firefighter or EMT or something. He was a cop—a detective, actually—in New Orleans for a few years, but when George, the cop here, retired, Zander stepped in. That way, he could stay close and take care of the town and his friends and family."

"Wow. Is that why you're a fix-it guy?"

"Exactly why. I wanted to help out, and someone always needs something fixed."

"Fletcher became a teacher, so he could stay close too?"

"The idea of teaching the kids here, being involved with the school and district here, part of making it better and giving these kids the best education they can get, is a big deal to him."

"That's all really impressive."

Mitch reached over and pulled her bottom lip from between her teeth with the pad of his thumb. He stroked over her lip, causing tingles. "Sometimes, you have to figure out what the place where you want to be needs from you. You should do something that makes you happy, of course, but there are a lot of ways to fit."

She thought about all of that. Was she taking care of cats because that was all anyone would let her do? Because cats kind of didn't have a choice? Because she wasn't confident enough in what she wanted to do to push any harder?

She *loved* her cats. She really did.

But she did go overboard when it came to determining if someone would be a proper adoptive cat parent. Her questionnaire had been called ridiculous, and the fact that she insisted on an in-home visit at the six-month mark to be sure everything was okay was maybe a little over-the-top.

"I'm not giving up my cats."

"But you're going to plan these weddings?"

"I guess I could make a few phone calls."

Mitch's answering grin made something deep and hot in her belly clench, and she sucked in a little breath. God, making him grin like that made her want to do it over and over and over. And it really wasn't hard. He was thrilled she was getting involved with his family.

But in spite of the trepidation she'd felt and the yearning for peace and quiet she'd been convinced she needed, she'd had a great day.

"How did Garrett propose to you?"

Mitch's out-of-the-blue question made Paige sit up a little straighter. "What?"

"We're on the subject of weddings. I want to know about you and Garrett."

Oh. That was fair, she supposed. "Okay, but you have to tell me some stories too."

"I've never proposed. Or been proposed to."

That was good to know.

She frowned at that thought though. She wasn't supposed to care how Mitch lived his life before her. Or after her. This was temporary. And casual.

But even in her own head, she knew that they'd already blown past casual. The part that still remained to be seen was the temporary part.

The fact that she was already less certain about that only spoke to how dangerous Mitch Landry was to her plans.

And potentially to her heart.

If she and Mitch thought this was something more than it was—or if it *was* more than they'd intended it to be—and then she left in August as planned, she'd break his heart. And, she knew too well, breaking other people's hearts didn't just hurt them.

She still wasn't over how disappointed and sad her parents and Garrett's family had been over their canceled wedding plans. She'd never forget the hurt in Garrett's eyes. She could still feel her own jab of pain now, four and a half years later.

"Have you ever been in love?" she asked. "Had your heart broken?"

"Maybe at the moment," he said after thinking for a second.

"The in-love part?"

"Yeah. Michelle Dillson."

"Wow." Paige was shocked by how much she hated Michelle Dillson.

"It was pretty serious."

"Huh." Paige decided she didn't want to talk about Michelle.

"We had lunch together every day. For like two weeks."

Paige narrowed her eyes. "Two weeks?"

"Yeah. Well, maybe eight days."

"Which is just one day over one week."

"Well, five days a week in a school week, so..."

Paige realized what he was saying. "When did you date her?"

"Fourth grade."

She shook her head. "Got it. So no, you haven't really been in love."

He took a couple of seconds to answer. He was watching her intently. It made her heart turn over in her chest.

Please don't say anything like "until now" or something.

"I guess not," he finally answered.

The stab of disappointment she felt was stupid, and she was irritated at herself. She made herself nod. "Me either."

"But you were engaged." He didn't say it as if he was surprised that she was confessing to not being in love with her one-time fiancé.

"Right. Because we'd dated for over a year at that point, and our families really wanted us to be together forever. Our moms were best friends. Even before we were dating, we had holidays and took vacations together once in a while. Once we were together, our moms talked about how amazing it was going to be to share grandkids and things like that."

Paige studied the bottom of the boat. It seemed like all of that had been a lifetime ago, yet she could still remember how she'd felt sitting at the dinner table listening to their families talk as if she and Garrett were already married.

"They caught us in his bedroom one night when we thought they were all out. They didn't even care." She gave a soft laugh, but she wasn't amused. She hadn't been that night either. "I think that was when I realized that I was in *way* over my head. They'd caught their seventeen-year-old son having sex with his girlfriend, and they were almost happy."

Paige looked up at Mitch. "I think that was when I realized that Garrett would eventually propose, and I'd say yes, and we'd get married, and... my whole life was already mapped out. It was just expected."

Mitch's jaw was tight, and he looked like he was trying not to say something he shouldn't.

"How did he propose?"

She thought about it. That night in his bedroom, and then the day she'd stared at herself in the fitting room mirror in a *wedding dress* at age eighteen and thought, *what the hell am I doing?* were more etched in her memory than the proposal.

"It was at my graduation party," she said. "He asked me to go over by the garage with him. And..." She shrugged. "He asked me to marry him."

"By the garage?"

"Yeah."

"Did he have a ring?"

"No. He said we should pick it out together."

"Did he say something sweet about you being the love of his life, and he couldn't imagine the future without you or anything?"

"No."

Mitch clenched his jaw again but didn't say anything more about it. "How did the next guy propose?"

"Which one?" She gave him a little teasing smile. It wasn't mature or probably even nice, really, but she liked poking him about her plethora of proposals because she liked his jealousy.

He gave a growl and said, "The *next* one. The one who thought he should ask twice."

"Oh, Adam." She grinned. "He asked me in his car in front of my apartment after a date the first time. The second time he showed up at my door with roses and a fruit tray." She smiled. "That was sweet. At least he knew enough to not bring me candy that I wouldn't eat."

Mitch gave a resigned sigh. "Yeah, he gets points for that."

She laughed. "Number three, Stephen, proposed at a candlelight dinner. With a ring in the middle of a lava cake. The whole thing. Everyone in the place was in on it."

Mitch narrowed his eyes. "Which you hated, right?"

"*So* much."

He studied her, and she felt like squirming. Mitch had seemed to figure her out easily from the very beginning, and it was weird. No one *knew* things about her that she didn't *let* them know.

"But you're not opposed to public displays," he finally said.

"It's not that. That isn't why you hated it."

She studied him back. Then she nodded. "Right. I hated that he really thought that's where we were. That he didn't know that was way too much, too soon. Or ever. You don't propose, and certainly not publicly, unless you're *sure* of the other person."

Mitch nodded. "Right. It's more of an announcement to the world then. The public display isn't so much about the question itself because you know the answer, but it's about making it memorable and letting everyone around you in on it."

Paige realized she was leaning in. Their noses were only a few inches apart. "And you'd never do it in a restaurant full of strangers. You'd do it at a family gathering or in the middle of Ellie's or something."

He nodded. "Yep."

She swallowed. That was how it should be done.

She knew that public proposals weren't everyone's jam. Hell, *proposals* weren't *her* jam in general. But at that moment, sitting and looking at Mitch Landry, she knew that the only way he'd ask a woman to share his life would be with his whole family gathered around in some meaningful way.

And the jolt of jealousy and ache she felt thinking about him doing that with someone else wasn't just a little prick of pain near her heart. It was like a knife slicing through her gut.

Dammit.

Leaving him was going to hurt so much.

"And then Carter proposed standing by my car in the freezing cold after we'd danced a few times at Josie's wedding reception."

Mitch's eyes widened. "Just blurted it out?"

"Yep. Out of the blue. Just 'hey, I was thinking.'"

"Jesus."

She shrugged. "I'm sure he'd heard that the roses and lava cakes hadn't worked. He figured why go to all the trouble."

"You go to the trouble because it fucking matters. But you go to the *right* trouble. You don't do it because some cheesy movie did it or because you want to make a big public spectacle of how great you are. You make it meaningful for you as a couple and for..." He pulled in a breath and sat back suddenly. "Never mind."

Yeah, they should both never mind all this talk. For sure.

"Should we head back?" he asked. "I can show you one of the pontoon boats."

She nodded. "That'd be great." She actually wanted to stay out here with him for a few more hours. Or days. Or forever.

So, yeah, they should definitely get back.

14

"We'll have to walk a bit down to the far dock for the pontoon," Mitch told her as they coasted up against the dock.

But it was immediately evident that their plans were about to change.

Maddie, Tori, Juliet, and Kennedy were coming down onto the dock.

Well, fuck. He was about to lose her. "Or we could make a break for it," he said dryly.

Paige laughed. "We're outnumbered."

He just sighed.

"Hey girls," he greeted as he jumped from the boat to the dock to tie it up.

"We need Paige," Tori said.

"You'll have to get in line." He meant that. She was his. At least for tonight. As much as he loved her helping out with the weddings—and he really fucking did—he wasn't into sharing her tonight.

"Nope," Tori said sweetly.

Dammit. Tori was the hardest one to be firm with. Juliet was second.

He could absolutely be an ass to Kennedy and Maddie. No problem. But Tori and Juliet hadn't grown up on the bayou, and it showed. They were *nice*. And it made everyone want to be nice to them right back.

He finished securing the boat and straightened, planting his hands on his hips. "What do you need her for? It can't wait?"

"It can't." Maddie held up a few sheets of paper. "We found these."

"What are those?"

"Oh crap." Suddenly Paige was beside him on the dock. "You weren't supposed to see those."

"Yet," Juliet said. "I hope you mean *yet*. Because you better have intended to show these to us at some point."

"What are they?" Mitch pressed.

Paige sighed. "Some of my wedding notes. I thought I got them all when I left the office. Guess I missed a few."

"This is just *some* of them?" Tori asked her, eyes wide. "You have more?"

Paige pulled her bottom lip between her teeth and nodded.

"Oh my God, yes, we need to talk." Maddie reached for Paige and grabbed her hand, pulling her forward.

"I didn't mean to step on your toes," Paige said. "I was just thinking and jotted a few things down and—"

"Step on my toes," Juliet said. "Please. I will gladly hand over my binder and everything. This is amazing."

Mitch knew he was standing there with his mouth hanging open. He felt like he'd just been hit by a tornado. A very blond and brunette, nice-smelling tornado.

Tori, Maddie, and Juliet practically carried Paige up the dock toward Ellie's.

"Hey! It's date night!" he called after them.

Maddie looked over her shoulder. "What do you mean? You're just friends."

Then she gave him a wink. And kept walking Paige away from him.

He should probably save her.

But he felt himself smiling.

Paige needed a place to belong. She needed to be a piece that fit somewhere. She needed to take care of a few people.

So maybe he'd take his time about saving her.

"My God, you're head over heels already, aren't you?"

He looked to his left to find that Kennedy was still on the dock with him watching the other women go.

"How can you tell?" he asked, instead of denying it.

"That stupid grin on your face," she said. "It's how Bennett looks at me," she added with a stupid grin of her own.

He shrugged. "Yeah, I'm pretty much fucked here."

Mitch was no better off two weeks later.

In fact, he was far, far worse.

Not only was he crazier about Paige, but he was horny as hell.

Paige had been officially installed as the wedding planner for all three Landry weddings, and she seemed thrilled. She'd been glowing since the girls had whisked her off to Ellie's.

His family loved her, and they were including her in everything.

And that meant he'd been cock-blocked.

Repeatedly.

Ever since their swamp boat ride.

Okay, she hadn't exactly been *glowing* the next morning after their first official wedding consultation.

They—and "they" included the girls and their fiancés, Ellie,

Leo, Cora, and Zeke and Zander—had introduced her to Bayou Whiskey, i.e., the moonshine Leo made behind his house.

That was a not-very-nice thing to do to a woman you wanted to help you with the biggest day of your life, and the girls had been apologetic the next day when Paige had shown up at the tour office looking like, well, an Iowa girl who'd accidentally gotten wasted on moonshine. Or paint thinner. Leo's moonshine could be that too. It was also a great de-icer for windows when it got particularly chilly.

Thankfully, Cora had the perfect hangover remedy. That, along with some grits—yes, she'd eaten grits and loved them— had gotten Paige back to near-normal by noon, and Owen had declared her well on her way to being a bayou girl.

She hadn't even winced at that idea. In fact, she'd grinned, almost proudly.

And she'd been glowing since *then*.

That made Mitch want her even more than he had before.

Her being involved was one thing. Her clearly loving it was another. And his family embracing her and including her, even when *his* sorry ass was sitting at home alone—well, with grumpy Griffin and the five cats—made him want her with an ache that he wasn't sure he could ever fully relieve.

But he hadn't so much as seen her naked breasts since the day in the shower.

The girls had needed wedding planning consultations that ran very late and fell, not-at-all-coincidentally, on Tuesday nights and Saturdays. All-day long.

Last Saturday, they'd all gone to New Orleans shopping and had ended up at Trahan's bar in the French Quarter. Trahan's was owned by two of Josh's best friends, and the girls had ended up there on Erotic Book Club night, which they'd been invited to join. Along with half-price drinks, because they were Josh, Owen, and Sawyer's fiancés, the girls hadn't called Josh for a ride home until well after midnight.

It seemed when Paige's free time wasn't occupied with something wedding-related, Cora needed help with her plants or new cream recipes.

Both Friday nights since he'd taken Paige out on the bayou, Kennedy and Maddie had gotten Paige very drunk at the craw-fish boil, and she'd wanted to stay for the dancing.

Then last Friday, Paige and Ellie had gotten into a loud, fairly ridiculous argument about the inhumane treatment of crawfish.

But ridiculous or not, it had somehow led to Paige crashing on Ellie and Leo's couch and having French toast with them the next morning rather than spending the night in Mitch's bed.

He knew none of it was accidental. He'd made the mistake of telling his family upfront what Paige's plans were for her stay in Autre, and now that they sincerely liked her, they were going to help her *not* get any more involved with him.

Apparently, that included keeping her from spending too much time alone with him. And definitely included keeping her fully clothed whenever he was around.

His family was a huge pain in his ass.

"Damn, we should sell tickets for *this* encounter," Owen said. He was leaning on the new fence that surrounded the otter enclosure.

"You think anyone else would be as into it as we are?" Mitch slid his cousin a look.

Owen's gaze was firmly on Maddie. Where she was bending over in the middle of the grassy space that took up this end of the otter enclosure.

"I mean, I know I'm biased, but fuck yeah," Owen said appreciatively.

"Don't think yoga is supposed to be a spectator sport," Sawyer said with a frown. He was leaning in next to Owen. He was scowling.

Juliet looked as hot as Maddie did in her yoga gear. But that was probably what was making Sawyer scowl. He was more than a little possessive of his fiancée, and no doubt hated the idea of anyone else ogling her.

Not that it was keeping *him* from ogling her. At all.

Josh was next to Sawyer, his eyes firmly on Tori.

Kennedy and Bennett were leaning on the fence, too, watching the entire scene in front of them.

Otter yoga had finally happened.

The otters had moved into the finished enclosure two days ago. They'd been climbing and sliding and swimming and chattering to Griffin in what could only be excited gratitude every time he came in to feed and check on them. He'd said he'd never heard them louder. Griffin had said it with a put-upon tone—how Griffin said most things, especially otter related things—but Mitch had been quietly thrilled the critters were so happy.

There was enough flat grassy area for about eight people to spread out for yoga. That was also no coincidence. Mitch had asked Paige to stretch out on the living room floor, and he'd done some measurements from fingertips to toes in a variety of positions.

Which had led to some very fun making out. *Finally*.

Which would have led to some very fun more-than-making-out, if Fletcher hadn't called Mitch needing help with his lawnmower, and Maddie hadn't called Paige needing help with something she was trying with her hair.

He didn't believe those two calls had come in at the same time by chance.

Fletcher hadn't confessed, but he hadn't denied that he'd been paid in homemade pralines to make that phone call.

Everyone was in on the cock-blocking.

Mitch hated them all.

And loved that they cared enough to help Paige with what she thought she wanted.

He'd *really* love it if they'd all start talking to her about how staying unattached and eventually leaving Autre wasn't what she wanted at all though.

"Why aren't you in there with them?" Bennett asked Kennedy from down the fence.

"I'm afraid I'll lose my edge if I get too Zen," Kennedy told him.

Bennett snorted.

Kennedy did have an "edge," but it was mostly B.S., and Bennett wasn't a bit afraid of it. In fact, she was a lot softer than she'd been when she'd met the nerdy millionaire, and she knew it. Everyone knew it.

"Still, wouldn't mind watching you bending and stretching like that," Bennett said.

"*You* could join them." Kennedy nudged her fiancé. "I wouldn't mind a little bending from you either."

"Maybe we can just do bedroom yoga later."

She wiggled her eyebrows. "I call Downward Dog."

"Well, Downward Dog wouldn't work as well if Bennett was the one doing it," Owen scoffed. Then he paused. "Would it?" He paused again as if thinking that through. "Never mind, I don't want to know."

"Oh, you kind of want to know," Kennedy said, laughing.

"*I* don't want to know. At least not if my little sister is the one explaining it," Sawyer broke in.

"I'm surprised Paige got Bailey to do yoga," Josh commented about Chase's girlfriend, who was also in the middle of the otters. He was probably hoping to change the subject. Kennedy was *his* little sister too. "Bailey doesn't seem like the meditative type either."

Bailey was a sweet, adorable, klutzy bookworm.

Proven a moment later when she tipped over from the one-legged stance the rest of the girls were doing without any trouble.

The chuckles at the fence were completely affectionate. Everyone loved Bailey. She was another newer addition to the family. Hell, so was Chase, really. But it didn't take long for someone to be welcomed into the Landry fold. If one Landry loved you, all the Landrys loved you.

Mitch focused on Paige again.

He loved her.

He knew that.

He hadn't told her that. Of course. He didn't want her high-tailing it back to Iowa just yet. Or ever. But he loved her. He just wasn't so sure that *he* was the reason the rest of them loved her. It was very possible they all would have loved her anyway.

She was making potions with Cora. She was bullshitting with Leo in between his trips to New Orleans to pick up busloads of tourists. She'd had Owen, Josh, and Sawyer address wedding invitations in between their tours. She was handling every detail of the job in the tour office *and* putting together not just one wedding but three. Well, kind of one. But, also, three.

The three weddings were now one big happy shindig.

The ceremonies would each happen individually. Tori and Josh would get married on the main dock first. Then everyone would pile onto a pontoon and head out onto the bayou to watch Maddie and Owen say *I do* in "their" cove prior to coming back to witness Juliet and Sawyer's vows on the dock they'd built together.

Then there would be one big wedding reception at Ellie's afterward.

Nearly every problem had been solved. They were all sharing the same decorations and flowers and menu. The ceremonies themselves would be simple. The venues were, obviously, taken care of. And since the three couples shared so many friends and family in common, the guest list had already been nearly identical. Now the people coming for Tori's and

Juliet's wedding were just getting a swamp boat tour out of the deal too.

Because they'd moved everything back to the bayou, they'd decided to do all the food out of Ellie's. Tori and Juliet wanted to introduce their out-of-state guests to local cuisine, and that meant things like boudin balls, fried pickles, etouffee, and meat pies. They were going to have some beignets too, but, of course, planned a huge wedding cake.

Which had resulted in a call back to Iowa as soon as they found out that Paige's sister worked in a bakery. Josie was well-known for her wedding cakes, and she'd been thrilled to get on a video call with Paige, Ellie, and Cora about the cake. She was even sending some embellishments—whatever the hell those were—because they wouldn't be able to get them delivered in time from anywhere else.

Everyone was ecstatic about every fucking thing.

Except Mitch. He wasn't getting laid, and he was falling in love, and that combo was making him itchy as hell.

But Paige was happy. And he couldn't bring himself to say or do a damned thing that might change that.

He had broken their rules *one* night and snuck into her room, and they'd had quick, hot, dirty sex. But he'd tried to be good since then. They'd put those rules in place for a reason. And just because his family kept her busy, or drunk, or both, on their supposed date nights, he wanted to be a man of his word.

Finally, yoga was over, and the girls all headed for the fence, stepping carefully around the otters.

Paige approached him with a smile.

"So, it worked," he said.

"Yep, plenty of room."

"I'm glad."

Was it ridiculous that he'd built the enclosure with otter yoga in mind? With *Paige* in mind? Knowing that she was planning to leave? Knowing that every time he looked at the grassy space up behind the rock formations and water slide that he'd think of her? Probably. He'd done it anyway. It wasn't as if his heart was going to be any less broken without that yoga space.

"So, I have a question for you," she said.

"Anything."

Her smile brightened. Did she really not know that was where he was at?

"Will you be my plus one for all the wedding stuff?"

He huffed out a laugh. "Uh, yeah."

"Well, I know we'd agreed I'd be your date to Tori and Josh's wedding, but now it's turned into a whole thing with the three weddings and some activities for the guests coming in early."

He made himself take a deep breath before he answered. There was no *too much* this woman could ask him for, but he had to be careful not to spook her.

He reached out and caught her hand, tugging her closer to the fence. "I'm in. For all of it. You've done an amazing job with all of this, and you deserve to enjoy it when it all happens."

Her eyes darkened with desire and a harder-to-name emotion.

He loved how pleased she looked by the compliment and by realizing what she'd put together. "Well, the tour in New Orleans wasn't my idea. That was Tori. I guess Josh and Leo did that when her friend got married. And the crawfish boil the night before the weddings is the usual setup, just bigger. And—"

"You've made this all happen, and not only taken a huge weight off the girls, but actually turned this into a hell of a lot of fun for everyone," he said.

He ran a hand up to the back of her head and pulled her closer. With his mouth against her ear, he said, "It's hotter than hell to watch you enjoying all of this so much. Makes me want to throw you over my shoulder and kidnap you out onto an airboat."

"Yes, please," she said. Her voice was breathless.

"I'm thinking we—"

"Oh, hey, Paige." Juliet was suddenly beside Paige. "I was wondering if you could look at something with me. For the wedding."

Mitch pulled back with a sigh. Seriously?

His and Paige's gazes met. She gave him a smile.

"What do you need me to look at?" she asked Juliet.

"Um... my..."

Mitch glanced at Juliet.

Kennedy cleared her throat, and Juliet blew out a breath. "My... dress."

Mitch looked at Kennedy who was rolling her eyes.

"What's wrong with your dress?" Mitch asked.

"Oh, you wouldn't understand," Juliet said. "It's about the fit of the bodice."

Paige snorted, and Mitch gave her an amused look.

"I don't really do alterations," Paige told her.

"I just want your opinion on it," Juliet said.

Mitch finally laughed and straightened, dropping his hand from Paige's face. "I love that you're a terrible liar, Juliet."

She blushed. "I'm not lying. I do want her to see me in my dress."

"You're making up an excuse to get Paige away from me."

Finally, Juliet sighed. "You're the one who said it was important that you two don't get too close. We're just trying to help."

Mitch met Paige's eyes again. She lifted a brow.

He had said that to his family. They had said it to one another. It was true. Or it had been.

Ironically, all the things that had been keeping them apart —her working at the tour company's office, helping with the weddings, concocting with Cora, and hanging out and getting to know his family better—had made him fall harder for her than if he'd kept her to himself.

"Well, making me associate her with things like weddings and family gatherings rather than just hot, dirty, fling-sex isn't really helping your cause," he said honestly.

He'd addressed the words to Juliet, but his eyes were on Paige.

Hers widened, and he watched her lips part.

He heard Juliet sigh. "You know, I actually mentioned that to Kennedy the other night."

He grinned. Paige looked surprised but not shocked. Or spooked. Exactly.

"Maybe you need to let me take her out tonight, just the two of us, and stop with all the wedding cake and flower talk," he said. Again, more to get Paige's reaction.

"No. No, no, no." Kennedy came stomping toward them. "Dammit, Juliet, that was terrible. Your dress? Why would you ask Paige about your dress? You could have asked her about the cake, or the flowers, or how about the cream we talked about for your sore shoulder? Those are her wheelhouse. Way more believable."

"Your shoulder is sore?" Paige asked, seeming bemused.

"It was." Juliet rotated her left arm. "But actually, since yoga, it feels better."

Kennedy shook her head. "I should have sent Maddie. Maddie can lie. You and Tori suck at it."

Paige laughed. "I'm happy to get you some cream. *And* look at the dress."

Kennedy was studying Mitch now, her eyes narrowed. "But you're saying you might need to spend *more* time together so that you realize she's not so amazing?"

Mitch grinned at Paige. "Well, spending time apart isn't working. Maybe we should try it."

And damned if Paige Asher, the hardest woman on earth to woo, didn't blush.

"Deal. You can come with us to Ellie's and listen to all the talk about the food and cake and flowers and crap," Kennedy said, turning to start in the direction of her truck.

"Crap?" Juliet asked, falling into step beside Kennedy. "Is that how you're going to feel when it's you and Bennett?"

Kennedy grinned at her. "Bennett and I are going to elope. Just some weekend when we have time. Then we'll throw a big bash to celebrate after. But I'm not going to talk about flowers and shoes and music for weeks ahead of time. We'll just get a wild hair one Friday night, fly out to Vegas and do it, and then come back and tell you all when we're ready."

Juliet stopped walking, nearly causing Paige to plow into her.

Kennedy went several feet before she realized Juliet was no longer beside her, and she turned back.

"You and Bennett got married, didn't you?" Juliet demanded. "You already did all of that."

Kennedy shook her head. "I didn't say that. I said that's what we *would* do."

Juliet stalked toward her until she was nearly on Kennedy's toes and put her hands on her hips. "You and Bennett already got married. You didn't want to wait, but you didn't want to do it in the middle of all of *our* wedding planning, and you didn't want to say anything. So you went to Vegas. And you're going to tell us about it in a month or so."

Kennedy opened her mouth. She blinked. Then she sighed.

Juliet gasped. Then she threw her arms around Kennedy. "Oh my God! You brat! I can't believe you did that!" She pulled back. "And I can't believe you think *I'm* a bad liar!"

"I'm a *great* liar," Kennedy protested. "You just caught me off guard."

Juliet laughed and hugged her again, then pulled back. "Wow. That is so... you."

Kennedy finally grinned. "I know. We were just hanging out one night, and I turned to him and said, 'I really want to marry you,' and he said, 'Oh, I fully intend to marry you,' and I said, 'Prove it,' and we got on a plane."

"So you kind of proposed to him?" Juliet asked. Then she nodded. "Yeah, that's very you too."

Kennedy shrugged. "Two weeks ago. And yes, we're going to tell everyone and have a big party, but *after* this circus is over and everything."

"Oh my God, did you get married by Elvis?"

"Of course." Kennedy grinned. "And I had him sing 'Burning Love' to Bennett."

Juliet giggled.

"So"—Kennedy pointed a finger at Juliet's nose—"you have to keep this to yourself."

"I will. But I'm throwing my bouquet directly at you."

The women linked arms and headed for the truck again.

Mitch, grinning, started after them. He glanced back when he realized Paige wasn't beside him.

She looked like she was trying not to cry.

He immediately turned. "What's wrong?"

"I'm in love."

15

Mitch's heart turned over in his chest. "What?"

"I'm in love with your family."

Mitch sucked in a breath.

Fuck.

That had scared him for a second.

Except, scared wasn't *really* what he was feeling.

Paige pulled her gaze from Kennedy and Juliet to meet his. "They are loud and over-the-top and in everyone's business, and there really are no secrets, but I love them. The *way* they are in each other's business is so different from what I'm used to. Like that—" She waved in the direction of Juliet and Kennedy's retreating backs. "Kennedy and Bennett elope, and Juliet is just happy that they got married and notes that it's very *them* to do it that way. It's just supportive and happy. My family would have been disappointed and upset about missing it." She sighed. "Everyone here knows everything about everyone else, but they're all accepting of how each of you is unique and needs and wants different things."

Mitch wasn't sure what to say to that. It was all true. His family definitely kept track of one another, but there were no expectations of anyone being or doing things a certain way. As long as everyone did their part and supported each other and no one was a dick, then there was a lot of room for being whoever or whatever you wanted to be.

He wasn't sure he'd ever really appreciated that before. At least, he'd never put specific words to it before. That was pretty damned great though.

He reached for her hand and tugged her close. "That includes you."

She nodded. "I'm understanding that. If I want to hang out here and not marry you, they're okay with that."

His heart didn't flip at that. It squeezed painfully. But he nodded. "Exactly. Whatever you need. They still want you around." He pulled her even closer. "I do too."

She didn't say anything, but she let him hug her, resting her cheek against his chest for nearly a minute.

"Are you really going to come to Ellie's for wedding talk?" she asked, looking up at him.

"Sure. I mean, there's coffee and cinnamon rolls if nothing else."

She laughed.

He kept his arm around her as they walked to his truck. He never wanted to let go of her. That wasn't a new revelation, but every time it hit him, it felt stronger.

Even when they were seated at the end of the bar at Ellie's with the other girls spread out along the length of the scarred wooden slab, he kept a hand on her leg. He didn't want to stop touching her. She didn't seem to mind. She leaned into his side, watching and listening to everyone else talk and laugh as she nursed her cup of tea.

"My mom sent these." Tori held up a silver coin and a gold coin with a smile. "They're for my shoes."

Maddie leaned in. "What do you mean?"

"They're a Swedish tradition. You put them in your shoes," Tori said.

Paige shifted and sat forward. "Your family is Swedish?"

Tori nodded. "Yeah. On my mom's dad's side."

"Mine too. Actually, my grandma and grandpa," Paige said. "Both of my sisters wore coins in their shoes."

"What do the coins mean?" Ellie asked.

"It's luck." Tori looked at Paige. "I guess?"

Paige smiled. "It's a Swedish wealth blessing. The coins are presented to the bride before she goes to the ceremony. The silver coin comes from the bride's father, and it goes in her left shoe, and the gold coin comes from her mother and goes in her right shoe. It's a symbol from her family that she will never go without."

Tori sighed happily. "Oh, that's even nicer than I thought."

Ellie nodded. "I like that a lot."

"Your parents won't be there?" Paige asked Tori.

"They will, but they sent these along with a lace handkerchief from my grandmother to act as my something borrowed. They just wanted me to know I had these things ahead of time."

"I didn't know you were Swedish," Paige said. "Did you want to incorporate any other traditions?"

"Like what?"

"Oh, well, my sisters both walked down the aisle with their grooms rather than having their fathers give them away. It's Swedish custom that signifies the bride and groom are equals who are marrying out of choice rather than one being given to the other."

Maddie straightened. "Yes. I love that."

Mitch smiled at his cousin's fiancée. Her father was actually in prison and wouldn't be a part of her wedding. Her grandfather and brother had both passed away. She had talked about walking down the aisle alone. This was perfect.

"Yes." Juliet leaned over and hugged Maddie. "That's exactly what we should all do."

"What else?" Tori asked Paige.

"Oh, this one is maybe good for you all too," Paige said. "In Swedish weddings, there is often only one bridesmaid and one groomsman and many times none at all."

The girls all looked at one another. "Since we're all going to be brides too, we had tried to figure out how to do that. Maybe we should just not worry about it."

Kennedy slumped on her stool, letting out a long breath. "Yes. That's a great idea."

They looked over at her.

"Don't want to play the part of bridesmaid three times on one day?" Maddie asked her.

"No offense," Kennedy said. "But I'll give you a great group toast. Hilarious and sappy at the same time."

"I know you will," Maddie said.

"At Swedish weddings, the speeches and toasts go on for a *long* time," Paige said.

"Well, hell, maybe we are part Swedish way back," Ellie said. "This group definitely goes on and on."

Mitch squeezed Paige's thigh and was pleased and surprised when her hand came to rest on top of his. She gave him a little squeeze back, then slid his hand up over her slippery yoga pants to her high inner thigh.

God, he wanted her.

He'd wanted this woman since the moment he'd met her. It had taken one look, and he'd been in lust. One night in her bed, and he'd been addicted. One week of texting with her, and he'd been captivated. One day in her hometown around her crazy family, and he'd been smitten. Now, she'd been in *his* hometown and around *his* crazy family for less than one month, and he was head over heels.

"Anything else?" Tori asked Paige.

"Well, I know we already have a *ton* of food, but now I'm thinking you should include some Swedish wedding cookies."

"Oh, what are those?" Juliet asked.

"They're buttery cookies with pecans. They come in ball shapes and are rolled in powder sugar."

"Let's do it," Tori said with a nod. "You know how to make them?"

"I don't have a recipe, but my mom makes great ones," Paige said. "I can call her later."

"Call her now," Ellie said. "Put her on a video call. Then we can all meet her."

Paige looked startled. "Oh. Uh. You want to meet her?"

"Of course," Ellie said as if that should have been obvious. "We adore her daughter, so why wouldn't we want to meet her?"

Paige blinked at Ellie. "You... adore me?"

Ellie frowned. "Yes."

"*You* do? *You* adore *me*?"

Ellie tipped her head. "Yes." Her tone was impatient.

"But..." Paige looked at Mitch.

He lifted a brow. He wasn't sure what was going on. Why was she so surprised? Ellie Landry generally liked most people. No, that wasn't true. She had a low tolerance for blowhards and assholes and absolutely no trouble telling them that they were blowhards and assholes.

But she gave people a chance and more than the benefit of the doubt. She was incredibly forgiving of mistakes and even stupidity provided the person learned from the mistake and was less stupid afterward.

But Paige had no reason to think that Ellie didn't like her. Did she?

"But what?" Ellie prodded.

The other girls were all watching, curious now.

"You just..." Paige wet her lips. "You didn't seem to like me much. That's all. You've been standoffish. Which is fine," she added quickly. "You don't have to like me. I know I'm a pain with the weird food I eat and the anti-marriage thing and all the cats." She finished weakly with a wince.

Ellie crossed the space behind the bar, coming to stand right across from Paige.

"You're not anti-marriage. You don't want to get married, personally. At least right now. Maybe ever. But that's your thing. You're not trying to talk anyone else out of it," she said.

Paige nodded. "Right."

"And you're eating what you like for your reasons. But you're not telling other people what to eat."

"Well, except for our little disagreement the other night," Paige muttered, her cheeks red.

"You don't like how crawfish are cooked," Ellie said. "It doesn't bother me. We had a disagreement. That doesn't make you weird or a bad person."

"But I yelled at you."

"I yelled back."

"Yeah." Paige nodded. "So... I guess I thought that kind of meant maybe I wasn't your favorite person."

"Yelling is just a way of saying something you really want to be sure the other person hears," Ellie said. "And God knows, around here, yelling is simply the only option sometimes."

Paige gave her a small smile, and Mitch squeezed her leg again. She slipped her fingers between his, folding their hands together.

"And as long as you can feed and take care of all those cats, and they make you happy, it's nobody's business how many you have. Someone who loves animals is my kind of person." Ellie gave Paige an affectionate smile and then glanced at Tori as well.

"My mom thinks that I'm filling the gaps in my life and heart with cats when I should be loving people instead," Paige said. Then she frowned. "I don't know why I just told you that."

"People tell Ellie a lot of stuff they don't really mean to," Juliet said.

Ellie shrugged as if that was just common knowledge. "Is your mom right?"

"Yeah. Maybe. Some of it might be that."

"How come?"

"Because cats are easier to love and harder to disappoint."

Mitch felt his heart kick hard.

Ellie just nodded. "That's true. Seems like everything you're doin' makes sense."

Paige's eyes rounded. "Really?"

"Sure."

"And that's... all okay with you?"

"Why does it matter if it's okay with me?"

"Because..." Paige trailed off. "I guess because I like you all, and I want you to like me."

"Well, I like you just fine. You're not eating meat doesn't affect me. You having a bunch of cats doesn't affect me. You not wanting to get married doesn't affect me. As long as you're not hurting me or anyone I love, I can like you even if we disagree about crawfish."

Mitch was watching Paige closely and noticed how she swallowed hard before offering a weak smile. Was she thinking about him and how he felt about her not wanting to get married?

He didn't like it. He'd love it if she wanted to fall head over heels and stay here forever. But he wanted her to be happy. He wanted her to know that whatever she needed was fine with him. If she wanted to stay here and never get married, he could be okay with that.

The thought hit him seemingly out of the blue. But he really just wanted her around, to see her, laugh with her, watch her light up, and find her place. He didn't need to put a ring on her finger for all of that.

"Then why were you aloof when we first met?" Paige asked Ellie tentatively.

"Because I thought that's what you wanted," Ellie said. "Mitch said you weren't looking to get involved. And honestly, when people get to know me, it's very hard for them to stay detached."

Paige laughed. "Yes. I'm learning that."

Ellie gave her a wink. "But when I saw that the girls had pulled you in, I knew you weren't getting out of here without leaving some of your heart behind."

"Um, excuse me," Mitch said. "What about me?"

"What about you?" Ellie asked.

"You don't think *I* might have anything to do with that?"

"Thought you were trying *not* to have anything to do with that," Ellie said.

"Well..." He glanced at Paige. She was watching him with interest.

Fuck. He was supposed to be trying *not* to make her attach. This was her place to lay low. And maybe everything he'd seen in her—the happiness and contentment—really was about her new friendships, and the acceptance of his family and the fun of the wedding planning.

"I'd like to think I'm a little miss-able too," he said with a grin to try to lighten what he was thinking.

"Oh, you are," she said with a mischievous smile. "I'll definitely miss that hammock. And I love the shower at your house."

The shower. Right. The last time they'd really had sex except for the quickie when he'd snuck into her bedroom.

So she'd miss the sex with him.

Well, that was fair. It was amazing between them. Every time. That was what he could give that the others couldn't.

And the knot in his stomach at that thought was stupid. This was what he'd agreed to. It wasn't Paige's fault that it had taken him only two and a half weeks to fall in love with her.

"Call your mom," Ellie said, pulling Mitch and Paige's gazes apart. "I want to know about these cookies."

"Oh." Paige shook herself slightly.

Yes, her thoughts had drifted to Mitch's shower, and the last time they'd been in there together. But she'd also been thinking about how much she appreciated that none of these people were pressing her about how she felt about Mitch or what her plans were or saying things like "oh, you don't mean that" when she talked about not wanting to get married. They were completely accepting of her choices. Of *her*.

And it made her want to stay forever. With Mitch.

The other day the girls had been going through photos of themselves and their fiancés, putting together a slide show of them all through the years. One big, fun, loving slide show.

The photos went from Sawyer by himself to all of the boys together, including his friend and Maddie's brother Tommy, to photos of Maddie and Tommy together. There were photos of Maddie and Owen together as kids. Photos of Juliet and her brother Chase, and then photos of Chase with the whole group, including Bailey, his girlfriend. There were photos of Mitch mixed in too. As a little boy with all the others and as a grown man, grinning with his ball cap turned backward, flashing a thumbs up from the deck of an airboat with the other guys gathered around.

Paige had wanted the stories behind every single photo. And, strangely, she'd wanted to call her mom and ask her to send a bunch of photos of her and her friends and family so she could share and tell stories too.

"You all have an amazing history," she'd commented.

"It sucks you in, doesn't it?" Tori had asked with a smile. "I've only been here for a year, but I feel like they're all a part of me."

Paige had nodded. It had only taken about a week for them to soak into her bones.

"History is just the synopsis of the whole story," Ellie had said.

"What do you mean?"

"When you learn history, you learn the highlights. And those are always told from one viewpoint."

Paige had nodded. That was a good point. "You're saying there's always more to the story."

"Of course, there is. There's the Wednesday morning breakfasts, the arguments over why the faucet still isn't fixed, and the times you'd rather be apart than together."

"There are times you'd rather be apart from Leo than with him?" Paige had teased. She'd never seen two people more in sync than Ellie and Leo.

But Ellie had laughed. So had the other girls.

"If you want to be together twenty-four-seven, one of you isn't being real," Ellie said.

"Ellie and Leo even broke up for a while," Kennedy had added.

Ellie had nodded. "Yep. We divorced, and I dated Trevor for a bit. But Leo and I couldn't stay apart."

Paige had been surprised. But also touched by that. "I guess that makes sense, with a history like yours."

But Ellie had shaken her head. "History doesn't make you love someone. Loving someone makes you want to make history with them."

Paige had been thinking about that for days now.

It was part of why calling her mom for input on some of this wedding stuff felt so good. She would love to bring some of her people into this. Even her people that didn't accept her choices. They were still the ones she had a history with. And, after all, the history in her head was just from *her* viewpoint.

Dee Asher picked up the video call after just three rings. "Paige!"

Paige had been texting, and they'd video chatted twice before this, but she'd made sure she was alone when she talked to Dee. "Hi, Mom."

"How are you?"

"I'm good. Really good. I'm actually at Ellie's, the restaurant I told you about, with the three girls who are getting married." She'd filled her mom in on the fact that Tori was now sharing her wedding day with Juliet and Maddie.

"Oh." Dee was clearly a little puzzled as to why Paige was calling her right now if that was the case.

"Tori's family is Swedish too, and I was telling her about some of the wedding traditions our family has incorporated."

"Hi, Mrs. Asher!" Tori called.

Dee smiled. "Hello, Tori."

Tori slid off her stool and came to stand behind Paige. She waved at the screen. "My mom and dad sent the silver and gold coins for the wealth blessing, but Paige was the one who filled me in on the details."

Dee lifted both brows. "She's been paying attention, I guess."

Paige worked to not roll her eyes. "I even told them about the tradition of the bride and groom walking down the aisle together and having only one or no attendants. It's all going to make this triple wedding easier."

"Paige has been *so* much help in planning all of this," Tori said. "She has so many great ideas."

"You've been helping plan the weddings?" Dee asked Paige. "Really?"

Paige had to give her mom a pass on her obvious surprise. It really was out of character. Or so it would seem from the things Paige said about her own feelings about marriage. But she really was enjoying all of this. Bringing traditions together, making each ceremony reflect the specific couple, even in the midst of combining the three weddings, making it a true celebration of not just the vows between the two people getting married, but bringing the families all together and honoring everyone involved in their lives.

Yes, the Landry weddings had given Paige a new appreciation for what weddings were and could be. Or rather, they'd given her a chance to really reflect on it more objectively. Those things—the special touches, the traditions, the families coming together—had all been there in the weddings she'd been involved with in Appleby too. She'd just been more intimately involved there because they'd been friends and family, and she knew everyone was looking at her and wondering how she felt and what she was thinking.

Here there had been no pressure, so she'd been able to truly appreciate it all more.

"Yep," Paige told her mom. "I've been helping with the weddings here."

"She's been more than helping," Juliet said, joining Tori behind Paige. "Hi, Mrs. Asher. I'm Juliet. And Paige has truly been the one doing most of the work. She's made the guys do some of it. Like building an archway and addressing envelopes." She laughed. "But she's really taken so much off our plates."

Dee looked surprised but pleased. "Well, that's wonderful. Paige is very creative."

Now it was Paige's turn to be surprised. "I am?"

Dee laughed. "You are. You always have been. Don't you remember making those cat houses for the stray cats and decorating them?"

"How did she decorate them?" Tori asked, looking delighted.

"Well, she'd have some that looked like regular two-story houses, some that were log cabins, some that were tents. There was an igloo. There was one she painted to look like one of those old Volkswagen RVs." Dee laughed. "She said all the cats had different personalities and would choose different places to live."

Tori looked at Paige with wide eyes. Paige could feel her cheeks burning.

"You made cat shelters that all looked like different types of houses?"

Paige shrugged. "That was when I lived at home, and they wouldn't let me take them all in."

"And that's what led you to open a cat adoption center."

She nodded.

"And yoga with cats?" Dee went on. "Not just everyone would think of that. Hot chocolate massage cream for sore muscles? You can't get that just anywhere."

"Hot chocolate massage cream?" Cora had just come through the swinging door from the kitchen, wiping her hands on her towel.

Paige lifted a shoulder. "It's just regular body butter, but I added a chocolate and marshmallow scent. I did a peppermint one too. For the holidays. But I told people to use it for massage." She paused. "I'm using it as a gateway cream."

Cora chuckled. "Gateway cream?"

"If they like it, they'll come back, and I can maybe talk them into something with more healing properties."

Cora nodded. "Good thinking."

Paige looked down at her screen again. "Mom, this is Cora." She turned her phone, and Cora waved.

Ellie was next to her. "Hello, Dee."

"And that's Ellie."

"Nice to meet you both," Dee greeted.

"And this is Maddie, the other bride. And Kennedy, the soon-to-be sister and cousin-in-law to these girls, and, of course, Mitch." She panned the group, and everyone waved.

She faced Dee again.

"Mitch? The one who's *not* Tori's fiancé."

Paige grimaced. "Yeah. Tori's fiancé is Josh." When Mitch had been in Iowa just after Christmas, they'd told Dee he was Tori's fiancé so that she wouldn't get any crazy ideas about Paige being serious about him. But in their last phone call, Paige had come clean about all of that. "Mitch is... my boyfriend."

Dee's eyebrows shot up, and Paige felt Mitch's hand squeeze her thigh tightly.

Yeah, he'd like that. She knew that. And she knew what it meant to tell her mom that. But it was true, wasn't it? If Mitch wasn't her boyfriend, what was he? He was more than a room-mate. He was more than a hook-up. He was more than a friend.

She was very afraid that she was falling in love with him, in fact. If that didn't move him up to boyfriend status, she didn't know what did.

And he knew better than to pull out a diamond ring.

She was pretty sure.

"Well," Dee finally said after a long pause. "It's very nice to know you all. And to know that you're helping with the weddings. And that... you're happy."

"I am."

"I can tell."

Paige gave her mom a smile. "Yeah?"

Dee nodded. "Of course. I do want you to be happy, Paige."

She believed that. She knew deep down that's what her family wanted for her. She just knew that her family's ideas about what would make her happy was different than her own.

Telling them what she wanted over the years hadn't seemed to convince them. Now, though, it seemed she was showing them.

How had she not been able to *show* them when she was in Appleby, but she could in Autre?

She wasn't sure, but she knew she'd be thinking about that now.

"Thanks, Mom." She suddenly wished she could hug her mother. "I was wondering if you had any other Swedish wedding traditions to share with us? Oh, and we need a recipe for the Swedish wedding cookies."

Dee's face lit up. "Of course! Don't forget about the kissing tradition."

"Oh yes!" Paige grinned and looked at the girls.

Kennedy leaned in. "What's the kissing tradition?"

"Well, after the ceremony, any time the groom leaves the room, other men line up to kiss the bride. And if the bride leaves the groom alone, other women can kiss him." She laughed. "It's a lot of fun at the reception. Everyone watches for the first time the groom leaves. Often they get someone to trick him into leaving the room just for the kissing tradition."

Kennedy's eyes rounded. "Sawyer will hate that so much." She nodded. "We're totally doing that."

Juliet laughed. "We're not Swedish."

"Well, you're basically Cajun once you hang out with us long enough. I think that Tori and Paige's Swedish can rub off too, don't you?" Kennedy said.

Juliet nodded. "True. Why not? The more traditions in the family, the better."

Paige felt a swoop in her stomach. She was adding traditions to the family? Sure, it was for Tori's part of the wedding, but it still felt strangely good to be contributing.

Dee was rifling through her cookbook on her end of the phone call. "I can send you this recipe in your email, Paige. I'm sure they have great pecans down there. You'll have to send me some of the cookies when you're done."

"Oh, no, just read it off to me." Cora plucked the phone out of Paige's fingers and turned away, taking the phone with her into the kitchen.

Paige watched her go, her mouth open.

Mitch chuckled. "I think your mom and Cora are going to be very good friends by the time they're done baking together."

"They're just going to make the cookies now? Mom will just talk her through it?" Paige asked. But even as she said it, she realized that yes, that was probably what was going to happen.

Ellie reached over and patted her hand and, even without words, the gesture said *everything is great, and you're right where you should be, doing exactly what you should be doing.* Then she turned and followed Cora into the kitchen.

Tori and Juliet reclaimed their stools, and the girls started talking about the kissing tradition and how hilarious it would be if they could let the guests know while keeping it from the grooms.

Mitch leaned in, successfully pulling all of Paige's attention from everything going on around them. She looked into his eyes.

"It's fucking adorable that you made shelters for cats as a little girl," he said.

She smiled. She was glad her mom had shared that story. She was even happier to have heard Dee say she was creative. She wasn't sure she'd ever heard that from her mother before. "I built them out of all kinds of boxes and containers and scraps."

"Does your mom have photos?"

Paige wondered. "Maybe. I would have said no until today, but maybe if she thought that was cute and creative on some level, she did take photos."

"How did you feed all of the strays?" Mitch asked.

"I fed them out of a bag of cat food in our pantry that I bought with my allowance." She frowned as she thought about that.

Mitch lifted a finger and smoothed it over the space between her eyebrows. "What?"

"I just realized that I never had to buy more food after I bought that first bag."

He smiled slowly. "Huh. A bottomless bag of cat food. Wonder how that happened?"

Her mom, and maybe her dad, had kept refilling that bag of cat food. Paige felt her heart thump hard as the realization hit her. She'd been too young to really think about it. She'd just kept using that same bag. Her attention had been on sneaking the food out of the house rather than on why the bag never ran out. But it was clear that's what had been going on. Her parents had known what she was doing and helped her, silently anyway.

"Wow," she said softly.

"Not every family is as expressive and loud and blunt as mine, but that doesn't mean they're not encouraging," Mitch said.

She nodded. "I'm learning that."

"I'm glad."

She leaned in and pressed her lips to his, kissing him softly and sweetly. It wasn't hot and dirty and deep. But it still warmed her from head to toe, and the way his hand tightened on her leg again told her that he liked it. It wasn't about sex. It was about affection and connection.

When she pulled back, she studied his face.

She didn't want him to ask her to marry him. But she wanted him to ask her to stay. For good. To be a part of this. To make some history.

That wasn't fair, of course. This family was about marriage and commitment, and roots. He had the right to want more.

They had the right to want her to stand up in front of them all and to pledge to love him and be there for him forever.

It was selfish of her to want to be here for all the good parts but to not be willing to make a forever, for better or worse commitment.

"When I was a little older and had learned to sew, I made my own stuffed cats," she said. For some reason. "I had... a lot."

One corner of his mouth curled up. "Where did you get the supplies?"

"My grandmas and aunts and mom all sewed and had baskets full of scraps."

"And they let you have whatever you wanted."

She nodded.

"Tell me more."

So, she did.

They shared stories over etouffee that Cora had made for Paige with tofu instead of seafood.

Mitch even ate it with her. He even said it wasn't bad.

He was lying, of course.

And it made her fall a little further into not-quite-yet-but-if-I'm-not-careful-it-could-be love with him.

16

"This is such a movie cliché," Paige said from the top of the stairs.

"Come on, let's go. I want to see you all dressed up and looking sexy as fuck."

Mitch was in the living room, waiting for her to come down so they could head over for the weddings.

Paige took a breath. It was finally the wedding day.

In retrospect, she was glad Tori had been willing to move the wedding date. It had given them all time to really put together an amazing plan that included a week's worth of activities for guests who came in early. Like Chase, who was able to spend five days in Autre for all the fun.

It was now April, and they were still ahead of the bigger tourism dates, but the weather was warmer for the outdoor activities, including the ceremonies and the reception overflow from inside Ellie's.

Paige had been getting compliments for her part of the planning all week, and she had to admit she was feeling very proud of the way it had all come together.

And now it was time for it to all culminate in the big, happy day for this family and the three women who had become good friends in the time she'd been here.

Even more than she had at the start of all of this, she understood how important it was to have a big celebration like this. She was so excited to be a part of Tori, Maddie, and Juliet's day. To watch them pledge their love and get that pledge in return from Josh, Owen, and Sawyer. Now that she knew the guys better, too, it made it all the more special.

She had, of course, felt that for her sisters and their husbands. But this was different. She supposed because she was choosing to be here. Or because not every other person attending was looking at her and wondering when *she* was going to get her life together and settle down.

Or at least, she wasn't assuming that's what they were thinking. It was possible, she could admit now, a month and a half after leaving Appleby, that maybe not *everyone* in town had wondered what was wrong with her and when she was going to get married. She might have been projecting a little. Or a lot.

Paige pressed a hand to her stomach and took a breath. She also felt invested in these weddings because she'd worked hard to make it all special and unique for these couples.

She'd done a final check on everything that morning.

The tents were set up over the docks where Tori and Josh and Juliet and Sawyer would say their vows. The netting under Juliet and Sawyer's dock was in place. It was there to make Juliet feel better about standing out there over the water rather than to actually catch any guests, but according to all the stories, there really *was* a chance that Bailey and Chase could end up tipping over the edge.

The lights and flowers on the pontoon boat for Maddie and Owen looked amazing, and Ellie's place was decorated and ready for the reception. Though it still looked like a bar that had been decorated to look like a make-shift wedding venue.

Still, it was home for all of these people, and that's what

mattered. Paige actually hadn't wanted to make it look *too* different. Ellie's had been the site of birthday parties, holiday gatherings, and other celebrations, as well as just regular weeknight dinners, for this family for years. The guys had grown up there. It was *right* that this celebration be there, and Paige felt a deep contentment whenever she thought about how they'd brought this all together.

"Okay, I'm coming down," she finally called to Mitch.

"I'm ready."

She rolled her eyes. She was about to descend the staircase in her dress for the wedding. Mitch would be standing at the bottom of the stairs waiting for her. They'd see each other for the first time all dressed up, and they'd have that moment where they were struck by how great the other looked and realize their crazy strong attraction. Like in every romantic movie she'd ever seen. So cliché.

Yet, she still felt her stomach flip as she stepped onto the third step where he'd be able to see her.

She took another deep breath.

But he didn't say anything.

She looked at him.

And oh, *wow*. Okay, that movie moment was real.

He was staring at her as if she was the most beautiful thing he'd ever seen. Added to that, he looked *damn* good.

She loved Mitch in his jeans and t-shirts and flannels. But the button-down shirt with the tie was a new look, and she definitely approved.

The weddings were, of course, casual. No one here dressed up in a lot of lace or tuxedos. The *I dos* were being said on boat docks or *on* a boat, so everyone had agreed that the weddings' dresses would be simple and the girls would wear flat shoes while the guys were fine in jeans. It was too warm for jackets, but the men had decided on button-down shirts and ties to dress things up a little.

Mitch was in dark jeans with a dark blue plaid shirt and navy tie. "You look so great," Paige told Mitch, stepping off the bottom stair.

He came forward. "Holy shit, Paige. You're gorgeous."

She grinned. "I take back everything I've said about those cheesy movie scenes."

Her dress was a silky material in a soft peach color with an asymmetric hemline that hit mid-calf. She loved that she could wear the short, flared sleeves and sandals without needing a jacket or sweater as she would have in Iowa this time of year. She'd put her hair up in a twist and had borrowed gold jewelry from Tori.

"The reason they do this in the movies is because once the guy gets a good look at the girl, he's not thinking about getting to the wedding or party or whatever on time," Mitch told her, running one big hand down her arm from her shoulder to her wrist.

Paige tipped her head. "No? He's wondering how the hell she got her hair up like that?" she teased.

His gaze moved over her hair. "Okay, maybe that a little too." He moved his hand up her arm, over her shoulder, and to the back of her neck. He pulled her close. "But I like it like this. A lot. It shows off all this sweet skin that I love to kiss and lick."

He did just that, pressing his lips against her neck and then dragging his mouth up to her ear.

"And makes sure you can hear me say that if you have panties on right now, I want you to leave them here at home."

Her stomach flipped and, stupidly, Paige realized it wasn't the idea of going panty-less at his request. It was the use of the word *home*.

Uh-oh.

"Why would I need to do that?" she asked, leaning into his mouth rather than away, in spite of the *uh-oh* feeling.

"It will make things in the front seat of my truck a lot easier when we take a break from the reception."

She pulled back. "Are you telling me that we're going to sneak out and have sex in your truck?"

He didn't even blink. "Yes."

"Thank God."

She was *craving* him. It had been five days since they'd had sex. Things had been crazy in these last days before the weddings, and Mitch's extra bedroom was full, as was his living room couch, with out-of-town guests.

Yes, it had been nice to know they could share meals and flirt when he stopped in at the tour company office and exchange texts even if they weren't banging every night.

It also felt nice to hang out with his family and work on wedding plans and know he was working on the petting zoo without either of them feeling slighted. They both enjoyed being involved in the family's bigger activities and feeling like a part of making those important things happen. That was a pretty great thing to have in common.

She liked that things had progressed for them beyond the physical.

But she was horny. She couldn't deny it.

No, it wasn't all about sex anymore. But she was definitely ready for some fun-and-dirty with him tonight.

Paige gripped his arm and lifted a foot, balancing on one leg. She reached up under her skirt and hooked the top of her thong with her finger, pulling it down.

Mitch made a little growling noise as he watched.

She grinned up at him as she tossed the thong toward the steps.

Mitch let her go and stomped to the scrap of silk, scooping it up and tucking it into his pocket. "Griffin doesn't get to see that."

She smiled. "Griffin wouldn't even notice."

"Doubt that very much."

"I don't know. I don't have fur and four legs, so I'm not sure Griffin gives a damn."

Mitch shrugged. "He's a human male. I think peach thongs have a way of getting through even the most cynical shell."

Paige laughed. "Okay, then it's all yours."

"Damn right." He grabbed her hand, and they started for the door. "Let's go see some crazy Cajuns get hitched so we can get on to the fun."

"I *am* really looking forward to the wedding cake."

"Brat." He swatted her butt as she climbed up into the truck in front of him.

Paige knew she was grinning as if it was *her* wedding day as they drove to the docks. But dang, she really loved... all of this. All of these people. Everything about being here.

And she couldn't help but wonder if more people in Autre and the surrounding area would like some help with their wedding planning.

"I don't think you're ready for this."

"Oh, come on. I've basically been training for this for two and a half months."

"This is way bigger than meeting the family a few at a time," Mitch said, reaching for one of the wedding cookies on Paige's plate.

"What about all the tourists I meet?" she asked, amused.

"You know all their names?"

"Sure. Dave and Shelli and Max and Stephen and Donna and Jennifer."

He narrowed his eyes as he studied her face. "You just made all of those up, didn't you?"

She grinned. "The chances that there's been a Dave *and* a

Jennifer into the tour office in the past two and a half months are really good."

Mitch laughed and stole the last of her cookies. "Okay, I'll tell you who everyone is, but there *will* be a quiz later, and if you fail, I might have to punish you."

She gave a shiver that he didn't think was entirely fake. And it made him a little hard behind the fly of his dress jeans. Yes, his dress jeans. He had one pair of nice pants, and he saved those for things like funerals and more sophisticated weddings. Not that he could remember the last time he'd been to a sophisticated wedding.

"I'm willing to take my chances." Her voice was a little husky when she said it.

Mitch suddenly wanted to get some fuzzy handcuffs and a blindfold. The sex with Paige was hot. The hottest he'd ever had. But he was always willing to take it up a notch. Whatever she wanted and was willing to do.

And, thank God, they'd been having more of that hottest-sex-ever sex since his family had realized it was a lot of work to keep them apart and clothed, especially when they lived together.

Or maybe they'd believed him when he said he and Paige were getting closer even if they weren't sleeping together. He meant that. He was pretty sure Paige had realized it too. Sex was one thing, but they'd now been dating—he supposed that was the best word to use though it seemed weak—for longer than either of them had dated anyone in years.

They'd shared their stories. They'd spent time together working, having fun, hanging with his family, just relaxing in the hammock on his porch. The weddings and the tour office, and the yoga classes people kept requesting had kept her busy. The new barn and fences for the petting zoo, building an archway and installing a net under the one Boys of the Bayou dock, and getting Ellie's into shape for the reception—though

Paige insisted that it was perfect as is—and his usual job duties kept him busy. But they ate lunch together a couple of times a week, and he'd taken her to New Orleans twice for their Saturday night dates.

It felt so right, so I-could-do-this-for-the-rest-of-my-life, that he'd caught himself three times before he told her he loved her.

It was too soon. It was too much. It was definitely not what she wanted.

So he kept it to himself. Though he knew that his entire family knew. They'd known the before-Paige Mitch and now the with-Paige Mitch. They were two different guys.

Thankfully, *she* didn't know that.

"Okay, so you know my Aunt Hannah and Uncle Jerry, Josh and Sawyer and Kennedy's mom and dad," he said, pointing at a table across the room. "The people sitting with them are Owen's mom, Cassie, and my dad, Sean."

Paige sat up straighter. "That's your dad?"

"Yep."

She looked from Sean to Mitch. "You haven't introduced us."

"Do you want to meet him?"

Paige frowned slightly and glanced back at his father. "Maybe."

Well, that wasn't a yes. But it wasn't a no.

Mitch's heart kicked. His dad knew about Paige. The men saw each other at least twice a week at Ellie's, and Sean had already heard about Paige before Mitch could tell him a thing. But his dad had clapped him on the shoulder over bowls of gumbo and had said, "You know what you're doin', havin' her move in?"

Mitch had nodded. "Sure. She needed a place to stay. That's what friends are for."

"Ellie says she doesn't want to be tied down."

"That's right." Mitch had worked to seem nonchalant. But his dad knew him.

"You gotta respect that."

Mitch had nodded again.

"You don't push yourself on people, son. You know that."

Mitch had swallowed hard but nodded again. "Yes, sir. I know that." It was what Sean had taught him all his life.

Be helpful. Make yourself useful. Be grateful. Make people happy you're around.

He'd been brought up to always think about the people around him before he thought about what he wanted. It was why he was a jack-of-all-trades. He wanted to be able to help anyone with anything they needed. He was the guy they all knew they could depend on, and he felt a lot of pride and satisfaction over that.

But that meant being whatever Paige wanted him to be. And nothing more.

"Okay, then," Sean had nodded and turned back to his gumbo. "You're a good man, son. You always do the right thing."

That night Mitch had almost told Paige he loved her while they were swinging in the hammock. But he'd swallowed it as his father's words came back to him. He wasn't going to push himself on Paige. He'd said that from the beginning. He'd promised *her* he wouldn't push. So, he could keep his feelings to himself.

He pointed again, moving Paige's—and his—attention away from his father. "That's Andrew. Tori's best friend from childhood. The one who was getting married when she and Josh got together."

Paige's eyes widened. "I thought *he* ended up declaring his feelings for Tori and breaking up his wedding."

"Yep." Mitch grinned, as he always did when thinking about Tori as a heartbreaker.

She was so sweet and a little awkward and had, evidently,

gone through high school and even most of college without a boyfriend or even dating much. But she'd been the cause of his cousin becoming celibate for a year after meeting her, and she had broken up the wedding of the season between Andrew and Senator Darbonne's daughter Paisley. *At* the wedding. In front of everyone.

"It's nice they're still friends," Paige said.

"I'm not sure Josh feels the same way," Mitch said wryly.

"Okay, so who's the gorgeous blond who asked Griffin to dance?"

"Someone was brave enough to ask Griffin to dance?" Mitch spotted his other roommate leaning against the bar.

"Yep. He said no, but he's been watching her ever since

"Why are you paying so much attention to Griffin?" Mitch asked, but he was amused. And curious as well.

"Because I think he's way softer underneath than he wants anyone to know," she said. "A true grump doesn't like cats and otters."

"He claims he doesn't like the otters."

"He's lying." She gave Mitch a grin that grabbed him in the chest.

Yeah, he was in love with her. And the fact that this place and these people—*his* place and *his* people—made her so happy.

"Fred hasn't slept on my bed since we got down here," Paige went on. "But I caught him strolling out of Griffin's room the other morning."

Mitch chuckled. "I don't know that his fondness for animals extends to people."

"Well, he's feeling *something* for that girl."

"Which one?"

She pointed, and Mitch felt his grin grow. "Oh, that's Charlie."

"Who's she?"

"Charlotte Arabella Clementine Landry."

Paige's eyes were round. "Wow. That's a lot of names."

"It is. And Charlie handles it." He chuckled. "Of course, only the bayou Landrys get away with calling her Charlie. She is very much Charlotte at home in Shreveport."

"A city Landry?" Paige teased.

"A couple of 'em got away." Mitch winked. "Guessin' Charlie knows which forks to use for what at a fancy restaurant."

"Too bad Griffin is such a grump," Paige said.

"I'm not so sure that would get to Charlie," Mitch said. "She's super friendly and... sunny." He decided that was the right word.

Paige laughed. "Oh, God, Griffin's nightmare. But..." Paige was studying Griffin. "A hot hook-up never hurt anybody." She grinned at Mitch.

Right. They'd started as a hot hook-up. That's all it was ever supposed to be. And yet, he was sitting here right now, head over heels.

Griffin should probably stay far away from Charlie.

"And who's Fletcher dancing with?" Paige asked.

"That's Jordan." Mitch couldn't help but smile.

"They look *very* friendly."

"They are. Best friends. Since kindergarten."

"And more?"

Mitch shook his head. "Nope. She started dating her boyfriend, Jason, when they were fifteen, and they've been together ever since."

"*Fifteen?*"

"Yep. He asked her to the Valentine's Day dance, and that was it."

"Wow."

"Yeah. They're practically engaged."

Paige frowned. "Just practically?"

"Well, not everyone moves as fast as the Appleby guys do," Mitch said. He was teasing, but he couldn't help the eye roll.

Paige elbowed him. "Okay, okay."

"They're not officially engaged. But it's been ten years."

"Does Fletcher have bigger feelings for her?"

"If he doesn't, he's a dumbass."

"But he's never said he does?"

"Nope. Though, his brothers tried to break them up a couple of times, and Fletcher never protested."

Paige leaned in, clearly interested. "How did they do that?"

"They doused Jason's car with perfume and left a bra in his backseat so Jordan would think he was cheating."

"But it didn't work?"

"Nope. It backfired big time, actually." Mitch grinned at the memory. "Jordan snuck into Zeke's bedroom—because of course, it had been Zeke's idea—handcuffed him to the headboard, doused his sheets in perfume, left a bra and panties on the floor, and shut off his alarm, so his mother found him that way the next morning when she came in to wake him up for breakfast."

"Oh my God, that's awesome," Paige said with wide eyes.

"Jordan and Fletcher were eighteen. Zeke and Zander were only sixteen. And already, troublemakers. Zeke knew he would never have been able to convince his mom that *Jordan*, the daughter she'd never had, would do something like that. And that was in part because he hadn't wanted to explain what he'd done to prompt her retribution."

Paige was laughing now.

"Then he found a note on his car seat the next morning that said simply, *Don't fuck with me. —J.*"

Paige looked out onto the dancefloor at Jordan and Fletcher. "I want to be her friend. For sure."

For her and Jordan to be best friends, Paige would need to be *here*.

He could make that happen.

If he would just fucking *chill*. But if he told her everything he was feeling and asked her to stay, she'd probably pack her stuff and hit the road tonight.

Dammit.

Instead of saying anything at all, he cupped the back of her neck and brought her in for a kiss.

A hot, deep, sweet kiss.

When he let her go, her cheeks were flushed. "What was that for?"

"Just... happy."

"Me too."

"I'm glad."

They stared at each other for a long moment. Then Paige said, "Can we go out to the truck?"

Fuck yeah, they could.

But they had to make a detour on the way to the door.

17

Mitch tugged Paige toward where his dad was seated.

"Hey, everybody," he greeted the table. He looped his arm around Paige's waist. "Dad, I wanted to introduce you to Paige."

"Well, hello, Paige." Sean gave her a big smile and extended his hand as he came to his feet.

She took it. "It's nice to meet you, Mr. Landry."

"Oh, God." He laughed, shaking his head. "There're way too many Mr. Landrys around here. It's just Sean."

"Nice to meet you, Sean."

"And great to meet the girl who's been making my son so happy."

That was exactly the kind of thing that would spook Paige. Dammit.

Mitch squeezed her waist and said, "We're on our way out for some air. Just wanted to say hi," before Sean could say anything more. And before Paige could react. "See you later."

He turned and steered Paige toward the door. She went along willingly, but as they stepped out into the cool night air, she said, "You didn't have to do that."

"Do what?" He kept walking. His truck was parked around the back and several yards from the building.

"Whisk me off just as your dad was starting to tell me how happy you are."

He looked down at her as they crossed the packed dirt parking area. "That's the kind of stuff that freaks you out, and I need you to not freak out."

He *really* needed her to not freak out. He wanted her to stay. She'd said she'd stay until August, but he also knew that promises weren't her strong suit. She didn't want people to hold her to everything she said all of the time. So he knew that August was a general idea in her mind and that it could change at any time.

He wanted her as long as she'd stay. Even past August. He just needed to *chill*. About everything.

They stopped by the truck, and he opened the passenger door for her. She climbed up with a boost from him, but before he could shut the door and go around to the driver's side, she tugged on his hand. He turned back.

"I'm not freaked out by that."

Her skirt was bunched up on her upper thighs, she was on the edge of the seat, and he was standing between her knees. She was still holding his hand and put her other hand on his shoulder.

"I like making you happy," she said, her voice softer now.

Their clasped hands rested on one of her thighs where the skirt and bare skin met.

"Well, you do," he said simply. "Things are good."

She nodded. "They are. Really good." She wet her lips. "And you make me happy too. I hope you know that."

His heart beat a little faster. Paige being happy here, truly happy, with him, because of him, because of his family and hometown and the things she'd been able to do here, mattered more to him than anything he could remember. He knew his laid-back, whatever-happens-happens attitude was one of his best character traits. People valued that in him. That it could be exactly what Paige needed was amazing. He put himself out there for the people he cared about. He was there for them, whatever they needed. But with Paige, it felt different.

He *wanted* to want things from her, but he was able to be patient and take her as she was. That was important to her, and he loved the idea that *he* could be what she needed, exactly as *he* was.

He knew she'd been discontented for a long time. Misunderstood too. Her family had expectations that she couldn't or didn't want to meet, and he knew that frustrated her.

"I'm really glad," he told her sincerely. He leaned in and kissed her.

The kiss was soft and sweet. They'd come out here, presumably, to have some hot front-seat sex. He still had her thong in his pocket. But this didn't feel hot and lust-filled and needy. This felt... familiar. As if he'd been kissing this woman all his life. And more, that he would be kissing her for the rest of his life. And that kissing would be enough in some moments.

He needed to *Chill. The. Fuck. Out.*

Mitch pulled back. He was pleased by the satisfied, happy look on her face from the kiss. "Maybe we should head home and have some hammock time," he said, brushing her hair back.

The hammock was a place she seemed so contented. They would just lie there together and rock. Sometimes they'd talk. Sometimes they didn't. But it was just peaceful and sweet.

He was going to have to take the hammock down when she left. He'd never be able to be in there again without thinking of her. And never with anyone else. But the moments with her out there were worth it.

"We can't leave the reception," she said. "I love being here with everyone."

"Oh." He had to admit he hadn't expected that. He knew she'd enjoyed the wedding planning and seeing it all come together. He knew she genuinely liked and cared about Tori, Maddie, and Juliet, and the guys. But he'd figured by now she'd be over all the wedding stuff and the massive number of people and the noise.

Paige tipped her head. "You're surprised."

"I am." He shrugged. "There's a lot of people and noise and bullshit and crazy in that building."

She nodded. "Yep. But... I've gotten used to it. I guess I understand the noise now."

"Understand it?"

"The noise is about love and belonging and celebration." She moved her hand from his shoulder to his neck, stroking up and down. "Even on a regular Tuesday at lunchtime, it's about celebration. Celebrating being together. Celebrating the life everyone here values. Even when they're bitching or arguing, it's still a celebration of having people in your life that will listen and will care enough to argue with you."

Mitch was watching her carefully. He loved what she was saying, but he was definitely surprised. It seemed her touch on his neck was absent-minded. She was lost in what she was saying.

"Being here has helped me realize some things about home," she admitted. "All of the ways my family has been 'butting in' to my life has really been more about me than them."

"How so?" Mitch asked. He felt a strange combination of happiness and hope that Paige was figuring some things out down here and trepidation that she was figuring out that maybe she missed Appleby.

He didn't want her to *not* love her hometown. In fact, he really *did* want her to love home and her family and her history there. But if she started missing it, maybe she'd realize she didn't need to go to Colorado to be alone after all. Maybe she'd just want to head home.

"Breaking off my engagement and canceling the wedding did a number on all of us. My mom was definitely disappointed and worried. But I think *my* guilt was stronger than anything."

She pressed her lips together, thinking. Then continued, "I think I've been projecting a lot of guilt onto the things they want from me. Like when they want me to help my niece and nephew with projects. Or when Josie and Grant want me to come to dinner. Or when I'm at weddings of friends and family. I've been thinking that it's all about them wanting me to want a wedding and a husband and kids of my own, but..." She took a breath and let it out. "That's ridiculous."

"Is it? Remember, I witnessed how hard your family tried to find out what was going on with us when I was in Iowa," Mitch said.

They'd been pretty relentless there for a while about trying to figure out who she was spending the night with instead of participating in family time.

"Yeah, but of course they were curious, right? I mean, I'm so secretive about things. I don't let them in. I don't really talk about how I'm feeling." Paige gave him a small smile, but she looked sad.

"I've never actually talked to my mom about calling off the wedding, or how I felt or how I feel about dating and settling down. I say things like, "I'll just get another cat" or "it's none of your business." But I think it's because I've wondered if I'm wrong about not wanting that stuff and if maybe I'm weird or something. I didn't know *how* to talk to her about it."

Mitch felt his gut knot. Yeah, she was figuring things out, and that probably meant that she would want to go home and talk this stuff out. Which she should. For sure. He wanted her to be happy and to have as good a relationship with her family as she could. Of course.

Damn, he was going to miss her.

"How has being here helped you figure that all out?" he asked, hoping she wouldn't hear how tight his voice was.

"Observing wedding preparations and family interactions that had nothing to do with me. Just being able to watch and see all the sides."

She lifted a shoulder.

"I mean, of course, there hasn't been any talk about canceling the weddings or anything," she went on. "But I've talked to Ellie and Leo and Cora and even the girls' moms a bit and, since I'm not reading anything into it or feeling suspicious, I've truly seen that they all just want the girls and guys to be happy. They would be fine with whatever that meant."

She smiled. "They're thrilled about the weddings, but I really believe that if one of the couples wanted to postpone or if one or two of them had never gotten engaged or like Kennedy and Bennett did, they just took off and eloped, everyone would still be happy. They might want it to all go a certain way, but at the end of the day, it's really about them being happy."

She sighed and ran her hand up and down his neck again. Mitch loved the feel of her hands on him. Even when it was like this. It was more affectionate than anything. More as if she just couldn't *not* touch him.

"I think my mom really does believe that I'll be happiest if I'm married," she said. "But I also think if I was *totally* honest with her and not defensive or sarcastic or annoyed, she'd listen, and she'd want me to be happy. All of this time with your family has made me see my mom and some of her motivations differently."

She was studying the top button of his shirt rather than meeting his eyes as she shared her thoughts.

"I also think that if I wasn't constantly worried about them worrying about me and thinking they were inviting me over because they felt sorry for me or something, I could enjoy hanging out with my niece and nephew and making dinner with Josie and Grant. And other things. Maybe family game nights and watching movies with my mom and helping Josie with her baking."

"You think they invite you to that stuff because they feel sorry for you?"

She met his eyes and nodded. "And don't want me holed up in my lonely apartment with my cats, becoming a weird spinster recluse."

He gave her a smile and squeezed her thigh. "You need to stop avoiding time with your family. You need to be honest with them about what you want and what you don't want, and then you need to find a way to be with them without all the misunderstandings and assumptions."

She nodded. "I do. I need to get this chip off my shoulder."

"Let's go home for hammock time," he urged again. He liked this softer side of Paige, and he was so glad she'd figured some big things out. He wanted to keep her talking.

"I don't want to leave." She smiled. "Planning these weddings and then seeing it all come together today was some of the most fun I've ever had."

Damn. He wasn't going to get her alone again for a while. "My dad is only the first person to say something like I'm a better man with you around. There will be more of that," he warned.

She laughed. "I have nothing to do with you being a better man, Mitch. You're the best man I know. Already. Before I had anything to do with you."

He shook his head. "You do make me better. You make me more patient and more content and happier."

He'd always been intent on helping everyone around him, fixing the things that needed fixing, being there to haul and lift and carry anything and everything. But Paige had taught him that he couldn't always put his hands on things and *fix* them.

Sometimes he just needed to be there, standing by while the people he loved went through things and letting them know that how he felt about them wouldn't change.

Yeah, she'd taught him that, he realized. He'd learned how he could provide an opportunity for someone to get what they needed, but that he might have to stand by and let them take that opportunity and go through it mostly on their own, hoping that it was what they needed it to be. He couldn't *fix* everything.

Sometimes he just had to love people while they were fixing themselves.

Damn, he didn't *feel* patient or content, though. He wanted Paige to be in the same place he was. Now. Tonight.

He wanted *more*. The need to be patient was a daily challenge.

"Well, I'm glad." She moved her hands to loop her arms around his neck and scooted closer. "I like to think that I'm giving you something too."

He could make this dirty. Flirty. Sexy. He could say something about the things he wanted from her. The dirty, flirty things. Not the forever things.

But instead, he said, "You don't have to give me anything, Paige."

She frowned slightly. "But that's not how relationships work, right? You give and take."

"Sure. But just having you here is giving me a lot."

She gave him a sweet smile. "I'm glad. And being here has given me a lot too."

"I'm glad." He was. Even if it was going to take her away from him.

She nodded, "And I want to ask you something."

"Okay."

"I got a call earlier today from my friend Piper's boyfriend, Ollie."

"Everything okay at home?"

"Yes. It's really good." Her smile grew. "Ollie is throwing Piper a surprise wedding."

"A surprise wedding?"

"Yep. Like a surprise party, but with getting married."

Wow. That was ballsy. That was Landry family level grand gesture.

"Is Piper going to like that?" he asked.

"Yes." Paige laughed. "From Ollie, yes. Because it's completely in character for him. And because it might be the only way to be sure he remembers to show up to their wedding and be on time."

Mitch shook his head. "Piper doesn't care about planning her own wedding or anything?"

"Nope. Well, I mean, she's a planner. She's great at it. But she's all in on things like this when it has to do with Ollie being creative and following his heart. She'll love it. And they talked about getting married already. She said yes. She just doesn't know that he's going to set the actual ceremony up as a surprise."

The truth hit Mitch all at once. "You're going home."

Paige nodded. "Yes. I really want to be there. I've helped him with a few plans from a distance, but if I can get there the day before, I can help him pull it together."

"You really are turning into a wedding planner." Mitch couldn't quite summon a smile, though that was beautifully ironic.

She grinned. "I am. But this one is simple. They're going to do it at the campground that they've built together. Josie is covering the cake, of course. And Ollie is a millionaire. He can throw money at this to get catering and travel and whatever is needed even last minute." She gave a happy sigh. "I just want to be there."

Mitch swallowed hard. This was great. She needed to go home. She needed family time. She needed to have these talks with her mom and everyone. And she needed time to be there with them with these new realizations about them and their expectations, without feeling all the pressures she'd felt when she'd left Appleby.

"When are you leaving?"

"Tomorrow."

He choked slightly. "Tomorrow?"

She nodded. "He's able to get her family there with the private jet. I don't even know if his parents are going to come. But all of his and her best friends are already there. Except me. So, it can easily be on a random Tuesday." She grinned.

"Okay." Mitch wanted it to be okay. He knew he *should be* okay with it.

Piper was one of her best friends. Of course, she needed to be there for her wedding. Of course, she did.

And then she needed to stay and make things right with her mom.

But damn, he couldn't deny his chest was tight, and he had a horrible feeling of *she's not coming back.*

"I want you to go with me."

Mitch took a deep breath. "I... can't."

"I know it's short notice, and I know that could be a little bit of a problem, but surely we can figure it out? The others can help pitch in until we get back, right?"

Sure. Probably. Maybe. That wasn't the issue.

"I don't think I should go, Paige."

She blinked at him. "Oh. Why?"

"You need time back home by yourself. You need to *not* bring the guy you took off to live with out-of-the-blue two and a half months ago if you're going to have a heart-to-heart with your mom about what you really want and how you don't want to be serious with anyone and make any promises."

Mitch's chest got tighter as he looked at the stunned look on Paige's face.

"I thought you'd want to come." Her hand dropped away from his neck.

"I mean, it would be fun. We could party at the wedding reception and everything. But there's more you need to do."

"More than have fun and party," she said. Then she pressed her lips together and nodded. "Right. I guess that's true."

Mitch steeled himself against grabbing her in a huge hug and reassuring her that he did *not* think that all they did together was have fun and party. This was more than that. On his side for sure. And he thought on her side as well. But right now, she needed to concentrate on her family and home and helping them understand what she wanted and needed.

"So, you go to the wedding and...whatever. Just give me a call at some point, okay?"

"Call?" she repeated. "At some point?"

"Yeah." He shrugged. "Or text." He could be cool about this.

"I can call every night," she said. "I won't be gone that long anyway."

But he shook his head quickly. "Don't worry about it. Just do what you need to do. However long it takes."

That was exactly how he *should* feel about this. That was how a casual friends-with-benefits thing would feel.

He'd messed this up so badly.

"Mitch—"

"No promises, okay?" he said quickly. "Let's not do that."

Because, honestly, if she did get home and realized that's where she wanted to be after this break, he really didn't want to be on the other end of a broken promise. That would hurt a lot more than if he just let her go, and she just went, and they decided to figure out what came next later.

Paige swallowed. Then said, "I want to start making some promises, Mitch."

His heart beat hard, but he made himself say, "After you're home. After you have a chance to see how things are there.

Okay? Not before. You can't make any promises before you know how things are going to be there now."

"I've always been worried about letting people down and disappointing people or breaking their hearts when I couldn't do or be what they wanted. But I think I can communicate better about what I can give and what I want and what my boundaries are. And I want people to depend on me. I want people to ask me for things. And even if it's more than I've given before or think I *can* give, I want to try. Because I think *trying* matters, and the right people understand that."

God, he really was in love with her.

She'd grown and figured things out and started to believe in herself and in how she could take care of people and love them. And she realized she wanted to do all of that.

He still had to send her home without her making him any promises.

Even more now. Because now, if she made him a promise to come back or said she wanted more of a relationship and that she wanted to talk about the future, and then something in Appleby changed her mind, she would still try to keep that promise.

He wanted her to go, to be this new, more confident person back in Appleby, and *then* decide what she wanted from him. If anything.

"Please don't," he finally said. "Not with me, anyway. Just... go. We can figure out the rest, whatever it is, later."

She flinched. Mitch's gut twisted.

She was hurt. Clearly. And he wanted nothing more than to say he didn't mean it, and he'd go anywhere with her and to please never leave him.

But that wasn't fair. He knew himself and what he wanted and where he wanted to be. She needed to figure that out for herself, by herself, without him there influencing her.

Paige took a deep breath. "Okay."

"Paige..." He had no idea what he was going to say.

"No, you don't have to say anything else. I'll go. And we'll just... see what happens. No promises."

Yeah, that's what he wanted.

At least that was what he *should* want.

"Okay."

She nudged him back and stepped down from the truck seat. "We should go back inside." She smoothed her skirt, studying her dress instead of him.

They should go back inside. Because if they stayed out here or went home together right now, he'd end up saying all of the things he was barely swallowing now.

18

A snowstorm? In April? In Illinois?

But as Paige peered through her windshield and strove to keep her car on the road, the answer to all three of those questions was a resolute *yes*.

Followed by *son of a bitch!*

It was *April*. How was she in the middle of what seemed, by all definitions, to be a blizzard?

She made herself relax the grip on the steering wheel. Her shoulders were tight, and she'd had to stop crying and singing along with Taylor Swift and eating peanut butter M&M's by the handful nearly twenty miles ago.

She really needed to cry and sing and eat. She'd just had her heart broken and was driving back home *alone* for a wedding.

Alone. That word. It was one that she'd actually aspired to, something she'd coveted. And now, here she was. Very alone. Just as she'd said she wanted.

And it sucked.

She didn't even care that she was definitely going to regret the M&M's later. Her mostly-sugar-free diet made it tough on her stomach when she fell off the wagon. But she was going to be miserable later—and for the foreseeable future—so what did a little stomach pain matter?

Yes, she was being dramatic.

Mitch hadn't broken up with her forever.

But... he didn't want any promises from her. He didn't believe she could make promises. She'd finally convinced a man that she wasn't a good bet and... dammit, he was the one she wanted to be a good bet for.

She shook her head.

She needed to concentrate on driving.

Paige caught and held her breath as she saw the sign indicating the exit for Peoria emerge from the swirling white that had been her view for the past almost forty-five minutes. Yes, it had taken her forty-five minutes to drive twenty miles.

It wasn't as if snow in April was completely foreign to her. She'd grown up in Iowa. But damn, she didn't drive when it was blizzarding in Iowa. One advantage to living above her place of employment was that she didn't even have to scrape her windows in the morning before work.

Still holding her breath, she started to exit. The car slid, she shrieked, and nearly broke the steering wheel off as she gripped it tightly. But the car straightened a moment later, and she was able to ease onto the off-ramp.

Fuck, fuck, fuck, fuck. She couldn't see anyone behind her in the rearview mirror. Of course, another vehicle could be right on her back bumper before she'd see them clearly in the white-out conditions.

What the actual *hell* was she supposed to do now?

She eased up to the stop sign at the top of the exit. There was a slight incline, which helped her slow. Then again, she was only going maybe ten miles an hour at this point.

Of course, trying to start again while on even a slight incline when the pavement was covered in heavy, wet snow was another reason for lots of cussing. And breath-holding.

Her back tires spun, and she felt tears welling up again. These were not Mitch tears though. These were *fuck-I'm-going-to-get-stuck-in-the-snow-in-Peoria-Illinois* tears.

But the thought of how these tears were *not* for Mitch made her think of Mitch, and how if he was here, she'd be a lot less scared. He'd know what to do. He'd have stuff in the back of his truck to get them unstuck. Then again, if they were in his truck, they probably wouldn't get stuck in the first place.

But Mitch wouldn't know about driving in a blizzard, a voice in her head tried to helpfully point out.

The thing is, Mitch can do anything. He can fix anything. He can be depended on for any situation, another voice argued.

Oh, really? Any situation? the first voice asked. *How about the situation where you're in love with him and want him to go home to a wedding with you, but he sees it as just a chance to have fun and party and decides it's not worth the long drive?*

A horn blared behind her, and Paige jumped.

"Oh yeah, I'm just sitting here watching the beautiful snow come down!" Paige yelled. Not that anyone could hear her.

Still, it felt good to let go of some pent-up emotion.

"If I could move, I would, asshole!" she yelled, just because she could.

The horn blared again, and she tipped her head back and let a long, loud, "Arrrrrrgggggghhhhh!" out.

Then she got out of her car and went stomping back to the pick-up behind her.

It was stupid. She knew that even as she was doing it. She had no idea who was behind her and what they might be capable of.

But she didn't care. She hadn't had an M&M in almost an hour.

"What the *fuck* do you want me to do?" she yelled at the driver's side window of the truck behind her. "I'm *stuck!*"

The window rolled down, and a man in his fifties with a dark green stocking cap peered out at her. "What are you doing?" he demanded.

The snow swirled around her, and tiny ice pellets bounced off her coat—that had spent the past two-and-a-half months in the back seat because she certainly hadn't needed it in Louisiana... a thought that made her feel like crying all over again.

"I'm asking you what the *fuck* you think honking at me is going to do?" she yelled.

"Are you all right?" the man asked.

Paige felt her eyes widen. "Seriously? *Seriously*? What the hell kind of question is that? I'm..."

But instead of yelling about being stuck in the snow or stressed out about driving in a blizzard or being three hours away from Appleby and certain to miss Piper's wedding, she said, "I'm completely in love for the first time in my life, and he thinks it's all just for fun. Or rather, he thinks *I* think it's all just for fun. Because that's all I've ever wanted it to be before. But he's different, and I want to be with him, and it's okay that I'm going to this wedding alone. We don't have to do *everything* together. And yeah, I've got some shit I need to work out with my family, and maybe it's better if he's not there while I do that. But I still should have told him that I love him. But I didn't. I just left. I left and didn't tell him I love him."

The man was staring at her now, and Paige realized she had tears streaming down her cheeks.

"Do you need a push?" the man finally asked.

Did she need a push? She most certainly did. Apparently. She needed someone to push her to realize that she was going to have to be the one to reach out to Mitch. Even if he loved her —the thought made her heart flip—he wouldn't say it first. He wouldn't even come home with her to spend time with her family. He wouldn't do anything that might spook her.

"I definitely need a push," she told the man. Fuck, she was tired of being spooked. Of thinking that everyone had ulterior motives. Of worrying that someone was going to take something she said or did the wrong way.

The man in the truck sighed and pulled on gloves. Then he rolled up his window and opened his door.

"Okay, let's get you unstuck."

Unstuck. That was what she needed. She needed to be unstuck from all the fears about disappointing people and worrying about their expectations. She needed to get out of the rut of assuming people wanted more than she could give. Maybe she *could* give more. Or maybe not, and they'd just have to be okay with that. But she needed to not be afraid of it. She needed to be upfront and honest and trust that the people who loved her, would love her no matter what.

And if people asked her to marry them, and she didn't want to, she'd just keep saying no. Even if it happened twenty more times.

Of course, if *Mitch* wanted to ask, then she wouldn't have to worry about anyone else asking because she'd say yes.

That made her heart stop for a second.

She'd say *yes* if Mitch proposed?

But she realized instantly that yes, she absolutely would.

"Miss?" the man in the truck asked. "Do you have a shovel or sand in your car?"

She shook her head. "No."

The man frowned at her license plate. "You're from Iowa."

"Yes. But I've been staying in Louisiana."

"You should still know better than to drive in this weather without a shovel or sand."

Paige rolled her eyes. "I've been *in Louisiana*. I had no idea that I was going to hit this weather."

"You got a weather app on your phone?"

She narrowed her eyes. "Does that really matter right now? I need a push. You able to do that or not?"

The man sighed. "Well—" He looked around. "Is there anyone else who can push you?"

Not really. Her mother had been pushing her for years, and it had just made Paige dig her heels in. Her sisters too. She was *more* stuck because of the pushing rather than less. The guys she dated pushed for more than she wanted to give, and it made her turn and run in the opposite direction.

But there was one person who pushed her. In a really good way.

By not pushing at all.

She nodded. "Mitch."

She knew he didn't mean to push her. In fact, she'd bet he felt strongly that he *shouldn't* push her. But that was what she needed most. He made her want him, showed her everything she could have with him, and then sat back and let her come to her own realizations and decisions about what she wanted.

"Who's Mitch?"

"The man that I'm madly in love with. But I need to tell him that. He won't say it first. He never asks people for things. He never reaches out for help or even favors. He's always the one helping and doing favors."

Damn, she was so in love with him.

And he needed to know that he could ask for things. Ask *her* for things.

"So, he *is* going to be pushing your car out of the snow or not?" the man asked.

"Oh, no. He pushes me by *not* pushing me."

"Did you hit your head when your car slid?"

She frowned at the man. "No."

"And Mitch is *not* showing up right now to help?"

She sighed. "No."

"Then let's get this over with."

Ten minutes later, the man in the truck had applied sand to the ice under her tires and had pushed her car off of the slick spot. He'd also given her his card. His name was Timothy Rogers, and he and his wife ran a bed and breakfast about three miles up the road. Where he was headed as well.

An hour after that, Paige was checked into the most adorable bedroom she'd ever seen. She was wrapped in a fluffy bathrobe, propped up on eight—yes, *eight*—of the fluffiest pillows she'd ever felt at the head of a four-poster king-size bed. The mattress felt like it was a cloud from heaven. The towels had smelled like lavender and vanilla. And she was now eating a bowl of the best broccoli cheddar soup and a salad with a homemade dressing that made her willing to bring the Rogers family a cat when she came back through on her return to Louisiana.

Or maybe a beautiful *photograph* of one of her cats that they could hang on the wall.

Actually, she wasn't so sure *she* was even going to be able to take any of her cats back to Autre with her. The cats were all living at Didi Lancaster's mansion, where they'd been spoiled daily by Whitney's grandmother for the past two and a half months.

The news was on TV as Paige ate, and she groaned as the weatherman pointed to the screen behind him. It was clear that she wasn't going to be to Appleby in time to help set up for the wedding. Or maybe for the wedding at all. The snow was going to stop, but it would be blowing all night, and the roads would be a mess in the morning. It looked like they'd gotten snow in southern Iowa too, but the map didn't extend all the way to Appleby. She wondered if she'd drive out of it if she started in that direction tomorrow.

"Dammit." She set her dishes back on the wooden tray Mrs. Rogers had brought to her room and reached for her phone.

A minute later, her sister answered.

"Paige!"

"Hey, Josie."

"Uh, oh, what's wrong?"

"You can tell something's wrong from two words?" Paige asked.

"Yeah."

Paige smiled but sighed. "Well, I'm stuck in Peoria, Illinois. Huge snowstorm."

"What? No way. It's April!"

Paige laughed. "I take it that means things are okay there?"

She heard a clattering and shuffling on Josie's end of the line. "Yeah. Things are okay here," her sister said. There was a pause, and then she said, "Oh dammit."

"What?"

"I just pulled up the radar. Yeah, looks like it's all south of us. Davenport is getting hit too."

"I don't know if I'm going to make it on time," Paige said, feeling the disappointment settle into her chest.

"Well, you shouldn't try tonight for sure," Josie said. "I do *not* want you on the road alone in this. Especially, as it's getting dark."

"I'm at a B and B in Peoria. I'm okay right now."

"Good. Just stay there."

"But the wedding..." At one point in her life, she would have tried to drive through the snow to be there, but she did know better now.

"The wedding will go on," Josie said. "It would be awesome if you could be there, but they'll understand."

"Yeah." Paige bit her bottom lip. "It's not them. It's me."

"What do you mean?"

"I want to see Piper and Ollie say their vows. I want to be there for the celebration. I've realized that weddings aren't really about tying two people together in a way they can't get out of." She gave a little self-deprecating laugh. "That's how it used to feel to me."

"I know," Josie said, her tone dry but affectionate at the same time.

Paige nodded, even though Josie couldn't see her. "I've realized that a relationship is about the two people in it, but it's not *just* about them. At least not in families like ours. And Piper and Ollie are our family, even if it's not blood."

Paige heard Josie sniff, and she knew her soft-hearted sister was tearing up.

"So you're telling me that you've become pro-marriage?" Josie asked.

Paige smiled. "Well, it's helpful for a wedding planner to not be *anti*-marriage, at least."

Josie laughed. "True. You want to keep doing the wedding planning thing, then? I think that's great. And hilarious."

"I know." It was kind of hilarious. "But yeah, I really enjoy it. And I'm strangely good at it.'

"I don't think that's strange," Josie said. "It's not that you can't be sentimental and creative and family-oriented. It's that you've been choosing not to be."

Paige was quiet. She thought about that. Finally, she said, "Yeah. You're right. I consciously rejected all of that so that I didn't get anyone's hopes up."

"It worked."

"It did. But... I think I'm over that."

"Over what?"

"Over not getting people's hopes up. I want people to want things from me."

Josie didn't say anything for a moment. When she did answer, her voice was soft. "I'm happy and sad."

"Sad?"

"This means you'll be staying in Louisiana, right?"

Paige realized that was exactly what it meant. Or what she hoped it would mean. "It's not that I don't love Appleby."

"I know. But Autre was able to give you something we couldn't."

"Is that bad?" Paige felt a little guilty.

"No." Josie gave a soft laugh. "I'm glad Appleby could give Grant something Chicago couldn't. It's how it happens sometimes. I think Autre gave you the ability to figure out who you really wanted to be. In Appleby, you might have figured it out eventually, but there were a lot of people with ideas about who you were already. In Autre, you could start fresh. All of the ideas were just yours."

Paige felt herself nodding. "Yeah. That's it. For a place that has a ton of history and roots, the fact that *I* didn't have any there was exactly what I needed so I could figure out what I want my history and roots to be like when I look back."

"I'm going to miss you."

"You can come visit. And I can come home a lot. My brother-in-law is loaded and has a private plane."

"Yes, he does. And I am learning that I can talk him into almost anything."

Paige's laugh was loud. "You're just now learning that? Because we've all known it for a long time."

Josie's voice was full of love and happiness when she said, "It's all going to be great. But I think you're going to wait for that visit home until the weather is a little nicer between there and here."

Reminded of her current predicament, Paige groaned. "I really wanted to see the wedding."

"I can put you on a video call, and you can watch the whole thing from the safety and warmth of that B and B," Josie said.

Paige sighed. "Yeah, I guess. And *maybe* they'll get the road cleared in the morning, and I can make it *just* in time."

They chatted for a few more minutes, and Josie promised to

send photos of the wedding cake before they disconnected.

Paige was smiling as she sat back against the fluffiest pillows she'd ever met.

But she sobered after only a couple of minutes.

Was she going back to Louisiana?

Of course, she was. Most of her clothes and five of her cats were still there. This trip to Iowa hadn't been intended to be permanent.

But was she *staying* once she got there?

Mitch hadn't asked her to come back.

He was probably assuming she would. For the cats, if nothing else. Temporarily.

But they hadn't talked about *when* she would be back. Or how long she'd stay. If she'd stay past August. If she'd even stay *until* August.

He hadn't asked. He had been quick to say no to coming to Iowa with her. He'd flat out told her not to make him any promises.

How would he feel about her being there permanently?

She'd told him she was going to stay in Autre until August. He knew she'd intended to head to Colorado eventually. *That* had been the plan.

She *had* made him a promise.

To *not* stay.

To not get serious.

To not commit to anything or do anything long term or to even be there past August.

She was in love with him, but he didn't know that. And he'd certainly not said he felt anything like that for her.

He liked her. A lot. They had amazing chemistry. He was a great friend. One of her best. He understood her, he didn't judge her, he didn't... push.

He *wouldn't* push.

If she wanted more from him, *she* was going to have to ask

for it.

And what if he said no?

She had *never* asked a guy for something. Ever. Men asked *her* out, to go to dances and dinner, to go back to their place for the night, to meet their families. To marry them.

Hell, Mitch hadn't even introduced her to his family.

They'd totally introduced themselves.

She'd run into Kennedy before she'd even seen Mitch.

It wasn't as if she could have been in Autre for two and a half months and avoided them, but the only person Mitch had actually introduced her to had been his dad.

Wow, maybe she was really jumping ahead here.

She could very well ask Mitch Landry to marry her, and he might just freaking say no.

The phone rang, and when Paige saw the number, she immediately reached for it.

"Kennedy, what's going on?"

"Hey, Paige," Kennedy greeted. "I was hoping to just run into you, but I haven't seen you yet. I was going to ask if you would be able to pick up the balloons for us Tuesday morning."

"The balloons?" Paige frowned. What balloons? What was Tuesday? "I'm on my way to Iowa for a wedding."

There was a hesitation on Kennedy's end of the phone. Then she asked, "Iowa?"

"Yes. My friend Piper is getting married tomorrow. It's a surprise, so I didn't have time to plan for it much." She paused, but couldn't help but ask. "Didn't Mitch tell you?"

"I didn't ask Mitch about you. I needed you, so I called you directly." Kennedy sounded puzzled, which Paige had to admit made sense. If Mitch and Kennedy hadn't talked, then Kennedy had no idea that Paige was no longer in Autre.

"I'm sorry I'm not around to help. But what are the balloons for?" It occurred to Paige how nice it was that Kennedy was calling her for help. Over the course of the last couple of months with the weddings, she had become more directly involved, and people seemed to have gotten more comfortable coming to her directly. She liked that. She wanted to be involved, and she loved the idea that they were comfortable asking, knowing that she wanted to help out.

"The grand opening of the otter enclosure," Kennedy told her.

Paige sat straight up in bed. The otter enclosure? There was a grand opening planned? She hadn't heard anything about it. It was happening on Tuesday? "I had no idea that was happening."

"I guess I just assumed that you knew. It was crazy trying to plan it with all the wedding stuff going on, but you were handling all of that for us, so we were able to put together the grand opening when Mitch got the enclosure done ahead of schedule. Maybe no one thought to mention it to you because you were so busy with wedding preparations."

There was a long pause where neither woman said anything.

Then Kennedy voiced exactly what Paige was thinking.

"But Mitch didn't say anything to you?"

Paige shook her head, even though the other woman couldn't see her. "No."

Again, there was a pause. Then Paige and Kennedy said simultaneously, "Of course he didn't."

Paige sighed. Of course, Mitch wouldn't have mentioned to her that they were making a big deal out of something he had done. She'd known that the otter enclosure was finished and that plans had been underway to open it to visitors soon. But she'd had no idea there would be a formal event for it.

"Is Mitch with you?" Kennedy asked. "Because I'm going to kill him if he left town with this grand opening happening. That would be just like him, to skip out when we were trying to praise and acknowledge him."

Paige had to agree that that seemed very in character for Mitch. She thought for a moment. Was this why he had turned down going to the wedding with her? But she immediately knew the answer to that. Mitch would never put something of his own ahead of something of hers. In fact, he never put himself ahead of anyone else. But certainly not her. Even if he had been excited about the grand opening, which she very much doubted that he was, he still would have skipped it to accompany her to her best friend's wedding in Appleby.

"No," Paige told Kennedy. "He sent me to Iowa alone."

Kennedy let out a breath. "Well, that's good. At least he's still here." She paused. "But you left him? You didn't insist he go with you? You didn't stay for the otter enclosure opening?"

Paige frowned. "I didn't know about the otter enclosure opening. And he seemed very adamant about me going home to Iowa alone and working out my relationship with my parents."

"I told you not to hurt him," Kennedy said. "I like you. I don't want to have to kill you."

"I don't think I hurt him," Paige said, knowing that she sounded as sad as she felt. "I don't think he is as brokenhearted about us being apart as I am."

Kennedy snorted into the phone. "Mitchell Landry is madly in love with you, Paige," she said. "If you left town, he is for sure worried that you're not coming back, and he's brokenhearted about that."

Paige felt her heart flip. Not because she wanted Mitch to be brokenhearted, of course, but the idea that he was madly in love with her made her feel warm in a way she'd never felt before.

But in the next moment, she took a deep breath and felt everything in her calm. Much the way she felt after a really great yoga practice. All of the tension and worry and confusion flowed right out of her.

Of course, he was in love with her. They were in love with each other. And if he had a big opening of a huge project he'd been working on and everyone wanted to acknowledge and praise him, she needed to be there. In fact, she needed to be there and insist he show up so that he could be loved and lifted up.

"I will be there on Tuesday. Actually, I'll be there tomorrow," Paige told Kennedy.

"But what about your friend's wedding?"

"They have a lot of people there for them. They don't need me."

"Mitch has a lot of people here for him too."

Paige smiled. Yes, he did. But he needed *her* there too. "Yes, but Piper and Ollie are with their most important person on this big day—each other. If I'm not there in Autre, Mitch won't have his most important person."

"He won't?" Kennedy asked. "Are you sure?"

Paige knew Kennedy's question wasn't because *she* wasn't sure. Kennedy wanted to know that Paige was sure. "Yes. I need to be there for his big days. I help make those days even bigger. This is a part of his story, and I want to be part of every page. From here on."

Kennedy laughed. "Unintended pun with the whole page thing?"

Paige grinned. "Nope."

"Wow, that sounds like a commitment from the girl who was only to be here for a few months."

"Yeah. It is a commitment, and one that I'm very ready to make."

"Great. So how far is it from Appleby back here?"

"Well, it's about fourteen hours from Appleby to Autre," Paige told her. "But I'm not in Appleby. I only made it as far as Peoria, Illinois because of a snowstorm. I'm pulled up in a bed and breakfast, but I should be able to get out tomorrow morning. Especially if I'm coming back that direction. The weather and road should be fine."

"Great. So can you pick up the damn balloons or not?"

"I don't know. I might be kind of busy convincing the guest of honor that he needs to show up."

"Good point," Kennedy admitted. "And I know a little bit about convincing stubborn men that they need to do things differently than they think they need to. But if anyone can convince him. I know that it's you."

"Damn right."

"Okay, I'll see you tomorrow."

"Yes you will. And hey, thanks for calling, Kennedy."

"No problem. Like I told you in the beginning, Mitch is my favorite, and I feel like I just did him a huge favor."

The women disconnected, and Paige sat staring at the swirling pattern on the comforter on the bed. The room was very quiet. Very, very quiet.

Wow.

She was alone. For the first time in months.

And that was the last thing she wanted to be.

There were two places that she wanted to be. Two groups of people she really wanted to be with. She would rather be anywhere but alone.

She also knew exactly which of those two places she needed to be most. She needed to go to Mitch. She also knew if she turned around now and went back to Louisiana, she would not be leaving Autre again. At least, not for good. Mitch would know he had her heart and that she was not going to be taking it away with her ever again.

And, as supportive as he'd been about her going home, and as great he'd been about giving her space, she knew that once Mitch knew she was his, he was never going to let her go.

That thought made her all the more anxious to get back to Autre as soon as possible.

19

"Hey."

Mitch turned to find Kennedy approaching.

"Hey," he said softly, then put a finger to his lips, indicating she should be quiet. He pointed, and her gaze followed his finger.

She smiled as she noticed Griffin inside the otter enclosure.

"Is he talking to the otters?"

Mitch nodded. His roommate, and friend, talked to the otters all the time. But only when he didn't think any other human was around.

Kennedy leaned onto the fence, settling in to listen with him.

"I mean, yeah, she was kind of pretty," Griffin told the otter who was crawling across his lap where he sat on one of the boulders inside the enclosure. "But damn, she was talkative. You know how I feel about talkative."

The otter chittered his answer and stuck his nose into Griffin's open palm, searching for more treats. Griffin ran his hand over the back of the otter.

"Fine, she was more than kind of pretty." The otter circled around behind Griffin's back, squeaking.

Mitch assumed he was chewing Griffin out for not bringing more treats.

But Griffin replied as if the otter were asking about the woman from the night before. "I don't know who told you about the kissing, and I don't appreciate the gossiping, but, yes, we might've kissed."

Mitch lifted an eyebrow and shared a look with Kennedy. She was grinning as if someone had just given her their last candy bar.

The otter climbed back into Griffin's lap and looked up at him expectantly. Griffin petted his head again. "Yes, it was very good. But you can just keep that to yourself. You all talk too much, too."

Kennedy slid closer to Mitch to whisper, "*Who* is he talking about?"

"I have no idea. I assume someone from the wedding reception?"

"Well, she's not my type," Griffin said as he nudged the otter off of his lap and stretched to his feet. "And she's not from here, so I won't be seeing her again."

Kennedy and Mitch shared another look. It was clear that Kennedy was mentally going over the guests from the wedding just as Mitch was, trying to determine who Griffin might've had a rendezvous with. The number of guests who were not from Autre definitely narrowed it down.

Griffin moved off with his entourage of otters following him across the enclosure chattering loudly. Most of the people they talked to like that were the ones who fed them, and while they did love Griffin bringing them treats, they talked to and surrounded him like he was a rock star when he came to see them no matter if he had treats in his pockets or not.

"I really don't know who he could be talking about," Kennedy finally said, clearly perturbed by that.

"Well..."

Kennedy arched a brow at him. "Spill it."

"Paige mentioned that someone had asked Griffin to dance," Mitch said.

Kennedy waited for several seconds. Then she shoved him. Hard. "Mitch!"

He laughed, rubbing the spot on his chest where she'd pushed.

"Who was it?"

"Charlie."

Kennedy opened her mouth, then her jaw dropped even wider as she processed that. Then she grinned. "Of course. I didn't think of her. I mean, I guess she's not from here, technically. It just feels like she is," she said of their cousin, who had spent so much time on the bayou in spite of growing up in Shreveport.

Mitch shrugged. "I don't know if that's who it was. I'm just telling you what Paige said."

Kennedy glanced in the direction Griffin had disappeared. "Dammit, Charlie's already left. She's flying to Paris tomorrow. I might not be able to grill her about this for a while."

Mitch felt a weird tightness in his chest. "If she's leaving for Paris, it doesn't really matter what happened with her and Griffin one night here in Autre, does it?"

Kennedy focused on him again. "Just because someone leaves, doesn't mean they can't come back."

"She left for a big reason."

"Are we still talking about Charlie and Griffin?"

Mitch felt his chest tighten further. "Of course."

"Uh-huh." Clearly, Kennedy wasn't buying it.

Mitch gripped the top of the fence a little tighter.

"I called Paige a little bit ago," Kennedy said.

Mitch gripped the fence tighter. It was ridiculous how much he missed her already. She'd just left. She'd actually been gone when he awakened this morning. He supposed it was for the best since he had no idea what to say to her. Well, other than begging her to stay. Which was ridiculous. She was going back home for her best friend's wedding. It wasn't like she was leaving forever. Or taking off for Colorado. Hell, he was the one who said no to going with her. She'd invited him along.

But he knew there was a chance that when she was away from him and Autre, whatever spell he and his hometown and family had somehow cast on her might be broken. Once she was back in Appleby, she could very easily decide to stay there. Or, when she was back in Appleby, she could be reminded about how much she really wanted her Year of Aloneness. She could head out to Colorado after the wedding. In fact, for a girl who really had been seeking the path of least resistance when she headed to Louisiana a couple of months ago, that would be very in character.

Of course, there was a voice niggling at the back of his mind reminding him that the girl who had arrived in Louisiana a couple of months ago wasn't the same girl who'd gotten in her car this morning. All he could do was hope that the girl who had headed north to Iowa had left a piece of her heart with him in Louisiana.

"I can't believe you didn't tell her about this," Kennedy said.

"She has a wedding to get to."

"That wedding is not more important than you are," Kennedy said.

Mitch shook his head. "That's ridiculous. It's a wedding. Two of her best friends."

"And you're *you*. *You* are important too, Mitch," Kennedy said. Her tone was exasperated but also full of affection.

He swallowed. "She needed a chance to get away and see

what she really wants. If you love something, set it free and all that."

Kennedy laughed softly. "Landrys don't let the things they love get away, Mitch."

"Right. Sometimes they *drive* them away."

Kennedy couldn't argue with that. "Well, we do try our best sometimes."

Yeah, they did. He'd seen all of his cousins try to screw up the relationship with the love of their lives. He'd seen his grandmother screw up her relationship with his grandfather for that matter. But they'd all fixed it in the end. He felt a little flip in his gut thinking about that.

"She was very upset that she didn't know about the grand opening of the enclosure," Kennedy said.

Mitch looked at her quickly. "You told her?"

"Yeah. Accidentally. I had no idea that she didn't know about it. But I would have told her either way."

"It's just a fence and a couple swimming holes."

Kennedy straightened away from the fence and turned to face him, her hands on her hips. "No, it's not. You know this means a lot to me, and Tori, and Maddie, and Juliet. The otters are practically our pets. And this will help the family business. Plus, you did an *amazing* job. Way above and beyond. This thing is awesome. The city is giving you a Best New Initiative Award."

"Autre is giving their incoming mayor's family a Best New Initiative Award," Mitch said. "That's ridiculous at best, considering there haven't been any new initiatives in any other businesses in years, and a conflict of interest at worst."

Kennedy, the incoming mayor, waved that away. "The whole city council agreed it's awesome. The award was Knox's idea, not mine."

Knox was the city planner. He was a great guy. He'd grown up in Autre as well, hunting, fishing, and climbing trees with the Landry boys. Knox was a big, outdoorsy guy and the last one that any of them would have expected to turn into a guy who worked in an office and worried about things like stoplights and traffic patterns. But he had a nerdy side. And he got shit done.

"Knox likes me. Not the enclosure," Mitch said.

"Everyone likes you, Mitch," Kennedy said with an eye roll. "That doesn't mean you're not good at things and deserving of recognition."

He didn't respond to that. Because that was really nice. He was proud of the enclosure. He had to admit it looked amazing.

"And now that Maddie's posted it on our social media, that animal park outside of Galveston wants you to come help them expand their enclosure. And you got that grant, Mitch!"

He had to admit the email they'd gotten from the animal park in Texas had been pretty cool. He was happy to take a trip over there and consult on how they could add to what they had. It was crazy that anyone really wanted him to consult on anything, but he'd take the road trip and the fee they'd offered him. And yeah, the news that they had been awarded five thousand dollars from an otter protection organization was amazing. Tori had just told him two days ago. Then it had promptly gotten lost in all of the wedding hoopla.

"Tori got that grant," he said.

"Tori sent the paperwork in," Kennedy said. "*Your* work got that grant. This is a big deal."

"Well, so is a wedding."

Kennedy blew out an exasperated breath. "Paige wants to be here with you for big things like this. Hell, she wants to be here for the little things too. She talks about your hammock all the time. At first, I thought it was an innuendo for something else. But she actually likes your *hammock*."

Mitch felt himself smiling at that. Paige really did like his hammock. His literal hammock.

They had way better innuendos for the other things she liked.

"If *she* was asked to plan a wedding in Galveston because of a social media post or was offered a grant to do more otter yoga, you'd be thrilled for her and would want to celebrate that with her, right?" Kennedy asked.

He swallowed. "Definitely."

"And you also love every second of being in that hammock with her, right?"

"Yeah." His voice sounded gruff now.

"Yeah." Kennedy gave him a soft smile. "That's called being in love. She wants to be a part of your life, Mitch."

He wanted that to be true. He certainly wanted her here. He knew that she would be excited about the otter enclosure. He knew that she would make a big deal out of the grand opening. But it wasn't really *his* grand opening, and she needed to go to Appleby. He wanted her here, but he couldn't take her away from the other important things in her life. "I guess we'll see about that."

"Meaning?" Kennedy asked.

Mitch shrugged. "If she comes back."

"Oh, she's coming back."

"Maybe. If she doesn't remember that she was pretty set on being alone for a while. She might have had some fun here and enjoyed the hammock and the otters and the weddings. But she definitely hasn't been alone."

"Well... I mean, she's definitely coming back. She's getting on the road tomorrow."

He straightened and turned to face Kennedy. "What?"

"I told her about the grand opening, and she said she was going to be here."

He frowned. "You should've talked her out of that."

Kennedy didn't look a bit apologetic. Not that he'd expected her to. "She loves you, Mitch, and when a headstrong woman falls in love, no one can talk her out of that."

His frown deepened in spite of the way his heart squeezed hearing that Paige loved him. He knew she cared about him, but love? That's what *she* needed to figure out.

"You shouldn't have asked her to come back."

"Oh, I didn't ask her, she insisted."

"It's a long drive from Appleby. She shouldn't get right back on the road."

"Well, she didn't make it all the way to Appleby anyway. I don't know how far it is from Peoria to here, but at least it's a little closer."

Mitch's frown turned into an outright scowl. "What do you mean she didn't make it all the way to Appleby?"

"She got stuck in a snowstorm in Illinois."

"*What?*" Mitch shoved a hand through his hair. "What the fuck, Kennedy? That's the kind of thing you should've told me *first.*"

"Why? What can you do about it?"

"Go to her. Help her."

"She's fine. She got help, and she's holed up in a bed and breakfast until tomorrow morning."

"She got help? From who?"

"I don't know. I didn't ask. I assume someone with a tow truck or at least a shovel?"

Mitch's heart was hammering, and he felt tension climbing up his spine. "Fuck. I should've gone with her."

Kennedy tipped her head. "Yes, you should have, but I'm not sure what that has to do with the snow."

"I would have been there with her. It wouldn't have been such a big deal for her to be stuck."

Kennedy shook her head. "I didn't say it was a big deal. She couldn't go any further because of the roads, so she stopped and is spending the night in Peoria at a bed and breakfast."

"But she was alone in bad weather, on bad roads, and is now stuck in between here and home."

Kennedy nodded. "And she's fine."

"But she's alone." His words hit him in the moment after he said them out loud.

Alone.

Alone was exactly what Paige wanted to be. It was what she liked most in the world. It was what she was looking for when he met her and what her plan was for when she left Louisiana in August to go to Colorado.

He blew out a breath, trying to calm his heart rate. He looked at Kennedy. "She's fine?"

"Well, she's upset that she's not here for the grand opening. She's sad that you didn't tell her about it. And she's eager to get back."

He shook his head. "She's really coming back?"

"Yep. She's really coming back."

For some reason, that time Kennedy said it, it actually sunk in. Paige was coming back for the grand opening of the otter enclosure. Yeah, okay, it was kind of a big deal. They were getting some great attention from the area for it, which would no doubt help the family business. They had gotten the grant money. And above all, the otters were happy and safe. But, in the overall scheme of things, it wasn't a *big* deal. It was just a big deal to his family. To him.

It wasn't such a big deal that someone should skip their best friend's wedding and drive twelve hours back, alone, in bad weather, to be there for it. Especially someone who wasn't really that into being involved in other people's business.

The only reason it would be a big deal to Paige was if *he* was a big deal to Paige.

And the reality of that hit him hard. Directly in the chest. Right over his heart.

Instead of using the snow as a perfect excuse to stay put, or her friend's wedding as the perfect excuse to avoid this a-little-silly-not-a-big-deal-to-anyone-but-the-Landrys event, she was getting back in her car after a twelve-hour drive, onto potentially snowy roads, to come back to him.

Damn, maybe she did love him.

"I'm going to Peoria, Illinois," he told Kennedy as he started toward his truck.

Kennedy had to run to catch up to him, but she was already pulling her phone from her pocket as he rounded the front fender.

She lifted the phone to her ear. "Hey, Mitch is heading out." She paused, listening. "Well, I assume he's going to have to stop and get some things from his house or fill up with gas or something." She looked at Mitch with an eyebrow up.

He wasn't sure who she was talking to, but he put money down on it being someone with the last name Landry. He gave her a nod as he climbed into the cab of his truck.

"Yeah, I think that's a great idea." She paused again and gave Mitch a grin. "Okay, I'll tell him."

Mitch started the engine, but he waited for her to disconnect the call and tuck her phone back into her pocket.

"Who was that?"

"Chase." Kennedy smiled. "He's going with you."

Okay, so he'd been wrong about the last name of the person. Still, Chase was definitely Landry-esque. Mitch frowned. "Going with me?"

Kennedy nodded. "To Illinois. To get Paige."

"He doesn't have to come."

"Yeah, he does," Kennedy said. "You probably slept like crap last night. Driving that far by yourself isn't great even when you're feeling good, but when you're sleep-deprived, it's stupid. And I know you're Mr. Fix-it and can handle anything and everything, but if there really are bad roads and bad weather, it doesn't hurt to have someone along. He's already packed."

"How's he already packed if I just decided I'm going to Illinois?"

"I told him to pack when I told him where Paige was."

"You knew I'd go after her?"

"When you found out someone you love was stuck somewhere they didn't want to be, having trouble of some kind?" She gave a little *pssst* sound. "Of course, I knew you'd go. That's who you are anyway, but this is Paige. It's not like you're going to sit here, all reasonable, and just *wait* for her to get back."

"I just want to be sure she's okay."

"You can't do that by phone?"

"She wouldn't tell me if she *wasn't* okay."

"You mean, you need to see for yourself and then still fuss about her and her car and—"

"Did something happen to her car?" Dammit. He'd fixed the terrible noise her car had been making when she'd rolled into town—her brake pads had been shot—but what if something else had gone wrong? Or what if she'd hit something or ended up in a ditch...

"No! She's fine."

But she wasn't. She was alone. And yes, he knew she wanted that. And yes, he was going to give her as much of that as she wanted. But he didn't think she actually wanted to be alone in a town where she knew no one and had to rely on strangers for help. He didn't think she actually wanted everyone she knew to be an hours-long road-trip away. He didn't think she actually wanted to rely on phone calls and video chats and texting to stay in touch with the people she cared about.

She wanted to make her own choices and have those respected. She wanted to be a part of projects and groups, but she wanted to contribute her talents and interests, not just do what people thought she should do. She wanted to take care of other people as much as she wanted to be taken care of.

And yes, she wanted to, sometimes, go off alone and just be

by herself. And sometimes, she wanted to party at a crawfish boil and get drunk and loud. And sometimes, she wanted to cuddle in a hammock on a front porch.

And she could have it all with him.

He needed to finally tell her that.

"Besides, once you get to Paige you're not gonna want to be in two different cars for the trip back to Louisiana, are you?" Kennedy asked.

Mitch had to admit that that was a very good point. "Nope, you're right."

"I keep telling you people that, and yet, it doesn't ever seem to completely sink in," Kennedy muttered.

Mitch laughed and reached out to tug on the end of Kennedy's ponytail. "Thanks."

"Of course. Anything for my favorite cousin."

Mitch cocked his brow. "You like me even better than Charlie?"

"Are you kidding? Of course, I like you better than Charlie. In the summers, Charlie was always competition for all the boys' attention down here."

"You wanted the boys' attention? I figured you knew that you were too good for any of the guys here."

"I was always too good for the guys here," Kennedy agreed. "That doesn't mean I didn't want their attention."

Mitch laughed and shook his head as he shifted his truck into drive. He was pretty sure that Kennedy was his favorite cousin too.

He swung by his house, threw a few things into a bag, and was back in his truck ten minutes later. He'd text Griffin at some point from the road. He knew Griffin would take care of the cats even without a text, so Mitch didn't have anything much to take care of before heading out of town. He pulled into the parking lot at Ellie's and didn't even shut off the engine when he went inside.

Chase, Josh, and Owen were standing at the end of the bar talking to Ellie, looking as if they were waiting for something. Or someone.

"You driving first, or am I?" Mitch asked Chase.

"I'm up first," Owen answered.

"You?" Mitch asked.

"You don't think we're gonna let you head out of town with just Dawson looking out for you, do you?" Owen asked. He looked at Chase. "Hell, this guy doesn't even know how to pop a dislocated thumb back into place."

"I do," Chase said, rubbing a finger up the middle of his forehead as if his head was aching. "I just don't do it quite like you all do."

It was true that a lot of the "real" medicine Chase was learning in medical school didn't line up exactly with how they did things down here on the bayou. He liked Cora's creams and salves, but he got a little green around the edges when they talked about removing stray bullets from thighs and giving each other stitches. They embellished the stories, of course, because it would never not not be fun to tease the guy who'd made the very big mistake of telling them that he got manicures and had never broken a bone. It was open season on rich fraternity boys down here. Chase knew it. And accepted it. Kind of. It was the payment he had to make for Cora's etouffee and time with Bailey.

"Do we really need a whole posse?" Mitch felt obligated to ask.

"Yep," Owen said.

Josh nodded. "Yep."

"You both just got married."

"That was yesterday," Ellie said, leaning onto the bar. "This is what's happening in the family today."

Yeah, that was how things went here. Whatever needed to

be done just got done. If someone needed something, the rest of them stepped up. Period.

Mitch knew he should argue. His newly married cousins didn't need to come to Iowa with him. Especially if he had Chase with him. But it felt pretty good that they *wanted* to come along. And he wouldn't have to do any thinking or planning or fixing if they were there. He could just concentrate on Paige.

That sounded nice. He didn't do that much. Or at all. He was the one taking care of everyone else all the time. Maybe this once it would be okay to let them do the caretaking.

"Okay. Well, whoever wants to come, can," he said.

"I wouldn't say it like that," Josh said.

"Why not?"

"Because Fletcher and Zeke and Zander might decide to get in on the road trip too."

Actually, they really might.

Mitch chuckled. "I guess we could take one of the tour buses."

"Did your broken-hearted-wallowing-in-being-too-good-of-a-guy ass just *laugh*?"

Mitch glanced at Chase. "I'm wallowing in being-too-good-of-a-guy?"

"That's your problem," Chase said.

Josh, Owen, and Ellie all nodded.

"There's such a thing as being too good of a guy?"

"When it causes you to let the love of your life get away?" Ellie asked. "Damn right there is."

He focused on his grandmother. "Do you think she'll stay this time?"

That was what he wanted. It was clear to him now. He wanted Paige to see that damn otter enclosure grand opening. Because it was a little thing in the world, but it was a big thing in *his* world. And he wanted her to be a part of it. She didn't have to walk down any aisles with him, and if she still wanted to go to Colorado in August, he'd encourage it. But he'd probably ask if he could come along. And then work on talking her into coming back to the bayou with him after they hung out in the mountains for a while.

"If you ask her to," Ellie said.

"You think that's okay?"

Ellie leaned on to the bar. "You are the most laid-back person I know. You go with the flow. You let us all do and be whatever we want." She paused. "And it's annoying as hell sometimes."

Mitch frowned at her. "How can that be annoying?"

"Because going through life not caring enough about anything to fight and push and *try* means you're not really letting yourself feel," Ellie told him. "You need to have some passions. You *deserve* to have some passions. And to be able to really show them. And the people in your life need to know when you have passion for them." she said. "*Finally*, someone came along that made you care that much. I know it will take you some practice now, letting someone take care of you a little, but Paige owes you some patience. The best first step is going after her and telling her you want her."

Mitch swallowed. Then nodded. "I do want her."

"Tell her that," Ellie said.

"She might still leave anyway."

Ellie nodded. "She might. But you will have fewer regrets about that than you will about never telling her what you want."

Mitch took a deep breath. "Okay."

"And Mitch?" his grandmother asked.

"Yeah?"

"You don't have to *do* anything special or really, anything at all, to be loved. We love you for who you are, not what you do. You are not, nor have you ever been, a burden to any of us. And I could kick your daddy's ass for making you think that."

He stared at her. Ellie seemed genuinely upset. He swallowed hard. He could see the truth—and the love—in her eyes. He finally nodded. "Okay."

"You believe me?" she asked.

Ellie had never lied to him. Hell, she never even cushioned the truth. Whether it was to tell you that you were acting like an ass, someone had died, or that she loved you and was proud of you, Ellie just said it like it was.

"I do," he answered.

"Good. And now you need to let that girl love you too," Ellie said. "She needs to do it as much as you need her to."

He nodded again. "Yes, ma'am."

Ellie smiled. "Go get her."

"All right." Chase clapped his hands together. "And no bitching about the cold and asking for hot sauce everywhere we stop for food," he said, pointing at Owen.

Owen reached over and snagged a bottle of hot sauce off one of Ellie's tables. "Got it."

Chase looked at Mitch. "It's a good thing she stopped in Peoria. I don't think you want *this* showing up in her hometown."

Mitch grinned, feeling lighter than he had in days. He was going to get Paige. He was going to let her—and everyone else —love him. Just... that. Damn, that sounded nice.

And he kind of did want to show them all Appleby, Iowa.

"Well, we're not meeting her in Peoria," he said.

"That's where Kennedy said she stopped," Chase said.

"But she won't still be there twelve hours from now."

"Kennedy told her to stay put."

"You're assuming she'll listen to someone tell her to do something she doesn't want to do."

"Another headstrong woman who does whatever she wants." Chase sighed. "No wonder she fits in down here."

20

P aige, of course, couldn't sleep.

She typed out four messages to Mitch.

And deleted them all.

She dialed his number.

But didn't let it ring.

She wasn't sure what to say or what to do. She wanted to yell at him for not telling her about the grand opening. She wanted to cry, thinking that he didn't think she'd want to know about that.

Most of all, she just wanted to *be* there. She wanted to turn over in the hammock, take his face in her hands, and tell him that anything that was important to him was important to her. Anything that acknowledged how wonderful he was and how talented and hard-working and dedicated he was was something she wanted to be a part of.

She didn't need to be there for every project he completed or even every "good job, Mitch" he got. But *this*... this was a new chapter for the family business. This was something they'd entrusted to him, and he'd delivered on. Something he'd gone above and beyond on, and everyone was really seeing that.

Mitch was often in the background. She knew he liked it that way. He didn't need the things he did called out and praised all of the time. But sometimes, he deserved that.

She was so happy his family was seeing how much he truly did for them and how much he was contributing to this new venture. She was so thrilled he was getting the recognition he deserved for his hard work.

And she absolutely wanted to be there to help heap on that praise.

She suspected he was also pleased. He was humble, for sure, but she knew it meant a lot to him to *do* things for his family and to give them things. This had to be so rewarding for him. To truly have taken this kernel of an idea they'd had and turn it into something actual and amazing.

She just wanted to hug the stuffing out of him. And then give him a really hot congratulatory blow job.

That was definitely something she could do for him that no one else in the family could to thank him for a job well done.

She needed to be with him, and she was pissed and frustrated that there were twelve hours and six inches of snow in her way.

Finally, she called her mom.

"Hi, honey."

"Hi, Mom. Is it too late?" It was almost ten o'clock at night. She'd left Autre around six that morning. Between the slow down because of the storm, getting stuck, and then getting settled in the B&B, it had taken her longer than the twelve hours the online map showed between Peoria and Autre.

"Of course not. Josie told me where you are and everything."

Paige pressed her lips together. Why had she called her mom? What was Dee going to say? She wasn't going to care about a bunch of otters. Or that Mitch had done this really amazing thing. She might even be annoyed that Paige was choosing to go back to Autre instead of to Piper and Ollie's wedding.

Because Dee didn't really know Mitch. She didn't understand how this could be a big deal for him. Or for Paige.

And that was Paige's fault. She'd kept her family from getting to know him when he'd been in Appleby to visit, because she hadn't wanted them to think anything serious was going on.

Now she wished they all knew him. She wanted her family to understand why the big moments in Mitch's life were important to her too.

She was such an idiot.

"Yeah, I'm fine, and I should be able to get home tomorrow, but..." She blew out a breath.

"But? What's wrong?" Dee asked immediately.

"I want to go back to Louisiana."

Dee was quiet for a moment. "Oh."

Paige couldn't tell if the "oh" was twinged with simple surprise, or anger, or disappointment.

"Is everything all right there? Is *everyone* all right?" Dee asked.

Paige took a breath. "Yes. They're all good. In fact, they're opening up the new otter exhibit. It's a new part of their business." God, she hadn't even really told her mom about the tour company or the otters or the petting zoo. She swallowed. "The family has several businesses in town. One of them is a swamp boat tour company that I'm working for."

"Right. Boys of the Bayou."

Paige frowned. "You know the name?"

"I looked them up online. It's an impressive operation. They have wonderful reviews. A lot of them talk about how handsome and charming the tour guides are." Dee laughed lightly. "But they seem to do a great business."

Paige blinked. "You looked them up?"

"Of course. You're working for them. And it's Mitch's family. And Ellie's. I'm always interested in what's important to you."

"You..." Paige wasn't sure what to say. "You think they're important to me?"

"Of course, they are. It's like when you got into yoga. I looked that up."

"You *did*?" Paige knew she sounded shocked. She *was* shocked.

"I did. It didn't all make much sense to me, and it isn't my cup of tea, but I wanted to know what you were doing."

Wow. She hadn't known that. Why hadn't Dee told her that?

Maybe because you would have thought—and said—she was being nosy and intrusive.

She really probably would have.

Or maybe she would have told you if you hadn't shut down every conversation about yoga because you figured she was going to lecture you about doing more with your life.

That wasn't pure projection. They'd definitely argued about Paige's choices. But Paige hadn't worked especially hard to make Dee *understand*. She'd really just wanted Dee's acceptance. Which was a fair expectation from your mother. But in lieu of that, Paige could have probably tried harder to explain why she loved the things she did.

"Well," Paige said, trying to focus. "The otter encounter is an off-shoot of the company."

"Boys of the Bayou Gone Wild," Dee said. "I read about it on the website. That's funny. Those cute little otters don't look very wild. And the goats and llamas and the pot-bellied pig they have are so cute too."

"Actually, they're alpacas," Paige said, absent-mindedly. "You saw all of this online?"

"Yes. And they're having a Grand Opening for the otter enclosure on Tuesday."

Wow, Paige could have just looked at the website, apparently. "Yes. They are. And Mitch built that enclosure."

"You want to be there for him."

That sounded simple when Dee said it.

"Yes," she replied after a moment. Again, simple.

"You should be there," Dee said.

"I should? Really?"

"That's what you do when you love someone."

"You... you know I love him?" Paige asked, her voice suddenly scratchy.

"Honey, I've talked to you over the past couple of months," Dee said, a touch of humor in her voice. "I've never seen you happy like you are now."

Paige felt warmth spread through her. She did love him. She was glad Dee could tell.

And her mom hadn't said a thing about bouquets and hadn't emailed her a single wedding dress website to look at.

"Were you planning to talk wedding cakes with me while we were celebrating Piper and Ollie?"

Dee laughed softly. "No. You running away from home made the point loud and clear that you want to do things your way."

Paige didn't even think about denying it.

"I was really hoping you'd invite us to your wedding," Dee added a moment later. "But I think I would understand if you didn't want to."

Paige's heart squeezed. "Oh, Mom, I would invite you."

"You sure?"

Paige thought about it. "Yes. I might have, for a second, thought about not inviting you," she said honestly. "But yes, I would've invited you." She knew that for certain.

"Okay, good."

Paige smiled. Then took a breath. "So, I should go back to Autre? To be with Mitch?"

"Would you want him there if you were revealing something you'd built and were proud of, and that made you happy?"

"Absolutely." She didn't even have to think about it. "He already has been." He'd been there as she'd put the weddings together, and his encouragement had made her even more excited to share details with him every day. Having him beside her had made it even better when it had all come together, and everyone had been so happy and complimentary, and she'd felt so rewarded and pleased.

"Then you know the answer."

"Thanks, Mom."

"I'm always here."

Paige felt her eyes stinging. She knew that. She'd always known that. She just hadn't appreciated it.

"And," Paige said, realizing she really did have one more question for her mom.

"Yes?"

"I was wondering if you guys would be able to be there."

There was a beat of silence on Dee's end of the line. Then another.

"Mom?"

"Be there? In Autre? At the opening?"

"Yes. I... would really like for you to meet Mitch and get to know him. And his family. To see Autre and everything that's going on there."

"Oh."

Paige could tell *that* "oh" was pure surprise.

"And I know Josie and Grant will need to be at Piper and Ollie's wedding, but then, maybe Grant could fly you all down here Tuesday morning. I mean, he does have a private plane." There really could be some great advantages to having a millionaire for a brother-in-law if she was going to live a few states away from her family. Her family that she would like to see once in a while. Or even more often than that.

Dee laughed. "He does, doesn't he?"

Paige knew that Grant would do that for them. He was a good guy, and he loved her sister very much. "I would love to have you all here. The kids would *love* the otters and alpacas and goats," she said of her niece and nephew. "And you've already met Cora and Ellie on the video call. It would be really fun to introduce you in person."

Suddenly, her heart was beating hard. This really would be fun. She'd love to show her family everything she loved about Autre and the Landrys. But she'd also like to show her family off to the Landrys. Her family was pretty great.

She heard her mother sniff and then say, "I would love to come to Autre for the grand opening. Thank you for asking."

Paige was smiling widely even as she felt her eyes stinging. "I'm glad."

"I'll talk to Josie and Grant and everyone, and... we'll see you on Tuesday," Dee said.

Paige swallowed hard and sniffed herself. "Great. I can't wait."

T hey met at the Love's Travel Stop, a big truck stop off Interstate 55.

Paige had already been on the road for an hour when Mitch texted her at six a.m. to tell her they'd be in Peoria at eleven. When she'd told him to meet her at Love's, he'd thought that was incredibly appropriate.

His heart was in his throat when he saw her car pull into the parking lot. He was out of the truck and striding toward her before she'd even shut off the ignition.

When they met in the middle of the parking lot, she just

wrapped her arms around him and pressed into his body. Mitch enfolded her, nearly crushing her to his chest. And he felt like he could breathe again. As if he was warm, again. As if things were right, again.

When he tried to pull back nearly two full minutes later, she clutched him tighter, and with a happy exhale, he hugged her again.

It was at least another two minutes before she loosened her hold even slightly.

When she did, she looked up at him. "When are you going to let someone love the hell out of you the way you deserve?"

His heart knocked so hard against his chest wall that he had to work to take his next breath. But he looked her directly in the eyes when he said, "How about I start right now?"

Her smile was swift and bright. "That was a very good answer."

He swallowed hard. *Marry me* was right on the tip of his tongue. He gritted his teeth, keeping it in.

After a long moment, Paige finally spoke softly.

"Ask me, Mitch."

He shook his head. He shouldn't have been surprised she knew what he was thinking.

"Ask me."

"I've got all I need right here," he said, hugging her close.

She squeezed him back but said against his chest, "Fine. Then I'll ask you."

He took such a deep breath, he knew she felt the rise and fall against her cheek.

Paige looked up at him. "Mitch?"

"Yeah?"

"Can I keep staying with you?"

The air lodged in his chest. Finally, he nodded. "Yes. Please."

"Even past August?"

"Yes. Absolutely. Forever if you want to."

Her eyes flickered with emotion. For a second, Mitch wondered if that was too much.

But he didn't care.

He couldn't keep swallowing how he felt about her.

"Paige—"

"I love you, Mitch."

He stared down at her.

"I can't not say it anymore. I love you. So much. I can't believe how much. I didn't know this kind of love really happened. But it's real and, it took four weddings and a swamp boat tour and a bunch of otters to make me realize it, but... I really, really, really love you."

He kept staring at her.

She loved him. She *loved* him.

"No, that's a lie," she went on before he could speak. "I loved you before any of the weddings. And I'll be watching the fourth one in the car back to Louisiana anyway. And I would love you even if there weren't otters. I'm not saying this just because you're now an award-winning otter enclosure builder."

She just watched him for several seconds.

"Mitch?" She blew out a breath. "Am *I* pushing? Am I going too fast? Is that even possible with a Landry?"

Finally, he crushed her to his chest and dragged in a long, shaky, deep breath. "Jesus, Paige," was all he managed for several heartbeats.

When he thought he could speak, he pulled back and looked down at her. "I love you, too. So much. I... need you. I never want you to leave. Stay. Or I'll come with you. Or whatever. But I love you, and I want to be with you. We don't have to get married or anything. That's not the important part. Just be with me. Let me be with you. Let's just... make memories."

"History," she said with a smile. "Let's make some history."

He nodded. "Yeah. Let's have some stories to tell in fifty years."

"Yeah." Her eyes were watery. "But there's just one other thing."

"Anything."

"Would you let me propose to you? Eventually? In maybe a year or two? I mean, I'll obviously do it at Ellie's in front of everyone and make a big production out of it. But would that be okay?"

"I..."

It took him a second to really *hear* what she'd said.

He was fully prepared to say yes to anything she asked. But this one definitely snuck up on him.

"Are you proposing to propose to me?"

She nodded. "Yes. I mean, we're not ready for that. We haven't known each other that long, and it's a big step. But eventually, I think that's a question I would definitely like to ask you. And you never ask anyone for anything, and hell, I don't either. Because I don't want people to ask me for stuff. And I thought that made us the perfect match. But the thing is, I need to say yes to things. I need to be involved. And I want that. I've realized that."

"Well," he said, his heart drumming hard and his mind whirling and happiness spreading through him. "I think if you need to start saying yes to people, then *I* probably need to start asking people for things."

Slowly a smile curled her mouth. "Yeah, I guess you have a point."

"So, maybe I should ask you something right now."

Mitch watched her take in a huge gulp of air. Now would be the moment when he'd expect her to bolt. Or at least push him back. Or start shaking her head, at least. He knew exactly what she was thinking he was thinking.

But she did none of those things.

In fact, she put her hands on his chest and gripped his shirt in her fists.

She met his gaze directly and took another deep breath. "Okay. I'm ready."

His heart expanded, almost painfully. "Will you be my otter enclosure grand opening planner?"

She didn't even blink.

She said nothing.

"With the weddings, everything with this has been kind of thrown together on the side, and we've got like cookies and balloons and that might be it, and... I've decided I want it to be a big deal." He really did. Now that he'd admitted it, it felt good. "And you'd be perfect at it. You have a gift. It's not *that* different from a wedding, right?"

She took a breath. But still said nothing.

"Okay, it's different from a wedding. It's not *that* big of a deal, but—"

"Are the cookies at least shaped like otters?"

He stopped. Frowned. And then shook his head. "Regular round cookies, I'm pretty sure."

"That will *not* do," she said. "I'm going to have to see if Josie knows where we can get an otter cookie-cutter shipped overnight, and then we're going to be up baking in Cora's kitchen late tonight."

Happiness and love spread through him. "We've got plenty of hands to help out."

She nodded. She was playing with the front of his shirt, but clearly, her mental wheels were turning. About the party. Not about how her hands on him drove him crazy.

"I think we should tell the story about how Gus became part of the family," she said.

Gus was the first otter who had adopted the Landrys. He'd been orphaned and had lived under the Boys of the Bayou dock. Everyone had a Gus story.

"I think we should take people down to the dock and show them his first home. Then we can take them out on a boat tour and show them how otters live in the wild. We then come back and tell them the story of Juliet braving her fear of the water to save Gus. And how the otter babies brought Bailey and Chase together." Paige was smiling now. "I loved hearing all those stories. The visitors to the grand opening will too. We need to tell everyone how the otters are a part of the Landry family stories. That will help them understand why this enclosure is a big deal."

Yes. That's exactly what they should do.

He took that all in, feeling amazed, in love, and relieved. "You sat up last night writing down all the stories everyone has told you while you've been in Autre, didn't you?"

She smiled up at him. "Well, not *all* of them. Just the otter stories. So far."

He felt his eyes stinging again as he looked down at the woman he was certain was the love of his life.

"That all sounds perfect."

She smiled. "Then let's go home."

Home.

That was almost as good as the L-word.

They needed five of the big airboats to get everyone out onto the bayou for their tour of the otters' natural environment.

The grand opening was a huge success. Of course, the Landry family could fill five airboats up, but they'd left the boats to their guests from the town and surrounding area. And Paige's family.

Paige had started crying the moment she'd seen her family. Mitch had been clearly choked up as well as he shook her father's and Grant's hands and accepted hugs from Dee and Josie. Her other sister and her family hadn't been able to get away on such short notice, but she'd promised to come visit when she and the kids had a break from school.

It really did help to have a brother-in-law who had a private plane sometimes.

She'd been incredibly touched, as had Mitch, that they'd come for this. Even knowing they'd be there, it was emotional to see them. They'd come without really knowing Mitch and only briefly meeting any of the Landrys over the phone.

But she understood that they'd come for her. And for the man who would, probably, someday be a part of *their* family.

Paige sat with her mom and dad as they observed the huge gathering of people at Ellie's after the boat ride and walking tour from the docks to the new enclosure.

Because Griffin had refused to do a public talk, Tori had led a presentation about the otters and everything that was included in the enclosure for them, from the shelter to the swimming areas to enrichment activities. And she'd definitely singled Mitch out as the creative genius behind it all.

Right now, Josie and Grant were chatting with Kennedy and Bennett across the room. Kennedy was, no doubt, telling Grant all the reasons he should donate to Bennett's foundation. Which he really should.

"This is quite the place," Dee said.

There was food everywhere, including otter shaped cookies. And drinks, of course. And music. People were talking and laughing. It was family and friends, coming together and commemorating another piece of their history.

"It really is," Paige agreed. "And they are quite the family." Paige glanced to where Mitch was accepting congratulations from more of the guests. He was flanked by Tori and Josh on one side, and he'd insisted Fletcher and Zeke stand with him since they'd done a lot of the manual labor for the enclosure too.

She loved that he was getting so much attention. And was accepting it. Or at least tolerating it.

"Well, I'm here to support you as you support Mitch," Dee said. "And I'm thrilled that *this* is where you landed."

Paige smiled at her mom. "I really did it, huh? I finally let my guard down a little, and I ended up with all of... this." She looked around the bar, full of people that she knew were already a part of her heart. And her future.

Dee squeezed her hand. "Well, I don't know if you really let your guard down. Seems these people can get past even a seemingly well-protected heart."

Paige nodded. "True."

It really was. She wasn't sure if she'd finally opened her heart or if the Landrys had applied a crowbar, but it was wide-open now, and she knew it was never going to be shut... or empty... again.

"So, Mom," she said, her eyes on Mitch again. He looked over and caught her gaze. He gave her a little smile, and she knew he was okay. But that he needed a hug and maybe a few words of "you're doing great" from her soon.

"Yes?"

"Before you all leave on Wednesday, I'd like to take you down Main Street and show you a couple of little shops. There's a great pizza place where we could have lunch."

"Are we allowed to not have lunch here at Ellie's?" Dee asked, picking up one of the meat pies that she'd earlier declared one of the most delicious things she'd ever eaten.

"Well, it's next door to an available space that I'd love your opinion on."

Dee smiled at her. "A possible yoga studio-cat café?"

"And a wedding planning business."

Her mom nodded. "Absolutely."

"And..."

Dee lifted a brow.

"I do happen to have some wedding dress catalogs now."

"For the business."

"Yes," Paige said. "But... maybe we could flip through a couple of them together."

Dee's face lit up. "I would love that."

Paige laughed. "I know. And I'm not actually *getting* a dress for a while," she cautioned. "But..." She looked over at Mitch again. "I *am* getting one. Eventually."

Mitch gave her a smile, then tipped his head in a "come here" gesture.

She nodded. "Be back in a bit," she told her parents, getting to her feet.

"We're fine," Dee assured her. "Go take care of Mitch."

Paige watched Mitch watching her as she crossed the room. His eyes on her filled her with a mix of love and comfort and heat and happiness that she wanted to feel for the rest of her life.

Yeah, she was getting a freaking wedding dress.

And as he wrapped his arm around her and tucked her against his side, she couldn't help the thought that danced through her head.

Maybe even tomorrow.

Thank you so much for reading Paige and Mitch's story! I hope you loved this trip to the bayou!

Have you read what happened in Iowa before Paige made the trip to Louisiana?
You can check out that part of their story in the
Hot Cakes series novella, **Oh, Fudge!**

And if you want even more from the Landrys and Autre...
there's lots more to come!

Check out the
Boys of the Bayou- Gone Wild
*Things are going to get wild when the next batch of bayou boys fall
in love!*

Otterly Irresistible
Heavy Petting
Flipping Love You

Find out more at
ErinNicholas.com

And join in on all the FAN FUN!

Join my **email list at**
http://bit.ly/ErinNicholasEmails

And be the first to hear about my news, sales, freebies, behind-
the-scenes, and more!

Or for even more fun, join my **Super Fan page** on Facebook
and chat with me and other super fans every day! Just search
Facebook for Erin Nicholas Super Fans!

IF YOU LOVED THE BOYS OF THE BAYOU...

If you love the Boys of the Bayou, you'll love the connected series, Boys of the Big Easy!

The Boys of the Big Easy

Easy Going (prequel novella)-Gabe & Addison

Going Down Easy- Gabe & Addison

Taking It Easy - Logan & Dana

Eggnog Makes Her Easy - Matt & Lindsey

Nice and Easy - Caleb & Lexi

Getting Off Easy - James & Harper

If you're looking for more sexy, small town rom com fun, check out the

The Hot Cakes Series

One small Iowa town. Two rival baking companies.

A three-generation old family feud.

And six guys who are going to be heating up a lot more than the kitchen.

Sugar Rush (prequel)

Sugarcoated

Forking Around

Making Whoopie

Semi-Sweet On You

Oh, Fudge

Gimme S'more

———————

And much more

including my printable book list at

ErinNicholas.com

ABOUT THE AUTHOR

Erin Nicholas is the New York Times and USA Today bestselling author of over thirty sexy contemporary romances. Her stories have been described as toe-curling, enchanting, steamy and fun. She loves to write about reluctant heroes, imperfect heroines and happily ever afters. She lives in the Midwest with her husband who only wants to read the sex scenes in her books, her kids who will never read the sex scenes in her books, and family and friends who say they're shocked by the sex scenes in her books (yeah, right!).

Find her and all her books at
www.ErinNicholas.com

And find her on Facebook, Goodreads, BookBub, and Instagram!

CPSIA information can be obtained
at www.ICGtesting.com
Printed in the USA
BVHW030514150221
600137BV00001B/28